The Wisdom That Comes With Winters

A Novel

By

Thomas Hofstedt

Table of Contents

Prologue

The Beginning: January 1961

They had little in common except that they were cold, afraid, and too young for the tasks they had set for themselves. They were separated by a vast distance and their shared ignorance of each other's lives, escaping from different demons and afraid for different reasons. However, they were alike in that they did not think about the future but, if they had, would have perceived it as a bleak and inhospitable place, governed by hostile forces.

A Frozen Lake in Minnesota

It was as if they were being compressed between two planes of blackness. The ice, jet black beneath them, but a shiny hard black, unlike the soft cottony blackness of the night sky, moonless and starless, that they could feel descending to meet the ice at that precise point where the white lines seemed to originate, the stress fractures marking where the ice cracked from temperatures approaching twenty-below zero and proceeded arrow-like toward the ragged opening in the black ice, that small rectangle of watery blackness absent of ripples, now perfectly still as though accepting the reality that it must again revert to a solid state, a polished slate-black cover for a grave, but one without inscription or ornamentation.

They followed the jagged white line, not because it led them where they wanted to go, but because it was the only marker in the blackness and it led away from the accusing shimmering hole in the black ice. They moved side-by-side, straddling the line and using the awkward sliding gait required for moving quickly on icy surfaces. The metallic tips on the short poles they carried made clicking sounds as they struck the ice in rhythm with their panting breath.

Near Wittenberg, East Germany

Five thousand miles away, the Elbe River did not freeze during the East German winter, as if resigned to its role as the watery barrier between the communist east and capitalist west for the ninety-five kilometers between Lauenburg and Schnackenburg. As a barrier, it lacked the solidity of the wall that was even then being built in the city of Berlin. And even worse, it enabled the citizens of the East German Democratic Republic to see the beckoning lights of the far more prosperous west just a few hundred yards away in the predawn darkness. Those lights signified a new life.

The young man waiting in the drainage ditch forty yards from the slowly moving current thought only about the story he would tell the border guards on the far bank. He did not think about his abandoned classes at Martin Luther University a few miles from where he sat. Nor did he think about the family that he was leaving behind. Or of the dozens of men and women like him that had drowned or been shot by the patrol boats while trying to do exactly what he was about to attempt.

My name is Horst Weber. I want to live in the West. I am educated in law and economics. Tell the Americans that I am close to Markus Wolf.

The patrol boat and its probing searchlights moved past his position within a minute of the time he had calculated, headed east. As soon as it passed, he sprinted for the water's edge with his homemade kayak under one arm, canvas stretched over a wooden frame and painted black; a crude craft designed for a single trip. He had made it in his bedroom from materials stolen from a construction site. His paddle was an oar cut in half.

He picked a light on the other shore, visualizing the vectors of the slight breeze and the current, and started paddling. He had six and a half minutes before the patrol boat came back on its westerly leg.

His instructions were short and simple. "That is enough time to get well past the midline of the river, which is the official border. But the GDR patrol boats will fire on anyone anywhere on the river until they're picked up by the West German border patrol. Do not stop once you start across."

He paced himself, fighting the urge to flail furiously at the stubborn water. He quickly developed a cadence by reciting, very softly because sound carried on the water, what he had come to think of as his catechism.

My name is Horst Weber. I want to live in the West. I am educated in law and economics. Tell the Americans that I am close to Markus Wolf.

The Ending: December 2007

The gun had no menace to it. It was merely a dull gray metallic object that could easily have been a paperweight, carefully centered on the two-inch high rectangle of white paper that was in turn precisely placed in the center of the table, each edge exactly parallel with its corresponding table edge.

I considered the objects.

A still life study in a beginning art class, maybe? Surely, it would be given a pretentious title ... 'A Juxtaposition of Possibilities' or some such thing. Requiring the student to master shadow and perspective. The manuscript, the stack of paper, would be the simple part for a beginner. A polyhedra. Specifically, a rectangular prism. Easy to draw. The gun much more difficult with its curvatures and all that symbolic weight to be captured in a few lines.

Ironic, because the stack of paper is where the real menace is. Two hundred and eighty-seven single-spaced pages, ninety-five-thousand words, sixty-one years of randomness spiced up by serious errors in judgment. Although, to be fair, the first ten years or so were probably not my fault. Surely children should not be held accountable for their failures until some agreed upon age of accountability. It was always hard for me to accept the argument of the evangelicals that infants were condemned to eternal damnation because they had 'not accepted Christ,' that god damned – in every sense of the word -- bright line that divides the saved from the unsaved.

"You can use it, or I will."

The man sitting opposite me, the person who had stepped out of the past and gently placed the revolver on the papers, the muzzle aligned ever so slightly in my direction, spoke in a conversational tone, one suitable for commenting on the weather or the dwindling chances for the Giants in the pennant race. Somehow, the very blandness of tone made the threat even more imminent, as though the absence of feeling conveyed the man's genuine indifference to the manner in which I died, like a bored medieval hangman asking whether I had any last words.

He added, "You didn't have to do this. You know that, don't you?" The man made no gesture, looking straight at me, but both of us knew what he was referring to – that damnably innocent looking stack of paper with its neatly aligned edges.

I wonder if that is so, that I actually had a choice?

Questions From Grandchildren

"Did you ever fight in a war, papa?"

The question was a natural one, the innocent result of a ten-year-old boy's curiosity triggered by the radio newscast with its thirty-second coverage of one of the several vicious little wars raging in the Middle East.

It was eighteen months ago. I was driving my grandson Daniel to Bakersfield, where he would participate in a soccer tournament. We were three hours into the tedium that was Interstate Highway Five and the Central Valley and I had turned on the radio to catch the on-the-hour newscast, mostly to help me stay awake. I no longer listened to the network news broadcasts, finding them both dispiriting and simpleminded. I had been too close to the newsmakers for too long and could no longer stomach the ignorance and oversimplifications of the media.

I did not answer him immediately, recognizing that Daniel's question, although innocent and even appropriate in the circumstances, was what his mother Melanie would consider as 'a teachable moment,' one of those rare opportunities for a parent – or a grandparent, in this case – to impart an important cultural or moral tidbit to a child.

She would attempt to turn Daniel's off the cuff question into a Socratic dialogue, stuffed with trite admonitions about the horrors of war and the violent proclivities of men, continuing long after the boy had stopped listening.

I tried for the middle ground. "No, I was either too young or too old when the wars happened."

Simple truths to obscure the lying by omission. Safe enough, I think. And even true in a hair-splitting fashion. If one is referring only to those conflicts that meet the formal definition of 'war.'

"Uncle Robert was in a war once, wasn't he? He showed me his scar and said that it came from a war that he was in."

He would do that. Robert viewed the scar as a badge of honor, not something to be covered up or dismissed as an accident of youth.

"Yes, he joined the army when he was eighteen. He was in a lot of wars." *And wars do leave scars, some of them invisible.*

He went to war and I went off to college. It was the beginning of a separation that would become permanent, a fact that we both acknowledged and regretted without being moved to do anything to remedy the split.

"Did he fight with the Arabs? In Bull?"

"It's Kabul that the man was talking about, with a 'k' at the beginning, not 'Bull.' It's in a country called Afghanistan. When Uncle Robert was in the army, America was fighting in a country called Vietnam. It was a long time ago. He was still very young."

"Did we win?"

Such a complex question. I wonder how Melanie would answer that one? Or Robert?

"We quit. And said that we won."

"Did Uncle Robert get shot in Vietnam? Is that what the scar is from?"

"I think you should ask him."

"I did, but he said he didn't want to talk about it."

He would say that.

Daniel seemed content with that and resumed his watch for out-of-state license plates, part of our made-up game to make the time pass more quickly. That left me to deal with all of the memories that Daniel's innocent questions had stirred up. Much later, I would recognize that what I came to think of as *the project* really began on that bleak stretch of Interstate Highway Five in the Central Valley.

It began as a fantasy, triggered by Daniel's simple questions and then helped along by ego and the many circling doubts that afflict a man about to celebrate his sixtieth birthday.

What if I told Daniel about all of the dirty little wars I've been a part of? Or how Robert got that scar? All that time I've spent in grubby little rooms with scheming people, some of whom were genuinely evil? Would he even believe me, and if he did, would it make me a hero or a monster? I wonder what he thinks of me? What am I to him other than a genial old man that is nice to him? What does he tell his friends about me?

The questions would not go away and I used my time in Bakersfield and on our return trip to begin to answer them. I was able to verify that Daniel had no idea who I -- his grandfather -- really was. It was a very gentle interrogation, one that he was unaware of. But at the end of it, it was quite clear to me that he did not find me remarkable in any way. I was just another adult in near-orbit. To a ten-year-old, I lacked drama and depth, a figure without consequence, neither feared nor respected. My vague awareness that all ten-year-olds viewed nearby adults in approximately the same way did not allow me to stop thinking about it.

Daniel's simple question -- "Did you ever fight in a war, papa?" – stayed with me long after our trip was done. The fantasy it triggered would not leave me alone, keeping me from falling asleep and the first thought in my head when I woke up. Inevitably, it led me to think about all the other questions that I couldn't answer, innocent questions freighted with threat, conjuring up images of other scars that could not be talked about.

I can't pinpoint the moment that fantasy became possibility, but there came a time – approximately eighteen months ago – when I thought, "Why not write a memoir?"

Past, present and future. That's all there is.

The latter is unknowable and for me, at my age, whatever future there is will be fairly limited in both scope and duration. That future is the proper province of science fiction writers, most of whom will choose grim, apocalyptic themes, or else the time-indeterminate fairy tales with their sugary "and all lived happily ever after" assurances.

Some smug philosopher will point out that the present is always becoming the past, so it is impossible to capture. In any case, it's uninteresting. "Today, I woke up and went to the office. It's raining and the dog is dying. I feel sad."

The kind of stuff best left for the Twittering crowd.

That leaves the past.

Even then, there are huge swathes of my past that I do not wish to remember or revisit. My childhood, for example, which I think of as the time when I had parents. And I most certainly do not want to write about them, although it might serve as catharsis. Virtually all of my memories of my parents are of drunkenness, vicious quarrels, shame (mine and theirs), anger, helplessness and sadness.

My father was a drunk – maudlin and self-pitying ... until he turned mean and vindictive. Mother would match him drink-for-drink. It always escalated to a brawl, with loud invective, sometimes ineffective blows, and – worst of all to a child -- hideous accusations. Intervention at any stage was hopeless and it ended only when an alcoholic stupor would set in. I do not recall, nor do I think it mattered very much, what the shouting was about. Certainly, the interaction of alcohol and poverty would have provided ample subject matter

Both of my parents died long before their actuarially appointed time. Mother was a heavy smoker and she contracted cancer of the throat and had her larynx removed, losing the ability to speak. She continued to smoke, a ghastly endorsement for the emerging anti-smoking league. She would hold the cigarette to the open incision in her throat so that she could inhale, demonstrating either the power of addiction or the indomitable human spirit. The frequent drunken brawls became dark comedy as she was forced to scribble her rage on little pieces of notepaper and hurl them at dad. She would die on Christmas morning in 1965, 52 years old.

I remember much time in bars, being terrified in a car weaving from shoulder to shoulder, hearing drunken accusations hurled back and forth, and the notoriety of my family among 'decent folks,' which often reflected itself in acts of charity directed at the children. Interestingly, that notoriety did not ever lead to a social worker dropping by. Children in small towns had few designated protectors in those days.

The telltale is what I do not remember – birthday parties, family dinners, school conferences, or any of the trappings of a normal childhood. Perhaps we did these things. But I do not remember them.

But there is more to life than childhood. All of us, I think, harbor the ingrained belief, probably with equal conviction throughout our lifetime, that if only "they" understood me, they would appreciate me more, without ever getting very specific about who 'they' are.

Most people deal with it and go on. Some sublimate the feeling into a generalized moroseness that can pass for worldliness; some sit down to write the great American novel; still others buy assault rifles and go out in a lunatic flash. Then there are those that don't trust the historians or obituary writers to fully understand or render the motivation, context or extenuating circumstances – the failed politicians, genocidal generals, falsely accused criminals, first wives, steroidal athletes, defrocked priests, and other casualties of their times and flaws. They write memoirs.

It seems I shall be one of them.

Consultation With An Expert

A week later, I was sitting in front of my desktop computer, staring at a Word document on the twenty-seven inch screen. The only words on the page were centered at the top — "A Memoir."

The blinking cursor was like a warning light.

This is a radically stupid thing to do, a product of having too little to do, feeling misunderstood, and bearing vague grudges that – at my age – are unlikely to be worked out. Maybe what's motivating this venture is turning sixty; one of those milestone birthdays ... a big deal in some circles and cultures. One of those passages that is said to trigger reflection and nostalgia.

It shall be, I think, a relatively purposeless essay, an undertaking of dubious merit except it is a task of interest to me, like a retired person taking up watercolors knowing full well that he has no artistic talent whatsoever. Deborah would attribute the whole enterprise to some long-suppressed Nordic drive to demonstrate a residual humanity, a sort of healthy sublimation that would otherwise show up as excessive drinking or ethnic moroseness.

I called Ashley Grimes. She had been the editor and publisher of the three previous bestsellers that I had authored and probably was at least as much responsible for their success as I was. She shaped me as much as she did the books, beginning with our very first visit.

It was 1974. I was a brand new professor of economics, bearing a PhD thesis that I thought the world needed to know about. She was a veteran editor at one of the major New York publishing houses, perhaps ten years my senior and vastly wiser. I had mailed her an outline and the draft of an introductory chapter, which was open in front of her. From my side of the desk, I could see handwritten notes in the margin, arrows, exclamation marks and numerous slashes through whole paragraphs. I was hurt, feeling like a first grader who'd shown his very first finger painting to his mother and she'd pointed out all the flaws. I was to learn that most of the manuscripts Ashley received were returned unmarked, as pristine as the rejection letter that accompanied them.

She saw the look of dismay and understood it quite well. "You're a classical academic, Brian. If you write what you want to write, in your own style, you'll sell a hundred copies ... to friends and relatives. Let me help you."

So I wrote, and she edited. Ruthlessly and with a laser-like focus on separating the relevant from the merely interesting, the provocative from the arcane. We each made a lot of money from the collaboration. And she became a friend. Now she was retired and living with her daughter in Santa Fe.

"You want to write a memoir? That's a surprise." But she didn't sound surprised, and I wondered how many of her best-selling authors had come to her with the same impulse.

"To me too. I thought you might try to talk me out of it."

There was a slight pause and I remembered her habit of hesitating before criticizing some flawed piece of prose.

"Actually, I think it's a good idea. You've led an interesting life, one that has some teachable moments for others."

"If I did, would you –"

"Brian. I'm retired. Really retired. But I know an editor that would do it justice. One that will put up with your quirks."

She sounds tired. We're both getting old. Maybe that's all this is: acting out a belief that we have learned something ... something that should be passed on to coming generations ... that wisdom comes with age?

"Any hints? About how to write a memoir? If I decide to do it."

Again, that hesitation, longer this time.

"It's got to be about you."

I started to say, "Well, of course!" but I knew that Ashley was trying to tell me something important.

"You mean ... like personal stuff ... family, doubts, roads not taken ... that sort of stuff."

Her voice took on a new resonance. "Absolutely. Otherwise it's just a chronological listing of people and places, the detailed resume you might provide to support your application to an exclusive country club."

"I thought I might provide a new perspective on some of the really dramatic changes in our lifetime. Maybe a title like *Behind the Scenes* or *The Itinerant Economist*?"

"That's called 'journalism,'" she said scornfully. "It works in book form only for ex-presidents and maybe their mistresses."

Then the questions came, rapid-fire. "Did you actually *like* those dictators that you advised? Did you ever have any doubts about whether the ends really did justify the means? Have you done any bad – really bad – things? Or the right things for the wrong reasons? Why did you marry Deborah? How did you *feel* – really feel – when she died? How did you pull yourself out of that two-year long experiment with booze and pills? Do you like the kind of person you've become?"

Her barrage of questions depressed me. Or maybe it was fear, aroused by the prospect of trying to answer those questions for myself, let alone write about them for an unknown audience.

Why can't it be a simple form of history, a recounting of dates and events with an interpretive overlay? She wants something more like the infamous "black box" that remains intact in a plane crash and is used to analyze what went wrong. Is my purpose to preserve a legacy or write an extended apology to those around me?

I tried again, knowing that I was whining and that I was not going to win this particular debate. Not with Ashley.

"I was thinking more along the lines of 'a witness to history' kind of document, something for posterity."

This time, her tone was the one she used when I was being particularly obstinate about retaining a particular paragraph or thought that offended her professional sensibilities.

"Isabel Allende said that posterity is what happens when you no longer care." Then, abruptly, "Call me back when you can answer a simple question: *Why* do you want to write a memoir?"

And she hung up.

I called her two days later.

"I *feel* misunderstood, undervalued … and I want to know if those are legitimate feelings or just the vanity of an old man that has been coddled for far too long. I have this fear that I won't know unless I write down who I am, where I came from, what I've done and why I did it. All in one document."

"Make that – what you just said -- your first paragraph. And then just keep writing. And Brian?"

"Yes?"

"Be prepared for surprises, not all them good."

I should have paid more attention to Ashley.

I have everything I need within twenty feet of where I am sitting. In my mind, all of the documentation can be separated into two categories – the professional and the personal. There is a third category, but that is not for the public eye.

My professional life, spanning the last four decades, is chronicled in the bank of filing cabinets on the opposite wall – papers written, diaries and calendars, reference letters, awards received, expert testimony given, congressional hearings. It is cataloged by year and cross-referenced by events and countries. Given the revolution in information technology, much of the last dozen years is fully annotated and easily accessible in electronic form on the one-terabyte hard drive in the credenza.

That's the easy part. My personal life, what Ashley meant when she said, "It has to be about *you*," will be much more difficult to document and to write about. I have come to view it as two distinct eras— Deborah and post-Deborah.

The 'Deborah Era' is represented by the impromptu cube sitting at the side of my desk. Beginning with our joint adolescence, Deborah began documenting our lives, saving news clippings, letters, photos, hand-me-downs from her parents .... All of the vast paper trail that we mistakenly believe will be of interest to our descendants. She was indiscriminate in deciding what to keep, but she erred on the side of preservation, as through she recognized that she could not know what a cultural anthropologist would find interesting a century later. She called it 'her stash' and stored it in a garage cabinet.

When she died, I gave away or tossed every tangible bit of evidence of her presence, a manic emotional purging, but I have left the contents of that cabinet undisturbed, except to move it with me to California several years ago. Yesterday, I reassembled the contents of that cabinet in my study. The 'Deborah Cube' is made up of eighteen book-sized plastic boxes. It's not really a cube, three layers of six boxes each, physically symmetric and arranged with the newest material on top. It will be like an anthropological 'dig' moving downward through layers of time and memories. The boxes have snap-on lids and each of them has an index card taped to the cover listing the contents, sometimes as a time period – '1979' – or an event – 'Indonesian Trip' or a social group – 'My Family.' It sits there with the weight of the sixteen years that have passed since Deborah's death.

But the cube only takes me to 1991, the year that she died. For the thoughts, feelings and motivations after that – the post-Deborah era -- I am reliant entirely on my memory, with all its imperfections and biases.

But I have a brother, sister and daughter as resource material. And a second wife. They know me better than anyone and have shared much of my life up to this point. Why not tap them? They can be the fact-checkers and second opinions for my memoir.

I had yet to learn the first reality of memoir writing: that my version of the past could threaten others. Caroline was the first of the four of them to make it clear to me that they opposed the project and would not collaborate.

The Insecurities of Second Wives

"You're not going to leave that in the middle of the floor, are you?"

I looked away from the accusative blank page on the screen to see Caroline standing in the doorway looking at the Deborah cube. Her expression was one of casual interest, the one she adopted whenever the subject of 'Deborah' arose.

A confrontation of sorts between the first and second wives, the former represented by eighteen plastic boxes. They never met, but they would not have liked one another. There are just too many differences.

Some of those differences would have been professional in nature. Deborah was a nurse, a classic enabler who disliked confrontation and did her best to keep everybody happy. Caroline is a divorce lawyer, a woman who thrives by stirring up strong feelings. She's one of the really good ones who can pick and choose her cases. Since she was a Stanford graduate who had married – and divorced in spectacular fashion– one of the major VCs in Silicon Valley, it's not surprising that she specializes in representing wives of wealthy high tech executives.

We met four years ago, as adversaries. James Rodin was a fellow Yale grad and the founder of the hedge fund where I was spending most of my time in those days as a high-priced advisor on country risk and similar issues. He was divorcing his third wife and it had turned into one of those scorched earth scandal-ridden cases that keep tabloids in business, with both sides making wild assertions about the other. Caroline was his wife's attorney and we first encountered one another in a deposition.

Supposedly the questions were limited to topics that would bear on the economic value of Rodin's firm as the key component of the community property, with the wife to receive half of its value. Rodin's attorneys portrayed it as worthless – a few desks, a little cash, not really very competitive, with an unpromising set of investments. The wife's attorneys said it was worth billions, the key player in the Silicon Valley M&A market. As usual, the truth – if 'truth' had been of interest to either side, which it wasn't – was somewhere in the middle.

Early in my career, I had published two papers having to do with the underlying economic theories governing the valuation of intellectual property, the very issue that was at the core of the deposition. I was also an occasional advisor to Rodin's hedge fund. Caroline's legal team didn't quite know what to do with me, so the questions veered between economic theory and the details of Rodin's portfolio of companies.

The deposition ran with six lawyers in the room – three on either side. Caroline was mostly a spectator, as one of her partners ran the deposition. His name was Raskin and he was a wicked combination of stupidity and meanness. His first question to me was, "You're a professor of economics and a partner in the hedge fund and a close personal friend of Mr. Rodin's?" Both his tone and his facial expression made the question sound like a statement of fact and an indictment, like a DA beginning his cross examination with, "So you're a child molester, Dr. Norquist?"

"No, no and no."

When he looked surprised, I added, "But what I *am* is busy and another thing I'm *not* is someone being paid $700 an hour to ask dumb questions. I'd appreciate your getting the facts right and stop wasting my time."

I saw Caroline smile. And when the trial ended – the wife got $200 million in cash – I called and asked her out to dinner. There had been other women since Deborah, generally amicable relationships that always segued from one to the next without regret or recriminations. Without thinking about it, I had reconciled myself to my role as a disposable companion for smart and attractive women who were averse to lifetime commitments.

I think it surprised both of us when we drifted into a married state. That was three years ago.

She was ten years younger and in better shape than me. She was a natural blonde who kept her hair long and either consciously or unconsciously used it the way a geisha would use a fan to hide or reveal her face. She not only looked good and liked to dress in tailored garments that clarified her shape, but she exuded a completely natural and innocent sexiness. Many people, on first meeting the two of us together, tended to see her as a trophy wife, but that would be a mistake.

We were content with one another. Each of us retained our old habits and friends, but we enjoyed our time together without imposing any expectations on one another.

So when she appeared in the doorway of my study, pointed to the plastic cube, and said, "You're not going to leave that in the middle of the floor, are you?" I asked her what she thought about the idea of a memoir, expecting her to be concerned about the role that she would play in such a document.

I was right about her being concerned, but wrong about its cause.

She looked at me like I had said that I wanted to enroll in NASA's astronaut training program. Later, I would recognize that her startled reaction was one of the perverse factors that made the project an imperative. I think that it was the first time that I became aware that others, particularly those close to me, saw me as limited, a once powerful figure but now with diminished capacities. It wasn't just ten-year-old Daniel.

"You want to write your autobiography?"

"I'm thinking about it. More like a memoir, really."

"What's the difference?"

"Mostly scope. An autobiography would cover from birth to death, chock full of details and chronology. A memoir is more selective, maybe focused on some critical years or incidents. It's more about psychology than history."

I watched her closely, easily able to track her steadily increasing skepticism showing up in the deepening furrows of her forehead, the narrowing of her eyes. It was even more evident in her voice, containing the first signs of worry.

"Why do you want to write about yourself? Are you thinking of trying to sell it?"

She was looking closely at me and it occurred to me that she was threatened by the prospect of me delving into my past. The idea offended me. *She has no right to be concerned. So little of that past is about her!*

"Sell it? God, no, of course not!   Actually, I thought that Daniel, or his children if and when he has them, might like to have such a story."

That's not true of course. Given who I am and what I've done, I am visualizing an impactful document, something that would transmit wisdom and change lives. Books like "Conversations With Morrie" or "Lord Chesterfield's Letters to His Son From Exile in Flanders" or, in keeping with my academic past, "The Last Lecture." It can be a brilliant moral narrative that will shape young lives, stir waves of nostalgia among my less-reflective contemporaries -- those who are still around to read it-- and, at the same time, communicate my own essence to later generations.

Face it! You don't even know who your target audience is! You're envisioning a yellow-edged, musty, leather-bound volume that's stored in an old steamer trunk in an uninsulated attic and discovered by happenstance by an ancestor decades from now, to be read sitting on the floor of the attic with soft late afternoon yellow light streaming through a dormer type window.

When I try to clarify what I'm visioning, it's my grandson Daniel, an attractive winsome individual in this scene; middle-aged and harboring faint grudges against me stemming from his imperfect appreciation for who I really was.

Caroline was staring at me, apparently trying to envision me as a vanity-press author. I was amused to realize that her skepticism was increasing my resolve, that what had started as a wishful sort of fantasy was taking on a real shape, that this was something I must do for my own sake.

The reality? Any such literary effort as this will simply demonstrate that my decades-long habit of keeping my thoughts to myself is – at a minimum -- prudent and – at best – a cautionary case study for those who, for whatever reason, think that they have something meaningful to say, and can say it in a manner that could hold the attention of a disinterested stranger, let alone an acquaintance or relative that long ago dismissed the possibility of having their mind changed by anything I have to say.

Ideally, this would be written posthumously; a difficult task. Next best would be to require that it be locked in a time capsule for, say, 50 years.

Then Caroline asked me the obvious question that I hadn't thought of. She was joking, I think, but her question threatened the project before it ever started.

"Don't you have to be famous – or, better yet, infamous – to write a memoir?"

Am I famous? How would I even know?

These days, there is almost certainly a scale of famousness, like the Forbes or Bloomberg's list of top billionaires, or Best Doctors, or Ten Best Places to Retire.

OK, you're supposedly good at empirical research. How would you construct such a scale?

My generation of academic researchers would start with a theory grounded in social sciences, specify the sub-dimensions of 'fame,' design a survey to quantify those dimensions, validate the survey, choose a carefully randomized sample, gather data and calculate confidence intervals.

But that methodology was developed in the days before social media. Today, such a ranking probably would be derived from a tabulation of Google statistics, supplemented by counts of your followers on Twitter and your friends on Facebook. My academic crowd would sneer at the result, call it 'non-rigorous,' but would eagerly test to see where they – and their colleagues – came out on the scale.

Feeling slightly guilty and disloyal to my academic heritage, I googled my name and got 257,000 hits, a number that seemed outrageously large. I scanned the first page of suggested web sites and was slightly dismayed to note that three of them linked to newspapers articles about Deborah's murder.

I typed in 'John Kenneth Galbraith' and got 411,000 hits. *And his wife wasn't even murdered!*

I was hooked. I entered "famous contemporary American economists" and was pleased to note that I was included among the twenty-three names on the most popular website that Google produced.

In my case, there are also the listings in 'Who's Who,' the long list of honorary doctorates from prestigious universities, the official bio with forty pages of references to papers written, talks given and professional honors received, three New York Times bestsellers translated into sixteen languages …

I think I can safely claim to be 'eminent,' without worrying about where I stand relative to the likes of Kissinger, Galbraith or Friedman. Surely, 'eminence' is sufficient justification for a memoir.

I could be accused of dilettantism, I suppose. After all, I have had four interlocked careers, each of them with lots of interesting offshoots.

There was the 'professor' phase, the one that I thought I would never leave. Approximately twenty-five years, not counting graduate school, at Princeton, a respected member of one of the world's most highly rated economics faculties. Some important research, maybe something– a few years from now when the theories have been properly tested -- that would put me in the serious running for a Nobel.

Would I still be a professor if the Soviet empire had not collapsed? Or if Deborah was still alive? I don't think so. The combination of two such cataclysms, one geopolitical and the other one highly personal, had to have an outlet. If I lived in the Middle East, I might have chosen jihad. But the choice was easy for a professor with bestsellers; I became a consultant – career number two -- and I've spent the last twenty years as a global advisor to governments and corporations. I have been close to major institutions in crisis and – more than anything else – have been an observer and occasionally a key player in what is arguably the defining event of the last hundred years – the rise and fall of communism.

The third career is really a blend of the first two, marked mostly by a change in location and title. I rejoined the university world, but this time as a distinguished fossil rather than a striving professor. In early 2000, I left Princeton and went back to Stanford as a "Senior Fellow" at the Hoover Institution on War, Revolution and Peace. There were no teaching or committee requirements, merely the expectation that one would do research and write papers that were related to Hoover's goal: "to advance ideas that support freedom and free enterprise."

Then there's the fourth career. The one that has run for the last thirty years, but cannot be talked about. Me and the Central Intelligence Agency.

Caroline knows nothing about that career. But others do, as I was about to learn.

Little Sisters

The most difficult conversation was with Kristi. Her status as 'kid sister,' with all of its emotional baggage, had always made it hard for us to get beyond the superficial. She was at the door the next morning, straight off the redeye flight from Minneapolis. I guessed that Caroline had called her and told her about my intentions. The fact that she had immediately picked up and flown to California was an ominous sign.

She looked good. She was two years younger than Robert and me and – as far as I knew – lived an uneventful life once she got out the chaos that was our childhood. She'd been looked out for by our neighbor, one of my high school teachers and a woman that was determined to make up for our train wreck of a family. Kristi went to the University of Minnesota and then moved back to the small town where we grew up, working as a schoolteacher and watching out for the next generation of kids needing rescue.

"You're – going – to – write – a – memoir?"

Each word was accented and separate and loaded with incredulity. Together, they conveyed disbelief, sarcasm, amazement and – if one listened closely and knew the back story – fear.

"Yes. Very selective. Very discreet. I was going to call you, but I guess Caroline got to you first."

"Doesn't the ... Don't *your people* have a rule against such things?"

She's guessing. She can't know for sure about that part of my life.

I tried for a puzzled tone. "I don't know who you're referring to, but – whoever they are -- they're not *my people*. And their rules don't apply to me."

The same response I'd been reciting to myself since deciding to go ahead with this idea of a memoir. I have never been an official member of the CIA, have not signed any "I shall never tell" kinds of Official Secrets pledges, have no security clearance, and I do not need their approval of anything that I write. Jacob Connolly has been my sole contact.

Very comforting. But then I always think of all those journalists and federal employees who are in jail for 'endangering national security' or 'leaking classified information.' But the most vivid doubts are evoked by my certain knowledge that the people I want to write about may not care very much about rulebooks, courts-of-law or good public relations.

Robert said it best. He was reminiscing about his early days in counter-insurgency operations. "It was really hard to tell the good guys from the bad guys. So we'd just kill 'em all and let God sort 'em out."

Kristi gave me a look that made abundantly clear what she thought of my argument. But I kept trying. I think that I was trying to convince myself as much as I was Kristi.

"It's not about them, and I'm leaving out anything involving … work … projects that I did for them. It's about my personal and professional life … a vanity press piece."

She waved away that defense. *"They* won't know that and wouldn't believe you if you told them."

"Kristi. You've seen too many James Bond movies. These are Washington bureaucrats. They'll call a lawyer and we'll fight about it with briefs and counter-briefs. At worst, I'll have to redact some sensitive parts."

She was shaking her head emphatically, from side to side with her hair swirling around her face.

"Maybe the world was like that before September 11, 2001. Since then, those 'bureaucrats' – your word, not mine – are also the folks who engage in waterboarding, involuntary renditions and indiscriminate drone strikes. And those are the things we *know* about. C'mon, Brian! You know how little they care about the rules. What they're afraid of is exposure to sunlight. And you're about to turn over the rock that they're under."

And you, Kristi? Do you want those forty-five year old rocks turned over? To revisit that day of Kennedy's inauguration? Is that why you don't want me to write about the past?

It was such a mean and petty thought that I immediately regretted it. But Kristi seemed to be clairvoyant.

"Most of the memoirs that I've read seem motivated mostly by a need to get even with other people close to the author… family members, partners, spouses … It's a vengeful branch of literature. Parents in particular get savaged a lot."

I tried humor. "I'll put it in a time capsule to be opened in fifty years."

She had withdrawn into herself, no longer trying to convince me. I wondered what kinds of mental pictures she was processing.

"Kristi. I promise. No family revelations. This is about me, not you or Robert. Or even them." We both knew who *them* referred to.

She had stopped listening, but nodded and turned away. "I'm at the Sheraton on El Camino. I'll see you later this afternoon."

She stopped in the doorway and looked back at me.

"Brian. You were … are … an economist. What do you call it when a particular policy or initiative has undesirable side effects?" She turned and walked out without waiting for my answer.

The law of unintended consequences.

Kristi had more foresight than any of us. I should have paid more attention.

Men in Suits

Kristi was right. What she called 'those people' inevitably would be heard from. I did not expect them so quickly, but they were waiting for me in the lobby of my Palo Alto office building just two days after Kristi had gone back to Minnesota. They looked like a pair of Mormon missionaries except that they were older and less hopeful looking. They had the leather briefcases, dark suits, white shirts, shined shoes and something in their eyes that said, "Here is a zealous person."

"Dr. Norquist?"

"Yes?" I tried to put as much impatience and annoyance into that single word as I could, figuring them to be lawyers and therefore the sort that I would not do well with, regardless of their mission.

They stood side by side. The slightly taller and younger one did the talking. The main role of his companion seemed to be to stare at me with what he probably thought of as a steely glare, but came off more as a painful squint.

"We represent a Washington DC law firm and the interests of an important client. We understand that you are undertaking to write your autobiography and we are here to advise you not to do so."

What the hell? That was fast. How could they know about my intentions at this stage?

"Do you have business cards?"

"Our visit here is entirely unofficial."

"The name of your client is ....?"

"They prefer anonymity."

"Can we discuss this in my office rather than the lobby?"

"That's not necessary.   We've said everything that needs to be said at this point."

I thought about saying "Central Intelligence Agency," but it was hard to break a thirty-year habit of not mentioning my occasional and unofficial sponsor. Instead, I tried the next best alternative.

"Did Jacob Connolly send you?"

There was no reaction to the name other than the one word response, "Who?" spoken in a tone so devoid of inflection and curiosity that it was a full statement in its own right.

"Never mind. But I'd like to know how you think you know I'm writing my autobiography."

"We're not permitted to say."

"What if I don't?"

The two of them seemed puzzled by the question, reminding me of the age-old student complaint, "But you didn't tell us that was going to be on the exam!"

"Pardon me?"

A trio of twenty-somethings – two men and a woman – entered from the street, headed for the second floor office where they sat huddled over their laptops all day long, perfecting some iPhone app that – according to them -- would change the world. I raised my voice to a pitch that made them stop and stare.

"What if I ignore your *unofficial* advice from an *anonymous* source and I do write my autobiography? What are the sanctions? Is there a fine? Will warrants be issued? Will you confiscate my printer? Does some no-neck thug come by with a baseball bat? Why in the hell should I pay any attention to you?"

The two men looked at one another and apparently agreed on a course of action. They turned and walked out the door, moving as a single unit, like a pair of synchronized swimmers exiting the pool.

The woman looked at me with concern. Her name was Becky and she had a doctorate in computer science from Stanford. She had pitched me on the possibility of funding their startup. "Are you OK, Dr. Norquist? Those guys didn't look real friendly."

"Thanks, Becky. I'm fine. They're just a couple of Mormon missionaries trying to fill their monthly quota."

The Early Years

I defined the forty-thousand word mark as a completely arbitrary halfway point in my mind, the literary equivalent of what the early trans-Atlantic pilots called 'the point of no return.' To my surprise, the words come easily and the act of writing seems to stimulate recall, activating some kind of sensory feedback loop that leads into deeper and deeper recesses of memory. I am beginning to think that the Freudians are right: Perhaps we can neither understand nor cope with our adult pathologies without going back to our childhood.

However, the word count and seeming ease of writing are deceptive. I have systematically ignored the troublesome topics. I am like the historian wanting to depict the horrors of war, but spending his time listing the names and dates of the battles. I have yet to consider the most important topics, the ones that devastate the innocent and thereby drive the sale of memoirs.

The concept of 'childhood' is difficult for me. Most memoirists spend a lot of time talking about their parents and there are entire cultures organized around the commandment "Honor Thy Parents." I regret that I cannot. And it cannot be done retrospectively; it has to be contemporaneous to be virtuous.

My parents were drunks. There is an entire literature devoted to the follow-on impacts of growing up in an alcoholic family. I am the *adult child of an alcoholic family,* a fact that apparently makes much of my current behavior transparent to the social work crowd. I have not looked at such characterizations, although the snippets I have seen or heard seem to be on the mark in my case. And there are numerous self-help groups to coach such people and to help them cope with the lifelong aftermath. However, for me, I choose to distrust anyone – and there are many – who assert that they can predict how I shall feel or act based purely on a biographical fact, even when it seems that they can.

There are benefits to this heritage as well as disadvantages. I believe that it inoculated me with an ability to accept what I'm given. The nagging fear is that – rather than a constructive, admirable acceptance – it's inbred a learned hopelessness that is triggered when some form of outrage would be both justified and useful.

So I have left the topic of 'family' to lie dormant, like one of those World War II bombs discovered buried in some London basement. Then, once more, my grandson Daniel provided the impetus to get serious.

He wandered into my study, clearly bored. I couldn't blame him. Melanie had dumped him on our doorstep for the weekend, saying something about a ballistics conference in Chicago that she couldn't avoid. Caroline was gone most of the time, leaving me to entertain a ten-year-old, a skill that had so far eluded me, even with my own daughter. The immediate and somewhat ironic problem was that I was caught up in writing. What Daniel had started with his simple question several months ago on that road trip to Bakersfield had become a near obsession.

He came in and sat down in the reclining chair. It was his favorite piece of furniture in the house and he always positioned it to maximum recline and then sat cross-legged in the 'V' formed between the lowered backrest and the raised footrest. It reminded me of a boy-king presiding over his court.

"Are you working on your biography?" He put the stress on the first syllable.

"It's a memoir, not a biography." I accented the 'og' syllable and in doing so was reminded of Deborah's long ago teasing: 'You can't stop being a professor, can you?'

Daniel took the criticism in stride. "I know that, but I can't say that word … mem… mem … whatever."

I thought about administering a French lesson but before I decided, he asked, "Are you writing about my grandmother?"

As always, the words 'my grandmother' saddened me. For Daniel, I was 'papa,' an affectionate diminutive that always pleased me. But he had never known Deborah; she died years before he was born, so she became the austere and distant ancestor that he thought of as "grandmother."

"Not yet. But I will. She's very important to my story."

"What was she like?"

It was a perfectly normal question, like a two-year-old asking 'Why is the sky blue?' And just as difficult to answer. Hard not because of any memory lapses, or lack of meaningful experience, or the sense of after-action disenchantment ("*Is that all there is?*") that makes it so deadly dull to write about the past, but rather the opposite. Hard because she has been so much a part of who and what I am, so major a force, so dominant a determinant of what I've done and not done, that any attempt to "describe" our time together is like asking a computer to describe the designer of the core operating system; to ask Pinocchio to describe Geppetto.

I went to the built-in bookshelves on the wall to the right. They spanned the entire space, from corner to corner and from floor to ceiling. They also were the object of a long-running argument between Caroline and me, the battleground for a second wife trying to expunge traces of her predecessor.

Her first attempt was based on logic. "Who needs bookshelves these days? Everything is digital."

My response gave away far too much. What I said was, "First, I like books. Second, that's my life on those shelves. My thesis, college texts, the Hardy Boys, ten years of subscribing to 'Great Books of the Western World' … and all those albums with pasted-in pictures from all those trips."

That's what I said, but I now know that what Caroline *heard* was, *"That's my life before you came along ... my life with that other woman. And I can't lose that!"*

It didn't help that one entire row – at eye level – was filled with framed pictures of that life, many of them including Deborah and me in exotic locations and looking happy.

Caroline's next try, a couple of months later, was based on aesthetics. "This room would be much lighter if we put some French windows on that wall."

I used the *'this is my lair and I like the room the way it is'* argument, but she saw through it immediately, knowing that I detested such appeals to authority as a form of debate. But the shelves stayed. Caroline's only guerilla act was to add several large framed pictures of the two of us at the end of one shelf. The large silver frames tended to draw the eye away from the older photos. Deborah would have called it passive-aggressive behavior.

So Daniel's complicated question 'What was she like?' was easy for me. I walked over to the shelves and took the fattest and oldest album from its place. The album covered what I thought of as 'the early married' years, a time period when Deborah was a lot like what Daniel's mother Melanie is now.

I carried it over to where he was sitting and put it in his lap. The cover was quite dusty and I realized that no one had looked at it for a long time.

Maybe Caroline is right. Maybe it's time for those shelves – and what's on them – to go.

"Here. The best way to know what she was like is to look at pictures. Then, if you like, I'll tell you the stories that go with the photos."

He opened the leather-covered album to the first page. It was a black and white eight-by-ten of Deborah standing in a arched doorway with a small bouquet. It was our wedding day.

There was always Deborah. Until suddenly she wasn't there any more.

I cannot remember our first meeting, but we would have been five or six years old. It was a small town and everybody knew everybody and everything significant about them. It was the kind of classless all-white village that Norman Rockwell documented on the covers of the *Saturday Evening Post*. Main Street was three blocks long and there was only one school, a red-bricked three-story WPA eyesore that housed everything from kindergarten through twelfth grade.

She was – literally -- the girl next door, the one who was part of a normal family; a family that had regular meals, parents to be trusted, a family that celebrated birthdays and went to movies together. Robert, Kristi and I became almost adjunct members of their family, using them as role model and occasional sanctuary. Today, such neighbors would call Child Protective Services, but in those days they simply were there for us, in the best sense.

She was a year younger than Robert and me and one year behind us in school, but the three of us were inseparable, especially in summertime. She was the third musketeer, our skinny, gender-free, tree-climbing best friend. A tomboy with pigtails who could run faster than we could and would never turn down any 'I dare you' challenge.

The setting was made for children growing up wild. We lived on an island, connected by a causeway to the shore. There were a hundred or so families living there, but the island was still heavily wooded and riddled with pockets of swamps and marshes, each with a local legend and enough seclusion to let us act out a Huck Finn kind of existence.

But Deborah was never a sometimes snippy, sometimes adoring Becky Thatcher to my Tom Sawyer. She was one of the boys, as quick to trade insults or initiate a footrace or punch your arm as either Robert or me. She would go to the Tarzan and Roy Rogers Saturday afternoon matinees with us and be just as snarky about the helplessness of Lady Jane Grey and Dale Evans as we were.

That all changed, of course, when puberty showed up, more or less at the same time for the three of us. That summer of 1961 was the dividing line. On those times we were together, there was a hovering uneasiness that we attributed to causes other than our growing awareness of gender differences.

There were other factors as well, that summer. Each of the three of us was working at a part time job, and the deaths of both her father – the local druggist – and our father seemed to require a seriousness that precluded playing in the woods or Saturday afternoon matinees with B-grade movies.

It wasn't just gender: Robert and I were separating as well. We were fraternal twins, but fault lines were beginning to appear. I was cuter, smarter and more athletic, much more likely than Robert to attract adult patrons, particularly teachers. He suffered from the comparison and from that summer on, he would introduce himself as "Brian's brother" rather than "I'm Robert," with a degree of sarcasm that precluded further talk. We began to move in different cliques, me with the college-bound high achievers and him with the borderline juvenile delinquents. We settled into divergent tracks that have continued for the last forty-five years.

I think Deborah saw the schism coming before Robert or me. That summer, she stopped showing up in the woods every morning, pleading 'other things to do.' Somehow, over the rest of that summer, she magically and without any warning morphed into an unattainable, incredibly wise, empathic creature who somehow understood – better than we did -- the hormonal cauldron that was a male teenager in the sixties.

The perennial problem in a divorce is who gets to keep the common friends, and so it was with Robert and me. Deborah was, in a very real sense, community property and each of us laid claim to her and – for the next three years – fought for exclusive access. Not overtly, but every phone call, walk in the woods, or random encounter in the hallways of the school had a 'Pick me! Pick me!' motif running through it. She treated each of us with the same cool neutrality – as a good friend – and finally reinforced that status by dating – the local dialect referred to it as 'going steady' – the quarterback of our high school football team.

The tipping point was a class party in August 1964, a gathering late in the afternoon. There were probably sixty kids from our class there along with their dates, including Deborah with her quarterback. It was the summer after graduation and the party formed in a wooded park on our island. Lyndon Johnson was talking 'domino theory' and ratcheting up the U.S. military presence in Vietnam. The army had opened a storefront recruiting center in our little town, with some success. So the gathering was billed as a 'going away' party for three boys from our class who had enlisted. One of them was Robert.

There was a lot of beer and some marijuana being passed around. But that had nothing to do with what happened.

I was watching Deborah, a practice so ingrained in the last three years that I was no longer conscious of it. I saw Robert approach her and pull her away from the three girls she was talking to. He said something to her that made her take a full step back and stare at him for at least ten seconds. Then she spun away and walked directly to me.

She said nothing, just grabbed my hand and started walking. She walked fast and stayed silent, but she radiated such purpose and intensity that I knew not to say or do anything that would divert her.

We had played cowboys and Indians in these woods and we knew every fold in the ground. She led us to one of our favorite spots. We had named it 'the roofless cave' because it was a small clearing – no more than a dozen feet across – in the middle of a pine tree cluster so dense that you could imagine the greenery to be as impenetrable as rock walls. We had carved the initials 'B+D+R" in the trunk of the massive tree that guarded the entrance to the clearing, as though to warn off trespassers.

It was near sunset and the light in our little clearing was fading fast. She dropped my hand and turned to face me. I remember that she took two steps back as if needing more space between us. Then she kicked off her sandals, pulled off her T-shirt and stepped out of the Bermuda shorts. She stood there in bra and panties – I remember that they were black – and simply looked at me, her hands at her sides.

Years later, we agreed on everything except who moved first to close that yawning six-foot gap between us. She thinks it was her, I say me.

I am sixty-one years old as I write this. I have had two wives and enjoyed a highly satisfactory sex life with each of them. During my unattached days – the last dozen years between Deborah and Caroline -- I have formed relationships with other women and have enjoyed a wide variety of sexual experiences. I have made love to attractive women on six continents and in a score of countries, in cars, boats, trains, planes, hot tubs, castles and tents, under the stars, on a tabletop. I have done it standing, sitting and lying down; slowly and in a frenzy; for love and for expediency; with intense pleasure and bone-deep regret.

But I have never since been with a woman in the way that I was with Deborah in the roofless cave on that summer evening. I have never since experienced such an abrupt change, the unbelievable gulf between the 'beforeness' and the 'afterness.'

I dabbled in meditation in my forties. The therapist leading the group advised us, "Think of a time or place that gave you pleasure, that was calm and you were at peace. Focus on that."

For me, that time and place was that day, in that clearing with Deborah. I still remember vividly the filtered sunlight, the pine needles in her hair, the way her freckles stood out against her skin, the way she laughed at me when I struggled to unsnap her bra.

I also remember how it started. The way Robert pulled her apart from the group and said something to her and how she turned to him and said something just before she started walking toward me so purposefully. Once -- I think it was an anniversary and we were in bed reminiscing about the early days – I asked her, "What did you say to Robert that day?"

She turned away for a second and I had the impression that I had frightened her. Then she turned back and snuggled against me, so close that I couldn't see her eyes.

"Nothing important, really. I don't remember."

Years later, I would ask Robert the same question. His answer was dramatically different.

The next twenty-seven years are documented in the photo albums that Daniel is paging through. Deborah is smiling in almost every photograph, while I look uncomfortable, as though expecting the camera to sting. As I watch over his shoulder, Deborah seems be unchanged by time, while I become stouter and more serious looking ... Her freckles and the tousled short hair that she would comb with her fingers, her shape – even after Melanie was born – and that smile.

Events move incredibly quickly from that day when she chose me over Robert, seeming to run a preordained course, one where the forks in the road are well-marked and easily selected. We are hopelessly young – she's sixteen -- and naïve. We talk of running away to Iowa or South Dakota to get married. Then I'm off to Yale and she's staying to finish high school.

We were formally engaged in 1967, as signified by the impromptu purchase of a $250 diamond ring (*"Only 36 easy monthly payments!"*) from a chain store jewelry store in Minneapolis. Both of us were still in college, me in New Haven and her in Minnesota.

Her family legend has it that we 'eloped' in the fall of 1969, and it is true that, if not planned, the wedding was certainly premeditated. She flew to meet me in Connecticut, her first time on an airplane. We were married on November 9, 1969 in New York City because the State of New York did not have a mandatory waiting period. We bought a dress for her and a wedding ring for me. The ring is in a drawer, just below the phalanx of photo albums.

After the Yale graduation, we stayed on the East Coast, working off of some unseen script that dictated what small-town kids should do after college. I worked for an economics consulting firm in Washington and Deborah got her master's degree in nursing at Georgetown. The future looked bright. And predictable.

I did not feel particularly exceptional. I had earned quite good grades, distinguished myself at Yale, but did not feel that I was off-the-scale or even particularly advantaged on any intellectual, social or occupational dimension. The reality was that both of us still had strong vestiges of our small town insecurities. Our expectations were lower than they should have been and, if we had acted on them – Robert Frost's *the road not taken...*, we would be in a very different place today.

If this was a Victorian novel, the probable phrase would be *"But Fate takes a hand!"* From that point forward, the reality has been far more exotic than any early scripts that we might have concocted.

"Adam thinks I should get a PhD in economics. He says I'm a natural academic."

Adam was my boss, the founder of the consulting firm and an ex-professor of economics from MIT. I was the newest and youngest member of his staff and we had become friends. He never said anything or behaved inappropriately to me, but it was clear that he was gay and still struggling with the idea. He would die of AIDS six years later.

I could see her thinking about it. She had a way of furrowing her brow and closing her eyes to better visualize the columns of pros and cons that she was meticulously constructing.

"I thought – you said – that we were going to buy a house, have a baby, get rich? Does all that go away?"

I thought about it. "No. At least, I don't think it does. It just gets deferred for a couple of years. And maybe we become only semi-rich."

"Would you teach? Do you want to be a professor?"

I said, "Yes" without thinking. But, as I said it, I realized that it was true.

The decision to enroll at Stanford was an easy one. We were attracted to Northern California with its absence of winter and quirky politics, and they offered a generous financial aid package. We moved into student housing and began to actively plan a future life instead of daydreaming. When we had a little extra money, we bought another piece of furniture, early American, from Sears. We acquired a Siamese cat, the first of three over the next twenty years.

I *was* a natural academic. I thrived in an environment where ideas were more important than ideology and any issue was subject to testing and debate. Lateral thinking was prized in a world where any question beginning with 'What if ...' was an acceptable, even interesting, question worthy of pursuit.

We became qualitatively different people during those five years of graduate school at Stanford. Part of the explanation lies in the classic broadening of horizons when provincial villagers move to the big city, or the minor league player to the big leagues. We learned, by simple osmosis, about a much bigger world. For me, it was big-time academics. For Deborah, I think it was the chance to be a fast-track nurse at a world-class medical center and to see herself juxtaposed with other smart women, more than a few of them married to obvious inferiors.

It was also the time and place where I met the three men that would shape the rest of my life.

Valentin

I met Valentin Aslanov at Stanford in 1974, my last year in the PhD program. We were each auditing a class labeled 'The Soviet Experiment.' The classroom was an amphitheater, seating about 100, with four tiers of horseshoe-shaped rows. Valentin and I sat at opposite ends of the highest row, with a dozen or so other students between us and separated by the width of the room. Because of the horseshoe layout, we sat directly opposite one another with the lectern midway between us, so it was both easy and diverting to watch one another. I wondered about him because he, like me, did not ask questions, although he was writing continuously, without paying any apparent attention to the lecture or anyone else in the class.

The course was co-taught by an ex-Ambassador to Hungary and a newly-minted Assistant Professor in the History Department. Unfortunately, their surnames were Abbott and Costello, and even more unfortunately, they managed, without any effort or intent, to act out their comedic roles as surely as though they'd been cast in a remake.

Costello, the history professor, was an ardent theorist, versed in dialectical materialism, thesis and antithesis, metaphysics, and mathematical models of sociological phenomena. He viewed history as the predictable outcome of large causal forces that could be parsed, calibrated and modeled. For him, it was more about social structure than human intervention. Actual *people* were of no interest, dismissed as 'noise,' no more relevant than individual atoms would be to a nuclear physicist.

Abbot was his antithesis, a classic 'good old boy' who was wealthy because his daddy passed on five thousand acres of West Texas grassland that happened to have ungodly amounts of oil under it. He donated enough money to LBJ and Sam Rayburn that he was made an ambassador and – by most accounts – did pretty well as an amateur statesman. Unlike Costello, Abbott's meta-view of history – if he had one – would be *only* about people; larger-than-life characters that changed the course of countries, started and ended wars, made stirring speeches. For him, 'the Soviet Experiment' was a series of anecdotes, colorful stories strung together to tell a more general story.

For me, the course was something to be checked off, to be taken because my thesis chairman thought it would be useful. He was a great believer in 'economic determinism' and I had learned to humor him on this issue. He told me, "You can't understand Marxian economics without knowing about the historical forces that gave rise to the Russian Revolution."

The statement seemed so obviously circular that I didn't bother to respond. And the course syllabus had some interesting readings, some of which I already had on my "some day" reading list. I could audit the class, so it was a painless choice. And after the first few sessions, I found myself caught up in the Abbott and Costello routine, drawn to the clash of styles and wondering if they were even aware of their competition to explain the massive, decades-long communist attempt to overcome human nature.

I dismissed Costello fairly quickly. He was enamored of his just-completed doctoral thesis and was essentially regurgitating it for his students. It also seemed clear to me that he was thoroughly steeped in the prevailing American view of communism in those Cold War years. For him, the 'domino theory' that justified our Vietnam involvement was perfectly compatible with his personal view of history.

At first, I thought Abbott was a likeable buffoon, but came to view him more like a modern-day Aesop. Each of his rambling stories had an implicit moral, and I felt that if only he told enough stories, it would form a grand mosaic whose pattern would reveal some great truth. I also liked him because it became clear that his rationale for choosing his lecture material --- which story he would tell on any given day – was to focus on an incident or event that would resoundingly contradict Abbott's explanation of events.

About two weeks in, after a particularly painful class in which neither Costello's 'socio-cultural algorithms' nor Abbott's long and seemingly pointless thirty-minute description of his luncheon with a semi-drunk Russian general waving a Makharov pistol while reciting Pushkin poems added to my understanding of why communism persisted despite its failings, I came across Valentin sitting at a table in a remote corner of the student union. He had an open book before him but his eyes were closed. His lips were moving and I distinctly heard Chinese phrases. I stopped and stood before him, waiting for him to open his eyes.

I would come to see Valentin Aslanov as the perfect chameleon. He was smart, but did not display it; asking questions instead of providing answers and keeping his opinions to himself. He was cultured, but his behaviors and apparent preferences always seemed to fit with those around him, whether they were student militants, redneck hillbillies or trust fund babies. Most of all, he was passionate about people and causes, but even that aspect was cloaked, to be revealed only at a time and place of his choosing.

That same ambiguity extended to his physical appearance. He was young – twenty-five when we met – but came across as a man twice that age. His nationality could have been Israeli, Turkish, Italian, Greek, Egyptian or from any of the Central European or Middle Eastern states. He wore baggy ill-fitting clothes that obscured an athlete's physique, that of a gymnast or an Olympic swimmer.

That day in the student union, he did not seem surprised to see me standing over him. I started to say, "I'm sorry to interrupt. I'm –"

"I know who you are – Brian Norquist, a very promising PhD student in economics and a fellow Abbott and Costello fan … an earnest student of the great Soviet experiment."

He gestured at the plastic chair opposite him. "Join me. I'm trying to decide which of them I would shoot first if I were the commissar in charge of the revolution of the proletariat – Abbott or Costello?"

Something in the way his eyes held mine as he spoke made his comment into a challenge, making me feel as though he was posing a small test. It annoyed me. I thought about responding in Russian, but that struck me as being showy, and Valentin didn't look like someone who would be impressed by such gestures.

"Costello is certainly the more irritating of the two, but Abbott is a populist, someone who could incite the peasants to riot. I suspect Nikolai Yezhov would happily purge both of them without worrying about the exact order."

I was showing off my knowledge of Russian history, but only a little. In the early seventies, not many people knew very much about Yezhov. He was close to Stalin and became head of the NKVD, Stalin's secret police and the forerunner of the KGB, during the Great Purge. It's estimated that he presided over the execution of well over a million Russians from 1936 to 1938, before he fell out of favor and was in turn executed as 'an enemy of the people.'

Valentin smiled. "Ah, Yezhov... A sad life. Not just because he slaughtered so many people, but then there was his alcoholism and his wife's suicide. And such an ironic end: to be shot personally by a future KGB chairman, in a room of Yezhov's own design. It had a sloping floor to make it easier for hosing away the blood."

I looked at him closely. The details of Yezhov's life and death, as far as I knew, had never been disclosed. He stared back, a bland expression other than the slight smile.

I sat down in the plastic chair opposite him. From there, I could see the title on the book in front of him – 'Quotations from Mao Zedong,' the famous 'little red book' from the People's Liberation

Army. It had been around for several years now, popular with some of the student activists.

When he saw me glance at the book, he said, "Two hundred quotes from the Chairman. I'm learning them in Chinese."

"Why?" Even as I asked, I realized that my one-word question revealed a great deal about my own political biases.

He didn't answer. Instead, he asked me a question.

"Do you think the Dean knew what he was doing when he assigned Abbott and Costello to co-teach a class on Soviet communism? Or is it his intention to confuse the students as a step toward their enlightenment?"

I nodded at the book in front of him. "Like Mao's cultural revolution, maybe? Chaos in place of education?"

He shook his head. "It's like taking a class to learn to swim. Costello lectures us about applied physiology, biomechanics, resistive forces in a liquid medium. Abbott takes us out in a dense fog and has us wave our arms about wildly."

It was such an apt characterization that I laughed out loud, forgetting about my need to impress this curious person.

"Who are you?"

"My name is Valentin Aslanov. I am a student, like you."

"From where?"

He leaned back, letting me stare at him. "Where do you think?"

But I was still young, from the American Midwest, lacking exposure to other races or nationalities except through books or TV news programs. At that time, I couldn't even distinguish between different European accents. To me, he merely looked exotic, faintly dusky, from somewhere far away.

He solved the problem for me. "I am a Kazakh. From Kazakhstan. One of the Soviet Socialist Republics that Abbott and Costello pretend to understand."

The Semipalatinsk Complex is there. Primary site for Soviet nuclear tests.

"But Kazakhstan is ... we are –"

He watched me struggle for a few seconds, and then said, "Yes, it is ... and you are. But your State Department and our Ministry of Cultural Affairs have worked out a modest exchange program. There are five of us in your country and five very earnest American graduate students in Kazakhstan. We study capitalism, they study cooperatives."

"You must be ... such a program must be highly competitive?"

Again that faint smile. "My father is Russian, a colonel in the armored corps."

He paused and then added, "He is the kind of person who hears rumors about secret executions of former NKVD members in the Lubyanka basement."

I was thoroughly hooked, eager to keep this strange conversation going. "How about a beer? Essential experience for a cultural exchange program?" Even as I said the words, I was thinking, *Kazakhstan is a Muslim country. Muslims don't use alcohol, stupid!*

But I was to be shown the first glimpse of the versatility that would be Valentin's hallmark feature for the next few decades.

"OK. One beer for each Mao quote that I can recite in Chinese. Let's go."

It turned out that he had mastered a large number of Mao's thoughts.

A Patron

Life was hectic in the extreme. I was in my last year of the PhD program, finishing up my thesis and interviewing for a job. Deborah was working at the Stanford Medical Center, part of a new hospital unit for children with psychosomatic disorders. Melanie was a one year old that we, like all first parents, viewed as a prodigy.

The academic job market for new economics PhD's was organized along rigid lines, a classic good-old-boy network whereby a half-dozen or so prestige departments competed for the dozen or so 'A-List' graduates that were identified and sponsored by a faculty patron who once had been on that same list. The system ran as a strange but effective blend of meritocracy and patronage.

And I had the right patron. My particular good old boy was Professor Grayson Griggs, winner of numerous honors and recently returned from a stint as Under Secretary of the Treasury for both Lyndon Johnson and Richard Nixon. If he'd been an Oxford don, they would have called him simply an 'old boy' or even a 'gray eminence.' He more or less adopted me early in the PhD program and served as my mentor.

It helped that the field of economics was in flux and in the news. The Bretton Woods currency system had been discarded, oil prices had quadrupled and inflation was running at double-digit rates. The mainstream economic models assumed relative economic stability and did not work very well in 1974. It was a time for new ideas.

I was surprised when Griggs invited us to dinner early in the second year of the program. I'd taken his 'Economic Policy' seminar and we had developed what I thought of as a friendly relationship, but one where we stayed in our respective hierarchal roles as faculty and student.

His wife had died two years earlier and he lived alone in a large house on the old part of the campus. Dinner was served by a couple that apparently lived in the house and took care of the domestic side of things. Deborah and I started out intimidated by both him and the setting, but by the time we got past the salad course, Griggs had charmed both of us into behaving naturally. The wine helped.

Deborah's comment set the tone for the rest of the evening. "You're not as stern as I expected. Are you sure you're a full professor?"

Griggs laughed and launched into a series of anecdotes, beginning with his own early days as a doctoral student at Harvard and winding up with a funny story about his first encounter with Lyndon Johnson in the Oval Office. The stories made him sound a lot like me – small town boy in the big city kind of stuff. By the time dessert was served, we felt that we'd known him forever. And we had told him a good bit about ourselves, probably much more than we realized. Looking back on it, it was a masterful piece of diplomacy on his part.

"So, what are you going to do for a dissertation?"

Deborah and I looked at each other, recognizing that the question was important.

"Uh, definitely something having to do with economic development," I said, trying for a note of tentativeness just in case he disapproved. "Something with empirical and theoretical innovations."

His tone was casual, but his eyes looked directly into mine. "How about modeling what the transition from a socialistic system to a market oriented economic structure might look like?"

Is that a question or a demand? Time to waffle a bit.

"Not much data to work with, is there? Maybe a handful of African and South American countries."

But Deborah had little stomach for indirection and said what we were both thinking. "Kind of headed the other way, isn't it? Looks like Vietnam is going to wind up on the socialistic side, and then the domino effect kicks in?"

Griggs shook his head and, for the first time that evening, became completely serious. "That's the past. There are going to be a whole flock of autonomous and clueless economies looking for economic models to help them make exactly that transition."

He's talking about the Soviet Union and its so-called federation of fifteen soviet socialist republics. Our arch enemy in the never ending Cold War. Does he think it's going to magically disappear?

For someone like Deborah and me, coming of age in the sixties, the idea seemed preposterous. It would be another fifteen years before Griggs' forecast would come true and, even then, the implosion would surprise everyone.

"Uh, that's a long way off, isn't it?" *I hope that comes across as respectful disagreement!*

He wasn't even listening. He leaned forward and raised his voice, gesturing to punctuate what he was saying. "The communist model is unsustainable – economically, politically and psychologically. Capitalism is highly flawed, but there's no question that the Soviet Union will collapse and that we – the western economies – will 'win,' and I think that's going to happen sooner rather than later. And when it does, all those new prime ministers and policy makers are going to be looking around for an instruction manual to help them with the transition."

His passion was obvious and Deborah suddenly looked a bit like a deer in the headlights. Griggs noticed and sat back, waving his hand as if to reassure her that it was a momentary lapse. "Oops! Sorry about that. Every now and then, I start thinking I can see the future. The condition seems to come on shortly after drinking too much wine."

Six months after that dinner, I asked Griggs to be my thesis advisor and sketched out a series of potential papers concerning a theory of developmental economics as applied to a sovereign decision to convert from a centrally planned to a market-based economy.

He seemed pleased, but he warned me as well. "You know that some of my colleagues will view you as if you were Noah before the rains came, shouting about the need to build an ark?"

He was right, of course. But he also told me, "But, remember: Noah was right. The rains came. If you do it well, you'll be famous."

He was right about that too.

Jacob Connolly

I first encountered Jacob Connolly at Stanford, in 1974.

There was nothing about him or our meeting that hinted at how intertwined we would become. At least from my end of the relationship. Certainly, our first meeting was perfectly ordinary, one of those many everyday chance encounters that acquire meaning only after the fact.

I know now that it was not chance, that Jacob had been pointed at me.

Sitting at my desk in the year 2007, it is easy for me to see why I was singled out by Jacob. I suspect that I was 'recommended' by Griggs, but by then I had published two papers in respected journals and had a foot on the first rung of the academic ladder. The papers were highly technical; econometric applications enabled by rapid advancement in computing technology and only somewhat related to the theory of transitioning economies that Griggs and I were fleshing out.

For Jacob, I suspect that I was at that point in our respective careers 'a prospect,' one of many that might have some promise. We met at a symposium on Marxist economics. It was lightly attended by faculty and doctoral students. After the Q&A session, Jacob appeared at my elbow.

"Kind of an oxymoron, don't you think? This thing called Marxist economics?"

The man was ordinary in every way except one. Maybe ten years older than I was, of medium height and weight with thinning fair hair. Dressed in a slacks and a sport coat whose pockets seemed to be filled with heavy objects, wearing a checkered blue shirt and tie. The clothes were slightly wrinkled and did not fit particularly well. He was carrying a yellow legal pad that seemed to be filled with incredibly elaborate doodles.

The feature that made him everybody's favorite uncle was his look of perpetual amusement, like a person anticipating the punch line of an overlong joke. Yet his mouth and eyes somehow combined to make it seem that nothing could surprise him, that he had seen everything and heard everything, that he had no expectations and therefore was incapable of disappointment. He was Buddha, absent every emotion except cynicism.

He was standing in the aisle, taking up enough space that it would be awkward to get by him, smiling as though to acknowledge that he understood his question to be simple-minded. Both the smile and the question provoked me, as was his intention. But I didn't know that then. I would learn that years later, in a bar in Helsinki.

But in 1974, in Palo Alto, at the workshop on Marxist Economics, I knew nothing about him. Jacob was merely a slightly annoying man standing in my way making trite comments about something that I knew more about than almost everyone else in the non-communist world.

"Marx was a good economist who got hooked up with bad politicians," I said, and tried to push past him.

He stood aside and let me get about five feet past him before he said, "Better than the alternative, don't you think? A good politician with bad economic advisors?"

I don't remember what I said, probably nothing. At that time, I was like most doctoral students deep into the recruiting season, thinking that I knew more than anyone else about my subject matter. I thought nothing of the encounter for another six months.

It was the week of the Stanford graduation and my thesis chair Professor Griggs had invited Deborah and me for another dinner at his house to, as he put it, "celebrate the beginning of an enormously distinguished academic career." He had promised to invite the two other members of my thesis committee, but when we got there precisely at six, we found the other invitees to be Valentin Aslanov and Jacob Connolly.

Griggs apologized as soon as he answered the door. "Grierson and Abelson couldn't make it, but they said to tell you how pleased they are with your dissertation and your appointment to the Princeton faculty. And they mean it."

Behind him, holding drinks and looking uneasy, Valentin and Jacob stood together, but with the telltale stiffness of two strangers sharing a long elevator ride in silence. Griggs took Deborah by the hand and said, "I understand that you know Valentin, but this is Jacob Connolly. He's a good friend of mine; an old ally from the never-never-land called Washington DC. He's in town for some professional meetings, so I invited him for dinner. And he's also very interested in the kind of possibilities that Brian is going to have everybody talking about."

"And exactly what possibilities would those be?" Valentin asked in a way that made it clear he already knew and disagreed with the answer.

Griggs turned to Deborah. "Mr. Aslanov is from Kazakhstan. He has been auditing two of my classes … and asking most uncomfortable questions … the kind that remind me of me when I was his age and listening to very old and obsolete professors teaching about a world that had changed without their realizing it."

He turned to Valentin. "I'm really pleased you could join us tonight Valentin. I wish we could have thousands of your countrymen visit us. This so-called Cold War would be over much sooner."

Connolly spoke very softly, almost apologetically. "Perhaps Valentin thinks it would end even sooner if thousands of Americans could see the merits of communism as it actually works in his country?"

"Have you been to Kazakhstan, Mr. Connolly?" Valentin asked.

Jacob looked at him with his usual amused expression. "Not very likely, is it, for a Washington bureaucrat to be roaming around Russian satellites? There's that very real obstacle they call the Iron Curtain."

Drinks went on for a long time. Griggs said something about his cook wanting to try something new. By the time we sat down to dinner, all five of us were slightly intoxicated and the conversation was animated, ranging over music and current events, including Richard Nixon's impeachment and resignation.

If there was a center of attention, it was Valentin. He was the exotic one among the four of us and, no matter what the topic, he seemed to have an informed opinion. After a while, Griggs, Jacob and I sat back and watched and listened as Deborah and Valentin shared funny stories about their respective histories and cultures. It made me realize that someone growing up in a small town in Minnesota might have a lot in common with a contemporary from a tribal culture on the other side of the world.

"So, a Kazakh man can steal a bride?" Deborah pretended to be shocked.

"Yes, but only if he has a very fast horse," Valentin said with a straight face.

Jacob had stayed on the sidelines until then, but he effectively ended the bantering at that point. "Your fast horse didn't help you with Stalin. He pretty well eradicated your Kazakh culture with forty years of collectivization, resettlement, gulags and nuclear tests."

It was such a sharp change in tone that all four of us looked at him in surprise. He pretended to be surprised. "Oops! Sorry. That was not –"

"Jacob." The single word from Valentin brought on a ten second silence and gave him the floor. "You have obviously studied our history. Very unusual for, as you say, a Washington bureaucrat. What exactly do you do in Washington?"

A good question, I think. I also am interested in what Mr. Jacob Connolly does.

Jacob waved his hand in the air. "I am in public relations. I tell stories and draw pictures in the air that make my clients look better than they are. I help people to want things that they don't need. I am the cornerstone of American capitalism."

"Mao Tze-tung clearly had you in mind," Valentin said. "He said that there are two revolutionary principles to follow. One is to focus on the actual needs of the masses rather than on what *we* think they need, and the other is to allow the masses to make up their own minds instead of *us* making up their minds for them."

He looked slightly startled at his own words. "And I am slightly drunk. I know that because I have started making speeches. I think I should go home now."

Jacob spoke up quickly. "Let me drive you. I promise not to talk about politics."

Deborah and I left at the same time as they did. For us, it was a pleasant tree-lined ten-minute walk from the old part of campus to the student housing high-rise where we had lived for five years.

"That was nice of Griggs," I said.

"Griggs is a schemer," Deborah scoffed. "A long range planner who plays chess using real people instead of pawns and rooks. You know that this dinner had an agenda, don't you? We just don't yet know what it is."

"Yes, there was an agenda. And, no, I don't know what it is." *But I don't think his agenda has much to do with us. It's all about Valentin and Jacob.*

We walked in silence for a couple of blocks. This would be our last night in Stanford student housing. Tomorrow, we started driving to Princeton and I think both of us felt that this was the end of an era.

"We've come a long way, haven't we?" Deborah said so softly I almost couldn't hear her.

That red brick schoolhouse ... The three musketeers living in the woods ... That house on the channel with the black ice. The roofless cave on that day ... It's an easy question to answer.

"Yes, we have. A long, long way."

She took my hand and tugged at me to speed up. "C'mon. I want to make love with you. Urgently."

I said, "Must be all that wine," but I started walking faster.

"Nope." And she did a quite accurate impersonation of Griggs, saying, "We're going to celebrate the beginning of a enormously distinguished academic career."

Robert

Caroline, as the second but current wife of a wannabe memoirist, is at some mild risk of embarrassment; and even that would probably arise mostly from her association with me rather than from any grand revelation about her.

But my brother Robert is a different matter. We grew up together, loved the same woman, and share far too many dirty little secrets. I owed him a chance to weigh in on the idea of a memoir.

He was easy to find, the corner booth at the 620 Club on El Camino. It was a seedy bar named for its street address and the interior was no more imaginative than the name. Most of the lighting was generated by neon signs advertising various beers. A mahogany bar with about a dozen stools ran the length of the room, the rest of the space was filled with tables and – on the wall opposite the bar – booths with backs high enough to make the inhabitants feel somewhat insulated from the others. The row of poorly lit spaces always made me think of the catacombs. All in all, it was a habitat for serious drinkers.

Robert was there on most afternoons. From the doorway where I stood, he seemed out-of-place … better dressed, more executive–like than what one would expect to find in such a place. It was easy to see him as the lawyer or accountant calling on the owner for some professional purpose, rather than an alcoholic who spent far too much time drinking in such an unpromising venue.

The effects of his cirrhosis were less visible in the dimly lit room. For a brief moment, I chose not to see the gauntness or the jaundice that were the outward markers for the willful destruction of his liver. He was committing suicide one drink at a time.

We'd talked about it only once, although I should have picked up on it two years ago, on the day he retired from the army. Even though it was forty-one years in the past, I remembered the day of his enlistment vividly, because it was the day that Deborah made her choice at our high school graduation party on the island.

He retired as a brigadier general, a high enough rank to warrant a small and informal ceremony at the Officier's Club on the base, some thirty or forty people. Kristi and I were there together, one of those rare times when the three of us were in the same place at the same time. Robert looked really good in his uniform, healthy and fit, but it was all for show.

"Congratulations Robert. You made it to the top." I'd looked it up. The number of brigadier generals is capped at 150 in the U.S. Army.

His smile was more like a grimace. "A long way from the top, Brian. But I've been told that I'm done."

"You're not even sixty years old. Just right for a few corporate boards, maybe a CEO of one of the major defense contractors –"

"Not for me." He glanced down at the substantial array of colorful ribbons on his tunic. "These medals? They're for doing the kinds of things that don't look so good after the fact. It seems that morality is both retroactive and contextual rather than absolute these days. Anyway, I'm not interested. I've had enough of hierarchies, whatever form they take."

Kristi asked the question for both of us. "So, where to? Back to Minnesota?"

He looked directly at me. "I was thinking of Northern California. I've been in too many cold climates."

It was unexpected, and I felt a small shiver of apprehension. *He's your brother. You've seen him – what? – maybe a dozen times in as many years? Why are you bothered by having him in the neighborhood?*

I think I reacted quickly enough that neither of them noticed the hesitation. "That's great! Come and stay with me. I've got plenty of room and can introduce you to some interesting people … Give you a chance to decide on next moves."

He stayed with me for three months. It quickly became apparent that he was struggling with something. He was gone during most of the day, long runs in the morning and off to meetings of an undisclosed nature in the afternoons and evenings. And he looked stressed. I was traveling a good bit of that time, so our relationship was more like that of landlord and tenant than that of two brothers with deep dark secrets that should have been talked about rather than left to fester.

The first real communication didn't happen until he was moving out. He'd bought a small house in the coastal hills, joking that "I can finally look down on you." I asked him, "Are you OK for money? Can you support your life style on a brigadier general's pension?" He'd triggered the question by saying something about needing a 'second career.'

I thought it was a safe topic, but it wasn't. The good news was that it broke through the invisible wall that we had tacitly accepted.

He thought about it. Longer than seemed necessary.

"I could, I suppose. Especially with the disability add-ons."

I was startled. "Disability? I didn't know you had –"

He went on in a rush. "Liver problems. Actually, cirrhosis. Hell! Call it what it is – alcoholism."

I realized that Jacob Connolly had told me as much, is his usual elliptical fashion. Maybe four or five years ago. One of those conversations whose purpose became apparent long after it occurred. "Your brother, Robert? He could go a long way up the Pentagon ladder if he paid more attention to his off-duty habits."

Not for the first time, I was surprised by his references to other members of my family. And, as always, I resented it. As though I could set boundaries around my involvement with the CIA. Back then, I tried to keep as much distance between Connolly and what I thought of as 'my normal life' as I could. As though I had any control.

Robert was looking at me strangely. I think he expected a shocked outburst. The best I could do was a lame, "Alcoholism? But –"

He just looked at me, very sadly. I think both of us at that instant were envisioning our father staggering across the frozen channel to that small-town bar, muttering over and over to himself about 'them.' It was an image that would not fade through time.

"Early stage liver disease. Too much booze for too long. But it can be arrested, maybe even reversed. If I can stop drinking."

There was a lot of emphasis on the word 'if.'

"Robert, if there's anything … anything … that I can do –"

"You already have." He gestured vaguely toward the window onto the street. "You've provided a halfway house. And I'm going to meetings. Hell, if I can live in a cave in Pakistan for two months eating goats and pretending to be a Muslim fanatic, I should be able to stop drinking."

It worked for a while. He went to AA meetings, even sponsored a few newbies, usually military types coming back from Afghanistan or Iraq. He got his realtor's license and worked as much or as little as he cared to. But there was a lingering darkness that hung about him. In the middle of a conversation, he would suddenly go quiet and seemed to be listening to something inside his head.

One of those times, I asked him, "Are you OK? You have this habit of disappearing without going anywhere."

All he said was, "I can stop drinking, but I can't stop the thinking."

It lasted about eighteen months. There was no dramatic single moment, no rash of DUI's or outbreaks of self-pity. He just started going to bars again. Our visits became less frequent and the intervals between them were long enough that the physical changes were quite perceptible.

He had his first heart attack three months ago, serious enough that Kristi flew in and both of us sat in the meeting with the medical team, one of whom was an gastroenterologist. She was a tough looking Chinese-American woman whose idea of a bedside manner had apparently been copied from a Marine Corps drill sergeant.

"You're going to die if you don't stop drinking. Your system can't take much more."

Robert smiled at her, as though she was the bearer of good news. "How long will it take ... assuming I keep drinking?"

She didn't blink. "Think of it this way. Your liver weighs about three pounds. Assume each glass of hard liquor kills a tenth of an ounce. You do the arithmetic. Then divide your answer by two, because you'll die because of the toxins that build up as your liver dies."

She smiled right back at Robert. They could have been discussing the weather. "It's your call," she said. "They'll write 'coronary incident' on the Death Certificate. But they might as well put 'Jack Daniels.'"

"Actually, I prefer scotch." And Robert walked out of the room, leaving Kristi and me to look at one another.

It wasn't scotch. Both Robert and the woman sitting opposite him in the booth had a bottle of beer – no glasses – in front of them. The woman seemed to be paying close attention to whatever he was saying.

He saw me watching him from the doorway and waved me over. "Hello, little brother. Are you looking for a broker? It's about time you began to think about downsizing ... something on one level ... close to good medical care ... I'll cut my usual commission in half for family."

The 'little brother' bit was standard for Robert. We were fraternal twins, but he was born ten minutes before I was and it's been a running joke between us. We inherited nothing but debts from our parents, so primogeniture has not been an issue

I pulled a chair away from the nearest table and sat down, placing it as if it was important for me to be equidistant from each of them.

Robert gestured at the woman. "This is Angie. She was asking me about whether she should get a broker's license. Angie, this is my brother Brian. He's the successful brother."

Angie smiled at me in a sad way that made it easy for me to construct an instant and entirely imaginary history for her. *In her early fifties. Recently divorced – dumped for a younger woman -- after a forty year marriage. The kids are gone and she's gotten a great settlement, but she "needed something to do" and since she had lived in the community for a long time and knew all the neighborhoods, why not get a real estate license? Work when you want. Meet new people. Make a little money. Maybe find another man.*

"Hello Robert. And Angie ... nice to meet you, but I have to warn you about keeping bad company. Robert here is –"

Robert put up a hand as though to physically block the words before they could get to her. "Pay no attention to him, Angie. He's been either a professor or a consultant ... knows nothing about the way things really work."

Some old mantra. The shrinks would probably call it a defense mechanism. Two brothers, fraternal twins, growing up in chaos. Same challenges to overcome, but he's a drunk and I'm one of the masters of the universe. I'm his worst enemy ... the benchmark against which he is constantly measured. Even after – what? – fifty years or so?

I know better, but it's always easier to keep to the same old dysfunctional patterns where Robert is concerned. "I haven't been a professor for a long time. But I do know how things work ... at least the things outside of bars."

It was stupid of me, particularly given what I hoped to accomplish on this visit. But it did serve one purpose: Angie picked up on where this was headed – which didn't require a whole lot of clairvoyance -- and slid out of the booth.

"I'll leave you two to work out all your old family rivalries. Thanks, Robert, for the advice. I'll catch you in the next day or so."

I took Angie's place opposite him. "I'm sorry, Robert. That was a cheap shot."

He leaned forward on his elbows, looking closely at me. Then he shrugged and leaned back again. "No harm, no foul. Anyway, it's a war I lost a long time ago."

I was never able to calibrate his degree of inebriation and I had come to believe that it was a constant, hovering just short of some magical tipping point that would transform him into an obvious out-of-control, in-your-face drunk, someone like our parents. For those who knew him well, the unpredictability made him seem dangerous, someone to beware of.

I tried for a conciliatory tone. "I wanted to get your input on something."

"That would be a first. What is it? Whether the Chinese should devalue their currency? Should Putin sell off some of the lesser state assets? Will the Euro survive the Greek profligacy?"

"I want to –"

"Or is it more about domestic policy? Time to raise the Fed Funds rate? Jack up infrastructure spending? To deregulate or reregulate? Whether or not to –"

"Robert. Stop."

The tone got through to him. He stopped talking and leaned back with his arms folded across his chest, the body language clearly signaling that he was not looking forward to what was coming.

"I want to – no, I'm *going to* – write a memoir. A short and selective history of me. I wanted you to know about it. No surprises."

I don't know what he was expecting. After all, our visits were infrequent and awkward for both of us. The conversations were stilted, limited to current events. Each of us tacitly accepted that we had little in common except our early childhood.

Which we would never talk about, ever.

But then he did.

"Will you write about our childhood? Our family? All those warm and cozy Ozzie and Harriet moments that characterized our growing up?"

Our parents were drunks. Our shared memories are of poverty, vicious quarrels, shame – public and private, ours and theirs -- anger, insecurity and sadness.

The quarrels would have been memorable if they were not so frequent as to become ordinary. By herself, Mom was a maudlin drunk – sloppy & self-pitying. Dad was a mean drunk – accusatory & vindictive. It always started with the two of them drinking together amicably, which, after a while, would lead to a mild disagreement. Escalation was slow at first but always accelerated to its final stage – an all out drunken brawl featuring shouting, invective, sometimes ineffective blows, and – worst of all to a child -- hideous accusations. I do not recall, nor do I think it mattered very much, what the shouting was about. Intervention at any stage was hopeless and it ended only when an alcoholic stupor would set in.

Robert was watching me closely and I wondered what particular videos he was viewing in *his* head. He had much better recall than I did, particularly about the nasty stuff.

That awful night on the black ice? Wondering how Kristi would find ways to cover up her shame? Or maybe all those times with Deborah and how she promised that she would find a way to marry both of us 'when the three of us grew up?'

I thought of lying, telling him that I'll confine the narrative to my adult and professional life. But then I remembered Ashley's 'It's got to be about *you*.' So I told him what – at that time -- I thought was true.

"I'll sanitize the story. We'll come off looking as wholesome as the Bobbsey twins."

"Would that be Nan and Bert? Or Flossie and Freddie?"

He devoured every book that he could get his hands on when we were growing up, whether it was the Hardy Boys or Churchill's six-volume chronicle of the British experience in World War II. I escaped from the chaos of our family through other people -- teachers and rescuers of other forms; Robert escaped through books. But he could not escape the family curse of alcoholism. He lost the genetic lottery.

"Robert, you're going to have to trust me on this. The reason I came, I wanted you to know about the project before you start hearing about it from others."

He waved his empty beer bottle at the bartender across the room, signaling for one more. Then he pointed it at me, like the barrel of a gun. "Be careful, little brother. You might discover some things about yourself, and maybe some other people, that you really don't want to know."

I was still smug at that stage, thinking that I knew all the dark spots, and even if I didn't, that I would be able execute a nifty little emotional sidestep around them as they appeared out of the past.

I was so wrong about so many things.

Melanie

The next day, I was in my office in Palo Alto, trying to make myself read the first page of a twenty-page document for the fourth or fifth time. I fooled myself that my lack of progress was due to the pretentious title – "The Art of the Memoir" – or perhaps because it was a narrative rather than a PowerPoint presentation, but the real reason I couldn't get past that first page was the absence of motivation. I'd come across the book in the 'used' stack on the table at the library and picked it up on a whim, knowing that I wasn't susceptible to advice.

Because of my occasional work with James Rodin's hedge fund, I had a very executive-like office on the third floor looking out at a quiet side street and the back entrances to several shops and restaurants on University Avenue. I spent a lot of time – especially when I was trying to avoid reading pretentious documents – looking out the window, mostly watching the homeless population sorting through the recycling and trash bins. Sometimes I would make up stories about the more interesting pedestrians, especially if they were female and good-looking.

The one just getting out of the Subaru SUV certainly met those tests. She was tall and athletic looking. Very blond and Nordic. It was easy to imagine her wielding a two-handed broadsword and wearing one of those horned Viking helmets. She was probably eighty yards away and her face was obscured by a floppy-brimmed hat, but I knew that she had startling green eyes and a wide mouth that laughed a lot. I also knew that she gave off vibrations that attracted small children but at the same time warded off easy intimacies advanced by either men or women and that she had an easily-triggered intolerance for stupidity.

She'd been my daughter for thirty-three years and I was constantly dismayed by her ability to surprise me.

I can tell from the way she walks that she has an agenda and is headed for my front door. I think I know what she has in mind and I make a small bet with myself: If I'm right about her intentions I'll buy myself the new laptop that I don't need and that costs too much. As is my custom, I carefully avoid specifying what I lose if I'm wrong. It's a sure thing bet.

As it sometimes did, such thinking triggered one of my fonder memories. It was the early days and Deborah and I were still getting to know one another. We were in bed together in some New England bed-and-breakfast and I had just told her about my habit of betting with myself.

She immediately zeroed in on the inconsistency. "Lemme see? If you're right, you win. If you're wrong, you don't lose?"

When I said with a straight face, "Asymmetric loss functions are constructive motivators in bilateral bargaining situations," she smiled, pulled the covers up over our heads, wriggled in a special way and said, "So, a 'bilateral bargaining situation,' that's kind of what we're engaged in here, isn't it?"

It was a pleasant memory and I was immersed in it, so I was startled by the single word, "Hey." Caroline had told me just last night that I was doing that more lately; 'zoning out' was her phrase.

Melanie stood in the open door. Actually, it was more like a vertical reclining posture, leaning against the doorframe with her arms crossed and the usual faintly concerned expression that reminded me of my age and the difficulty of children accepting their parent's increasingly evident mortality.

"Oh, good! It's my favorite FBI agent. But 'Hey?' Is that the same as 'hello' or 'hi' or 'good morning?'"

She pushed herself off and came in, sitting down at the conference table in the corner rather than in the chair facing my desk. And she closed the door behind her.

Oh, oh! This is not going to be one those bantering improv sessions that we both enjoy so much. She definitely has an agenda.

It quickly became apparent. "I heard that you're writing your autobiography."

It was not a question and her tone reeked of disapproval. I think that was the first time that I became fully aware of the emotional fallout that was possible. Later, I would wonder at my obliviousness. After all, literature from King Lear on is filled with pathological relationships between fathers and daughters.

"Not an autobiography, a memoir."

"Why?"

"For Daniel, I think. A few decades from now."

"He ask?"

"No."

"Finished it?"

"Nope."

"Do you really think that's a good idea?"

"Don't know yet."

I'm using the verbal equivalent of Muhammad Ali's famous 'rope a dope' strategy and she knows it. And she knows I can keep it up longer than she can. In fact, I learned the mechanics from her: It's an exact reversal of our roles when she was a teenager and I was her overly concerned protector.

She sighed, a quite loud and overly dramatic sigh, and pulled a tissue from the box in front of her and waved it back and forth over her head, the classic white flag of surrender. "I give up. No more uncomfortable questions. Whaddya think about the Giants chances for the pennant?"

We're so much alike. Genetics at its best. Or maybe worst. 'Never complain, never explain' as a way of life. Independence above all. A 'what will be, will be' view of a world that is almost always disappointing.

I left my desk and joined her at the table. "It's a memoir, Melanie. Very selective. Sanitized, saccharine and bowdlerized. A cure for insomnia… for both me and the readers, if there are any."

She planted her elbows on the table and leaned forward, signaling the importance of what she was about to say. She even dropped her voice very close to a stage-like whisper. Her playacting somehow dramatized the seriousness of what she said.

"You've led a very colorful life. Some people might feel threatened if you were to share stories about them."

How much does she actually know about what I did? In theory, the FBI and CIA worked independently, but Melanie had been around long enough and knew quite well what the rules of engagement were when Langley was involved with the mission.

The furrows on her brow got deeper. "Did Caroline put you up to this? What did she say?"

At first, whenever the topic of 'Caroline' came up, I listened carefully for any over or undertones of hostility or resentment about her stepmother. *The woman I had chosen to replace her mother!* But I gave it up when I realized that both of them viewed me as a shared reclamation project and collaborated with one another on the best way to go about it.

"Actually, she didn't know about it. But once I told her, she said that she thought it was a really bad idea."

"Did she say why she thought it was a bad idea?"

"Not specifically, but you know how she feels about people who talk about their feelings in public."

A definite taboo for Caroline. Well-bred folk keep their troubles to themselves. A 'what's in the family stays in the family' creed that gets reinforced by her clients over and over. Angry rich people getting divorced, spilling venom all over her shiny and uncluttered lawyer's desk.

I asked, without caring very much about the answer, "So who blew the whistle on me?"

"Uncle Robert. He said you asked him for some old files for 'your project.'" She paused and then added, "He also had the impression you were into some research about mom. It bothered him enough that he called me."

You were seventeen years old when she died. I wasn't there for you, but he was. He was Uncle Robert, the 'good family friend' who filled in as a parent figure while I was running around the third world as a salesman for capitalism, a Willy Loman with better suits and more degrees.

"Melanie, I –"

"Will she be in your book? How about that bit about how she died and it took you five days to get home to your teenage daughter because you were *busy?* "

That single word – *busy* – contained enough pent-up hurt and anger to remind me that some injustices do not dim with time, that fifteen years is not long enough to forget or – if you can't forget your grievances -- forgive them.

She thinks I was at an academic conference in Prague, too absorbed in my work to leave for a family emergency. The simple and unforgivable reality was that I did not know about Deborah's death. I was locked up in a safe house in Bulgaria, on an assignment for the CIA. Jacob didn't tell me about Deborah until after the Bulgarian central banker had been thoroughly debriefed.

Bulgaria (1991)

They called it 'the end of history.' With a few pen strokes, Mikhail Gorbychev had just officially dissolved the Union of Soviet Socialist Republics, triggering waves of euphoria. There was talk of disarmament, world peace, and the triumph of capitalism. It was disruptive innovation on a massive scale.

Among other things, chaos breeds opportunity. And if there are suddenly hundreds of billions of dollars of assets whose ownership is either ambiguous or slated for 'privatization,' the opportunists will be thick on the ground.

I was watching CNN coverage of street celebrations in various ex-Soviet satellites on the small television set in my Princeton office when Jacob came in. The screen was showing a half-dozen young Latvians waving flags and hugging one another.

He stood looking at the TV. "Happy, aren't they?"

"With cause," I said. "It's a brand new world for them."

"That's true, but it won't be what they're envisioning. They have no idea what's about to hit them."

I wanted to argue with him just on general principles, but I knew he was right. I was considered to be one of the world's experts on transitioning economies, and all of my research pointed to things getting worse, maybe a lot worse, before they got better. And those hurt the most would be those at the bottom of the economic pyramid. It was hard for me not to feel sorry for the kids on the screen.

I pointed at the TV before I turned it off. "I gather the reason you're in my office has something to do with that?"

"I'd like you to spend a few days in Bulgaria."

"Doing what?"

He sat down, clearly settling in for a more substantive discussion. He gestured at the silent TV. "What you see going on there means nothing. The real action is the feeding frenzy that's about to start."

I knew quite well what he was referring to, but said nothing. I was curious how he would characterize what was about to happen.

"As you know better than most" he said, "virtually all of the resources of ex-Soviet states are controlled by different parts of the state, often some branch of the military. A year or two from now, they'll have been auctioned off at fire-sale prices or given away. There's a huge 'first mover' advantage for all the generals, ex-party bosses and – not so surprisingly – the mafia."

"You've read my book." Chapter 3 was entitled 'The Big Selloff' and took sixteen single-spaced pages to make the same point.

"I have read it. I told you so, a long time ago. And I've also read Chapter 4."

Chapter 4: It is important to create competitive private markets quickly, even if such privatization is done inefficiently and, inevitably, with substantial corruption. The best way to minimize the longer run inequities is to get it done quickly and emphasize transparency during the transition.

Jacob pointed at me. "It's all about information right now. The person with the most and best information will be the big dog. Where's the real value and who do you have to know to get on the inside track?"

"And you just happen to know someone that has that sort of privileged information?"

"I have some leverage on a man named Vasily Boronov. He's essentially the chief accountant for the central bank of Bulgaria. He doesn't like his boss. Says that the fellow is about to give away state assets to his friends and relatives. He thinks that he can trade what he knows for a villa in Spain."

"What do you think I can do for you?"

"Debrief him. Get what he knows. I've tried, and I think I understand it from about the forty-thousand foot level. But I'm lost when he gets down to where it matters. He pulls out these balance sheets and ledgers, talks about counter-flows, second-tier accounts and mezzanine reserves. I can't tell if he's just an incurable nerd or whether he's trying to scam me."

So I went to Plovdiv, Bulgaria's second largest city; to a small house in the shadow of a Russian Orthodox monastery dating back to the Middle Ages and next to a bar that seemed to run on a twenty-four hour basis. He introduced me to Boronov and then left, not to return until four days later.

On the fifth day of the session, in the middle of long and tedious explanation by the banker about Bulgarian foreign exchange controls, Jacob suddenly declared the session over. He gestured for me to come outside.

"Do you think he's telling the truth? Can we use him?"

It was the question he always asked. I had come to believe that he had recruited me as a sort of portable Rosetta Stone, his means of decoding arcane languages. I was his second opinion on any and all matters involving data or theories that could be and often were used as straight-faced support for two diametrically opposed alternatives.

In this case, it was easy. "He's scamming you. His trade statistics are from a three-year old UN white paper and those so-called 'reserves' are as fictional as his conversion from communism. They were used to bail out two state banks that make a lot of uncollectible loans to his family members. The only true thing he said was that he wants to stop his boss from cherry-picking all the bank's assets, including the cash in the vault. That's because he wants to get to it first."

Jacob nodded, but he wasn't paying much attention.

"I've arranged for a military jet to take you home," he said. He wouldn't look at me and was uncharacteristically subdued. "Deborah had an accident and you need to get home as quickly as possible."

The flight from Plovdiv stopped once to refuel. I thought about asking the pilot to try some kind of communication link to my office or home so that I could find out the reality behind Jacob's cryptic "Deborah had an accident" sendoff, but knew that there was nothing that I could do about it even if I knew. And if I stayed ignorant, I could be hopeful.

It wasn't until I landed at the Naval Air Station on the east coast that I found out what had happened and learned that 'the accident' wasn't an accident and had happened five days earlier.

Traces of the hopefulness were still there when I saw Kristi waiting for me on the tarmac, a lone figure in the floodlights as the plane taxied to within twenty feet of where she was standing. But it ended when I saw the tears, just before she spread her arms and pulled me into a wordless hug.

We didn't speak until we were in the taxi. Only then did I finally say, "Tell me."

"It shouldn't have happened."

Kristi spoke woodenly, as though reciting from a creed that she no longer believed in. She looked like she hadn't slept for a week and sat slouched down in the taxi like someone trying not to be noticed, a messenger with unwelcome news.

"She was doing her usual Wednesday night thing – volunteering at the homeless shelter. She was at the door … checking them in … watching for contraband stuff … weapons, drugs, booze … "

Kristi was not in good shape. There were long pauses between the mumbled phrases and she kept her head down, focused on her hands that were twisted together in her lap.

"Kristi? What happened? You said she was at the door ...?"

She sat up straight and suddenly the words poured out of her as though she needed to tell me everything at once. "They close the doors at ten. She was done, walking to her car. She parks in a lot behind the shelter. He stabbed her. Over and over and over."

"He? Who was *he*?" A simple fact-based question, anything to stop the stream of images that was flooding into me.

"His name was – is – Anton Morris. He's a paranoid schizophrenic. He hears voices, has visitations from spirits ... refuses to take his meds. That night, he was on meth as well."

"Did the police –"

"He said *they* gave him the knife, said she was evil, deserved to die. Told him it was a good thing ... what he had done."

"He stabbed her because *they* told him -- ?"

She was shaking her head before I finished asking. "A ten-inch carving knife, the kind of thing you'll find in almost every kitchen."

Kristi leaned forward to say something to the driver. Whatever it was, he made a quick U-turn.

"Where are we going? I want –"

"Robert's here. I think you should see him first."

That's all I need. Another failed reunion with Robert. I can't do this now. Much later and to my intense shame, I would remember that Robert loved Deborah too and that he – like me – had lost a part of himself.

"Kristi. I can't –"

"He's been here for four days. With Melanie and me."

It was a simple factual statement, potent not for what it said, but for what was unsaid. 'You do not *feel*. Your wife is murdered and you don't even *call*. Your brother came from six thousand miles as soon as he heard. But *you*? Your precious *work* is more important to you than your daughter at such a time.'

I said nothing. What could I say? "The CIA kept me incommunicado for five days, closeted with a Bulgarian banker, but I'm not supposed to talk about such things. It's classified."

Robert was waiting for us at the hotel. He was in his uniform, looking like he hadn't slept for a week. When he stood up to hug me, he staggered slightly and I noticed that his eyes were red. I wondered if he was sober. Much later, I would learn that it was a giant sized combination of anger and grief. Anger at me because I didn't care enough to drop what I was doing and come home when my wife was murdered; grief for himself because he was mourning the woman he had loved since we were all small children.

It was only when he reached out for me with both arms that I began to sob.

Children & Memoirs

Melanie had thrown the question at me: "Will she be in your book? How about that bit about how she died and it took you five days to get home to your teenage daughter because you were *busy?*"

She sat quietly, watching me think, probably thinking that I was trying to think up a new way to answer an unanswerable question. In a way, it was a relief to have it out in the open instead of lurking behind every conversational corner.

"It was a screw-up, Melanie. I've told you that. And there's nothing I can do to change it."

But what about you, and all those things that you won't talk about? You were there. You knew what she was doing. But you said nothing.

Once on a long overnight plane trip, I fantasized about writing a book entitled *Imaginary Dialogues With My Children*. It would be a collection of wonderfully articulate dialogues instead of the dreary concurrent monologues that made up our reality. The talks would have no taboos and would always progress to real insights and an appreciation for one another's views. There would be no hidden agenda nor toxic aftermath. They would sparkle with the kind of brilliant repartee previously heard only in Neal Simon screenplays.

I also think that, when memoir-writers whine "*I wish they really understood me!*" the "*they*" that we have in mind are our adult children, not our spouses, business colleagues, mistresses, golf buddies, or – even, finally – the eulogists and obituary writers. Freud and the early Greek playwrights were right about a lot of the subterranean emotional stuff. The relationship between fathers and their daughters has lots of emotional baggage on both sides, murky stuff not easily overcome or even understood.

But sitting there and feeling Melanie's stated and unstated accusations hovering around me, I could not think of anything to say other than the clichés and platitudes that go with any discussion about tragedies in the distant past.

Melanie solved the impasse. She stood up and moved to the door. But she stopped in the doorway.

"If you decide to do this thing … write this memoir … and I hope you don't … you need to check with me before you start to write about what happened to mom. There's a lot you don't know."

A lot I don't know?

Melanie walked out of my office, but left all of the guilt and suppressed hostility behind, enveloping me. I knew it wouldn't dissipate easily and I remembered one of Ashley Grimes' questions: 'How did you feel when Deborah died?'

The first of the boxes in the top layer of the 'Deborah cube' in the middle of my office was unlabeled except for the 'August 1991" scrawled on the lid in fluorescent ink. Given the date, it would contain traces from the last month of her life. I moved it from the top of the cube, set it in the middle of my desk and sat there studying it.

It's been fifteen years. Is that long enough? Do I really want to do this?

I remembered Ashley Grimes' words about the wisdom of my undertaking a memoir, "It's got to be about you." And I knew that much of what was in those boxes would tell me something about me. So I pulled the box labeled 'August 1991' to the edge of my desk, pulled off the lid and looked inside.

It was only partially filled and contained three accordion type folders, each of them about two inches thick and with a handwritten file label indicating the contents. The top file was labeled 'clippings.'

I don't know what I expected ... wedding announcements, local newspaper articles about Deborah's various awards, pictures of Melanie's soccer team, book reviews ... but the dozen or so yellowed pieces of paper that I poured out onto my desk were from a much darker world. They were newspaper clippings about Deborah's murder.

All of them were dated within a two-week period, from both regional and national newspapers, with a great deal of overlap in the coverage. They fell into two classes, the first dealing with the murder itself and the brief investigation, and the second with follow-on articles about the killer, Anton Morris, and the 'deplorable shortage' – one reporter's words – in mental health treatment for veterans.

I found that I could read them with a level of detachment, the way one would read articles concerning the death of a distant relative in a far off city. That bothered me, and I wondered if Melanie had been right when she screamed, "You didn't care about mom!" or whether it was the elusive 'closure' that the therapists talked about.

The second folder was an accumulation of photographs, written testimonials and even some audio tapes from Deborah's memorial service. I had been there, but remembered almost nothing about it. I tried to picture myself as the grieving husband accepting condolences, but could not. I may have been drinking. I know that I did not participate in the eulogies. I read the obituary that was included among the papers and decided that it was written by someone who didn't know the real Deborah.

The third folder was a complete surprise. It was labeled 'Investigation' and contained approximately two-hundred official-looking pages, every one of them with a bold-face 'Confidential' stamped at the top. It was the police file of the investigation of Deborah's murder.

I riffled through the pages in about thirty seconds. A number of the pages had marginal comments, reminding me of all the journal articles that I had read at one time or another and marked up for later reference.

I looked at the last page. It was a memo from a 'forensic psychiatrist' at the Trenton Psychiatric Hospital in New Jersey. It was dated October 22, 1991 – three months after Deborah had been murdered.

Police reports are closely held, not given out to reporters or any non-law-enforcement types. And I put these boxes in that garage cabinet three weeks after she died, long before this memo was drafted. Somebody else has been adding to the boxes.

I looked at the handwriting on the file labels, and then picked up the phone receiver.

"This is Melanie."

I said only, "It's me." But I guess the tone was sufficient to warn her that this was not the usual 'keep-in-touch' connection. She said nothing, just waited.

"I'm going through Mom's stuff from the garage cabinet. There's a box that I didn't put in there. It's labeled 'August 1991.'"

"So?"

Maybe just a tad defensive. But no denial.

"Why?"

"Why what?"

More than just defensive. She really doesn't want to talk about this.

I ignored her attempt to stall. "Melanie, the official police report is in the box. I have no idea in hell how you got it, but it's got your handwriting in the margins and on the file label. What I want to know is why you're rummaging around in a murder case that was solved a long time ago."

There was a long silence. It went on long enough that I knew she was going to answer the question, but was thinking about the best way to do so.

"You know that I worked on the Bureau's task force on hate crimes? About five years ago."

"Yes, but what does that –"

"Just listen for a minute. Most of the men – they're always men, never women – are sick. They should have been locked up, in treatment, not out on the street. I interviewed a dozen of them, read their files."

"Your mom's murder was not a hate crime."

"I know, but there were some similarities ... and a lot of discrepancies in his story."

There was another long hesitation. Then she said, "And there are some other ... things ... that you don't know about. Things that led up to ... that night."

"Melanie, you've got to let it go. She's gone. There's nothing to be gained –"

"Dad, I was there. You weren't."

I had no answer for that. Because I thought she was still blaming me for that five-day lag between her mother's death and my arrival on the scene. I was wrong about that too. In any case, she wasn't waiting for an answer. Instead, she took us to a whole new level.

"I talked to Anton Morris."

I blanked on the name for a couple of seconds, long enough that she noticed and allowed some impatience to show through.

"Mom's killer."

"I know who he is. He's an out-and-out whacko. Did what his voices told him to do. Why would you talk to him?"

The FBI has no jurisdiction in local murder cases. She's on her own if she's poking into Deborah's murder ...

She didn't answer the question. Instead, she said, "The prison shrink has gotten him to take his meds. He's a lot clearer now."

"Melanie, he was standing over her body, holding the knife –"

"Oh, there's lots of evidence. It was an easy case to try." But she said it as though she was trying to convince herself.

The frustration that had been building throughout this strange conversation finally broke through. "So what in the living hell are you doing? Let it go!"

She responded calmly. All the early defensiveness was gone, replaced by the intensity of a person who is trying to say something important to a disbelieving listener.

"I won't ... I can't ... let it go. Read the police report and maybe you'll see why. I think this was an assassination, not a random murder by a deranged psychotic."

Melanie said, "Read the police report and maybe you'll see why."

The police report was interesting, but Melanie's written comments in the margin were the most troubling.

The knife was a problem. It was a quite ordinary kitchen knife, but it was not the brand used by the kitchen in the homeless shelter where her killer was seen. And it was new. The police traced the purchase to a Home Depot in a nearby town the day before Deborah was killed, but had no luck identifying the purchaser.

Then there was Anton Morris, her killer. He was a regular at the homeless shelter, well-known and thought to be harmless. He did not keep any weapons and had no recollection of where the knife came from, other than "my spirit guides gave it to me." He would have stood out at the Walmart store and the security cameras would have picked him out quite easily, but there was no sighting of him in the store on the day of the sale. He was a classic paranoid schizophrenic. He heard and talked to the voices in his head but had always been non-violent.

According to the toxology screen, he was loaded with meth, but he had no history of using the stuff. The police found none in his possession, and the known dealers denied even knowing him, let alone selling to him.

The police interviews with Morris went round in circles, an Alice-in-Wonderland exchange. Not so surprising given his mental condition. He seemed as bewildered as anyone else about why he had done such a thing. The court-ordered psychiatrist's report did not surprise anyone and the verdict was an easy one: Morris was committed to the state hospital for the criminally insane.

Melanie met with him three years ago, long after the crime. She introduced herself as an FBI agent, but never disclosed that she was the daughter of his victim. Her notes were mostly factual; quotes from Morris in answering her specific questions. But it was clear that, by the end of their three-hour session, she was skeptical about the official version of Deborah's death. Morris remembered nothing about the actual killing, although he accepted that he had done it and was contrite. By then, he was staying on his medication and the interview was eerily normal.

Melanie asked him, "Why did you kill her?"

"Because he told me to. He said she was evil."

"He? Who's *he*?

"My spirit guide."

"But he had never told you to kill anybody before. Why then? Why her?"

"I don't know. He was different, much louder ... angrier. And he told me to take the drug, gave me the knife and told me where to find her, and that I had done the right thing."

No one saw Morris in the act. He was standing there with the knife looking at her lying on the pavement, but had no recollection of the actual killing. He did not deny that he had killed her, but his refrain from then on, from 1991 through Melanie's interview, was always, "I don't remember, but I must have done it."

A determined criminal defense attorney might have gotten him off given the circumstantial nature of the evidence. There certainly was a case for 'reasonable doubt,' but Melanie went way beyond that. She said: *'I think this was an assassination, not a random murder by a deranged psychotic.'*

What else does she know?

The Formative Years

Critics say that Act II of a three-act play is the most difficult, both to write and to sit through. It is essential to the story, but lacks the novelty of Act I and the dramatic closure of Act III.

The Princeton years are like that for this memoir: essential to the story line, but lacking any dramatic intensity. Except for the interludes where I played spy, and I cannot write about those.

Some literary society sponsors an annual 'worst writing' award, with "It was a dark and stormy night" as their motivational example of how bad it can be, sort of like the lead-in footage for 'Wide World of Sports,' with the hapless ski jumper falling before reaching the end of the takeoff ramp and tumbling through the air like a manikin thrown down the stairs.

I cannot help myself. I must begin the chapter with 'It was the best of times and the worst of times.'

I would stay on the Princeton faculty for twenty-five years, going from an unknown to my present celebrity status. Melanie would grow up there. We did not know it then, but Deborah would die there.

But Princeton was hard for Deborah. Some of it had to do with geography. Princeton was not Palo Alto. It was Eastern, a small company town with town/gown tensions. It was cold half the year and gray all year. It lacked culture. The hospital where Deborah worked was old, not a medical center and the staff were provincial.

Then there were the omnipresent stressors for the upwardly mobile. We bought our first house, using 100% debt financing. Money became more important. The new house was 15 miles out in the country, on an acre of land. We moved to the country without becoming country people. Deborah had to drive twenty miles to her nursing job (which she didn't particularly like), often in terrible weather late at night.

It was the best and worst of a stereotyped suburban existence, oriented around the husband's career and the children's development. I became an assistant softball coach for Melanie's team, Deborah a den mother and driver for school events. We attended soccer matches, TGIF parties for adults and birthday parties in the park for children, and we went to church 'for Melanie's sake.'

Social life was limited to our university set, a highly self-selected set of couples that apparently came to Princeton for exactly the opposite reasons that we did. The social events tended to be wholesome picnics and dinners. It was common for people to bring musical instruments and there would be sing-alongs at the end. Faculty lived in old, drafty farmhouses that they renovated, and the faculty wore corduroy sport coats with leather patches sewn on at the elbows.

Arguments became more frequent and harsher. I do not remember the explicit causes, but I do remember the extended silences. Not really silence, because appearances had to be maintained for outsiders and for Melanie's sake. So it was more of an icy civility, with minimal interaction. On my side, my *never complain, never explain* mantra, and, on her side, an incredible stubbornness, would enable a slow-burning hostility to persist for interminable weeks.

We learned of major and contentious differences between the two of us. Some of it had to do with standards and expectations. For me, "new and different" was sufficient. 'Play the hand you're dealt. Do what you can with what you've got, where you are.' And so forth. If you're living in Princeton; the fact that Palo Alto is better is irrelevant. For Deborah, the standard would always be the highest and best of her cumulative history. For her, Princeton was an ordeal because it was not Palo Alto.

Deborah was a walking paradox, able to forgive others for their flaws and yet to have a crystal clear, instantly invoked, incontrovertible judgment of right/wrong about events, individuals and issues that were far removed. This made dialogue difficult. We would rarely talk about politics, economic policy, money, travel plans, movies, or many other substantive topics without running head on into this impasse. Yet, in matters requiring action, decisions or choice as opposed to analysis or argumentation, we would almost always agree on all but the timing; she favoring *do it now!* while I was usually *wait & see!*.

She spoke in absolutes, a language that does not allow for the shadings and nuances so important in characterizing the behavior of actors whose motives are unknown or ambivalent, perhaps even to them. I cherish ambivalence. She spoke as though all acts, people and problems can be characterized on a binary scale – good/bad, right/wrong, etc. – and that each failure has an identifiable cause and therefore an associated blaming.

There were some telltales, most of them stemming from the ambient conflict inherent in any long running, close-quarters relationship. It worried me that we could not agree on what I thought were basic questions. Once, when another faculty couple that we were close to was in the middle of one of those divorces where a murder-suicide seems the only solution, I asked her, "If we were to divorce, we could do it without falling into scorched earth tactics, couldn't we? We would still be friends?"

She looked at me with such intensity that I immediately added, "Deborah. It's a hypothetical question. I'm never going to divorce you!"

She was deadly serious. "Brian, if you divorce me, I will do whatever I can to destroy you. I will take Melanie, all your money and tell all my friends that you abused me!"

My job was stressful. I was saddled with high expectations about publishing groundbreaking research papers while earning high teaching ratings at one of the world's most prestigious economics faculties. I went into the office early and came home late.

I migrated more and more into consulting, giving me access to global companies in far off places. That also required me to be gone frequently, often for a week at a time. I was traveling, teaching, writing, consulting and busy. Deborah stayed home, engaged in a challenging career and attempting to work out in real time the irreconcilable conflicts between the new feminism and the embedded expectations that had taken us to this point – Gloria Steinem vs. Betty Crocker.

What to do? As a Texas friend says, we "money-whipped" it. We bribed Melanie by buying her a horse and enrolling her in a first-class private school. We upgraded our housing to a near-castle close to campus, bought a BMW and a Jaguar. We went on skiing trips to Vail, vacations to Hawaii, and numerous trips with Melanie around the U.S., always fitted into the gaps in my schedule

Slowly and inexorably, we became independent, capable of self-actualization outside of our relationship to one another. I believe that it was deliberate and inevitable, given our history up to that point and the classical centrifugal forces that operate on any American family of our times.

I asked her once, "Are you happy?"

"I want more of you," she said instantaneously, and I wondered if she had been waiting for me to ask.

I should have paid more attention. But it wouldn't have made any difference if I had. I was incapable of hearing at that time.

Several years after going to Princeton, we booked Melanie for a month-long summer camp and planned an extended European trip for the two of us. Deborah spent weeks planning the itinerary. The dining room table was covered in travel brochures, Fodor's maps, and guidebooks for virtually every country in Western Europe. Then I was offered a three-month Research Fellowship at Woodrow Wilson that was too good to turn down.

It was an inflection point in our marriage. I argued for rescheduling the trip. "We can go to Europe any time. It's only a few hours now with the SST."

"No, I'm going to go on my own," she announced calmly. "You'll always have another paper to write or meeting to attend or speech to write or award to receive or ..." Her voice was rising throughout this list, becoming almost hysterical when she stopped.

Looking back, I should have seen the line in the sand. But I didn't, so she went to Europe alone and that established the new normal for our marriage. Outwardly, we were the poster couple for one of those upscale society magazines; a beautiful couple who had everything – looks, money, status, relationship. But it was hollow at its core.

Our twentieth wedding anniversary was November 9, 1989, and we had planned a three-day stay in Manhattan. I had booked tickets for *Sweeny Todd* and *A Few Good Men* and both of us, I think, were looking forward to the time as a chance to get back to where we had been with each other. We were headed out the door when the phone rang. It was Robert. "Turn on the TV. You need to see this."

The picture was of the floodlit Berlin Wall, a section near Checkpoint Charley. What seemed to be thousands of people – men, women, children – were standing on the top of the wall while thousands more were streaming into West Berlin from East Germany while Soviet border guards stood by and watched.

We stood and watched, mesmerized. I remember that Deborah was still holding her small overnight case in her hand.

"Griggs was right," she breathed. "It's finally happening."

We watched the screen for an hour, long enough to appreciate that this had caught everyone by surprise and that what we were watching was one of the great historical events of the century. It also became clear that the talking heads on the TV networks were scrambling to keep up.

The phone rang again.   It was a deputy something-or-other from the State Department in Washington D.C.   I listened to him for thirty seconds while I watched Deborah watching the dissolution of Reagan's 'evil empire.' I said "OK" and disconnected.

"I have to go to Washington," I said.   Deborah looked at me.   I said, "They're sending a car," as though that was sufficient reason for cancelling our anniversary celebration.   She turned away, picked up her overnight case, and walked out of the room.

When I came home three days later, she was in the living room, sitting on the sofa watching television.   It looked like an infomercial for cookware, but the sound was off, so I wasn't sure. She didn't turn away from the TV, but said, "Do you remember what you promised me twenty years ago? That we'd buy a house, have a baby and get rich?"

I said nothing, just sat down beside her and put my arm around her shoulders.   But she leaned forward to pick up the remote control and turned up the TV volume.

Then she said, "I should have asked for more."

Varna (1978)

I didn't see Connolly for four more years after our initial encounter at Stanford. By then, I was an up-and-coming professor at Princeton, writing a series of empirical papers based on the theories I had advanced in my PhD dissertation. The University Press had published the thesis after some editing to, as my editor said, "make it understandable to those people who matter." Most of the footnotes, mathematics and carefully hedged disclaimers were taken out, leaving a best seller that the *Wall Street Journal* called 'seminal' and a *New York Times* literary critic described as 'a foreign policy primer for the Oval Office.' It helped that Jimmy Carter required all members of his campaign staff to read the book in the runup to the 1976 presidential election.

Academic politics being what they are, the book being on the New York Times bestseller list for a dozen weeks would have ruined my standing among my university colleagues, the crowd that favored rigor over relevance. In their cloistered world, *popular* books could not possibly be serious research. However, the empirical work I was doing – and publishing in all the right journals -- was quite rigorous and was actually confirming some of the more daring policy assertions that made the book so popular.

Among other things, the book's success meant that I became slightly famous early in my career. I became a regular feature on any talk show that was serious about economic policy in modern American politics. However, the widespread fame that Professor Griggs had prophesied was still in the future, awaiting the implosion of the USSR that was still unforeseeable. But I thought of his prediction every time a major east vs. west blowup occurred, and such incidents were frequent in the late seventies and throughout the eighties.

The book also was the impetus for my consulting and advisory career, the one that would take me to forty-seven countries, make me at least semi-eminent, and give me access to men and women that directly affected the lives of billions of individuals. And – the biggest surprise of all – Deborah and I were suddenly rich, at least by our modest Midwestern standards.

It would also lead me to this idea of writing a memoir. But that would be much later.

But the single most life-changing consequence was that it caused Jacob Connolly to call upon me once more.

President Carter was pushing hard to negotiate an extension of the reduction in nuclear arms treaty with Russia, the *Strategic Arms Limitation Talks* or 'SALT I' that Nixon had achieved. Michael Blumenthal, Carter's Secretary of the Treasury, had approached me to serve as an academic economist on a task force of American and Soviet economists during the negotiating sessions of the emerging SALT II treaty.

I was flattered, but I remember objecting, "I really wouldn't think economists have much to say about reductions in nuclear arsenals."

Blumenthal's representative – a disagreeable woman who disliked me for some reason I never figured out – shook her head. "They don't. But if we're going to get this done, both sides are going to want significant concessions on non-arms issues, and most of those will involve economic tradeoffs. We need to have an instant sounding board to decide what to ask for and what to give up. And we don't want academic gobbledegook!"

So much for glamorous presidential appointments.

She confirmed my thoughts. "We'll keep you in some grubby back room and expect informed opinions on demand. You'll have to work with your Russian counterparts on some of the issues. We've already set up your first meeting – in Varna, Bulgaria next month."

There was no public announcement. But a week after I accepted the assignment, Jacob Connolly showed up in my office. Actually, he was standing looking out my window when I came in that Friday morning.

"Good morning, Professor Norquist. You've come a long way since we last met."

When I stared blankly at him, he said, "Four years ago at Stanford, a workshop on Marxist Economics and dinner with Grayson Griggs. We talked about the dangers of good politicians paired up with bad economists. Or was it vice versa?"

He had not changed. The same lumpy sport coat and weary expression … the same way of talking as though skeptical of his own words.

"I'm sorry. I don't remember –"

"Jacob Connolly. I work for the CIA."

I was trying to look offended, but the absurdity of what he said made me laugh. "The CIA? Lemme see, isn't that the government agency that goes to great lengths to hide who it is that works for them?"

He handed me a business card. It had his name, picture and the title "Senior Associate Director," along with a very official looking Central Intelligence Agency logo.

He said, "We're a major worldwide employer and most of our staff are in the open. You're thinking of the covert operations types – what people call *spies*, We do our best to keep *those people* out of sight."

He took back the card. "Me? I tell most people that I'm a Vice President of Public Relations for something called Omni-Global Ltd." He smiled at me in a conspiratorial way. "I have a business card for that too. And if you call the number on either card, you will encounter my secretary – sorry – my administrative assistant. She also has multiple employers."

"So why are you revealing your secret identity to me? Isn't that a serious violation of the famous 'need-to-know' dictum of your employer?"

He shrugged. "Because you'd figure out who I worked for in the next five minutes, and then you'd be offended by my clumsy attempt to corrupt you and throw me out of your office in a self-righteous huff."

"And you? What does a 'Senior Associate Director' do? The one who works for the CIA instead of Omni whatever?"

"This and that. Right now, I'm part of a team gathering background data for the SALT II negotiators. Which is what I want to talk about with you."

"Mr. Connolly. I'm a professor of economics –"

"Who is going to be meeting with a group of prominent Russian economists in Varna, Bulgaria in seventeen days."

"I'm not a spy –"

"Neither am I. I don't tap phones, use miniature cameras, break into offices late at night, bribe bureaucrats, blackmail homosexuals, or pay informers. What I am is a person who collects and analyzes bits and pieces of information."

I would learn – the hard way, as they way – that in fact he did all of those things that he had listed, and more. But the knowledge would come too late, long after the time when I could feel revulsion or even a faint moral superiority.

"Mr. Connolly. I'm busy. Exactly what is it that you want me to do for you?"

"You'll be meeting with three fairly important Russian economists, two men and a woman. I'd like you to tell me what you think of them. That's all."

"What I think of them ... professionally? Personally?"

"Whatever strikes you. They're people, just like us. Smart about some things, naïve about others. Worried about their children, paying their bills, keeping their weight down, whether their colleagues like them."

What am I missing here? I tried for a hint of skepticism. "You don't want to know their views on the SALT negotiations? What they're in favor of or against? What they may know about their government's intentions or weaknesses?"

That made him smile. "First, they won't tell you. Second, if they tell you, they'll lie. Third, that'll show up at the main table, if ever. We don't need you for that."

"I don't –"

"I have only four arguments I can use to convince you. One is patriotism. The good of your country, the flag, American exceptionalism, blah blah blah."

He paused and looked at me closely, correctly reading my silence as distaste for any such appeal.

"Secondly, I could point out that if you cooperate, it could make a SALT II treaty more likely than if you don't cooperate. You grew up thinking that nuclear holocaust was inevitable, but it isn't. And this treaty will help.

"Third, there are no downsides. No risk for you. There is no good reason *not* to help me.

"The last hook, if I need it," he went on, "is that we both know your views on communism, that it's an evil system and that it cannot survive in the long run. Your cooperation in this small matter will shorten that long run."

"And how are you so sure of my views on communism, or anything else?"

He turned to leave, but just as at the end of our first encounter, he left on his own terms.

"Why, I read your book, of course. Nice preface by Dr. Griggs, by the way. Why don't you think about it. I'll give you a call in a couple of days."

In 1978, it took me almost twenty hours to get from Princeton to Varna. I spent most of that time thinking about Connolly's request. It was an endless internal dialogue of "Why not?" followed by "On the other hand ..." I was still undecided when my designated Intourist escort left me at the reception desk at the hotel. My room had a very nice view of the Black Sea, but that was its only positive feature. Everything else about the hotel made me think of a Motel Six in the wrong part of a hollowed-out Midwestern town.

I had not been to Bulgaria or any other Iron Curtain country up until then, but was intrigued by the country. It was one of the more willing members of the Soviet Socialist Republic states and Varna was reputed to be one of the more interesting resorts in the Soviet Union. All I knew about the city was that it was where the fictional Dracula sailed from when he left for Britain.

The meetings were held at the University of Economics, one of the oldest educational institutions in Europe. The two other economists 'on our side' – I couldn't help thinking of the venture in competitive terms – were unknown to me, one coming from a federal agency that I had never heard of, and the other from the Department of Defense. They were polite to me but were clearly unimpressed by what they called my 'theoretical point of view.'

The Russians were more interesting to me, partly because of the mystique associated with being from Russia, but also because they seemed curious about the west. Perhaps, like me, they also believed that their system could not survive and wanted to understand the alternatives.

Vasily and Lena were older, in their sixties. They were professors from the State University in St. Petersburg and I recognized their names from reading lists in my Marxist Economics courses. They were cautious, gray individuals, the kind that survive Stalinist purges and spend their time processing inflated statistics about wheat production in the Ukraine. They kept to themselves and said little during our meetings.

Nikolai Orlov was different. He was close to my age, whip-smart, fluent in English and intensely curious. He had a professorship in a Moscow research institute and – from what I could tell – some degree of freedom to study Western schools of thought. He had read my book and – with some effort – obtained copies of my published papers.

When I expressed surprise at that, he said, "Why? Capitalist economics is all about markets, and there are markets for everything – including vodka, ICBMs, organ transplants, and especially a market for ideas. If you suppress markets, you make people stupid."

It was such a blatant heresy that I actually scrunched down in my chair and looked around for a listening KGB agent.

Seeing my furtive look, Nikolai grinned and said, "C'mon, you've been reading too many spy novels. Tell you what. The Bulgarian beer is not bad and I know a little square where we can feed bread to seagulls and talk about your work. I have some questions about your methodology."

I was in Varna for three days. Our combined group spent the mornings meeting and reviewing the so-called 'economic impact' of the SALT I treaty. It was all very vague, short on data and long on speculation. I spent the afternoons and evenings with Nikolai, visiting the sights in Varna, but mostly continuously engaged in intense debate about the relative merits of some emerging theory or economic policy. However, the underlying motif of our dialogue was about the relative merits of capitalism and communism.

I was continually surprised by his outspokenness about the shortfalls in the socialist system. He was fond of referring to 'the worker's paradise' with sarcasm so thick that I feared for him.

After a few beers, he would talk about his family – a wife, also a professor, and a teenage daughter. We compared photographs of our families and agreed that our wives looked surprisingly alike and that his daughter looked unhappy in the photo. It was in these more personal arenas that he would show small signs of discontent.

"Your Deborah. Does she travel with you?"

"Sometimes. When she is interested in the place that I'm going. She likes London, for example."

He was so obviously depressed by my response that I felt guilty and tried to compensate. "But now, with a young daughter, she stays home most of the time."

"Melanie, yes? In Moscow, she would be 'Malvina.' Will she be a famous professor, like her father?"

"She's four years old, Nikolai. And I'm not famous. But she can be whatever she wants to be."

The conversation morphed into a discussion of the relative treatment of women in the Soviet Union vs. the United States. Even that ended badly.

"We treat men and women the same," Nikolai said with some bitterness. ""Each gender is fully empowered to choose the occupation that the state directs them to choose."

I left the next morning. I wouldn't see him again for more than twenty years.

The Varna trip had been totally anticlimactic on all counts, so dull and inconclusive that I think it convinced me that an occasional project on behalf of the CIA would be as safe as commuting from Princeton to New York City.

Another round in the continuing SALT II talks did begin two weeks after my Varna trip and continued intermittently until 1979. The two sides did reach an definitive agreement, but neither Russia nor US ratified the treaty due to the Russian invasion of Afghanistan. Our team of economists did not meet again, nor did I hear from Michael Blumenthal or his disagreeable representative. The entire sequence of events took on an Alice-in-Wonderland flavor for me.

But I did meet Jacob Connolly in Atlantic City shortly after returning from Varna and, over the course of a long lunch, shared my observations about the three Russian economists. He took no notes and seemed distracted throughout.

His parting comment was, "Not much there, although Nikolai Orlov sounds like someone to watch. But thanks for the briefing. Maybe I can find something more interesting for you to do."

Thinking back on those events almost thirty years later, it's easy to see now what I think of as Connolly's machinations to entice me into that first step on the infamous 'slippery slope.' But those same decades have created sufficient self-insight that I know it wasn't Connolly's manipulations, but my own over-developed sense of self-importance that was the cause.

Actually, it was summed up nicely by Nikolai Orlov, sitting in a sunlit square in Varna in 1978. We were deep into philosophy ... the merits of communism vs. capitalism. He was close to being drunk, but his words were true. "The communists are right about one thing. You and I? We think that we matter ... that we can make a difference. But they – the political commissars -- they know the truth. Individuals don't count. It's all about the system, the collective, the society. You and I? We're just sand in the gears."

The rebuttal was obvious. "So, why are we sitting here, two intelligent highly educated men debating the role of price theory in monopolistic markets?"

"Because we refuse to accept that we are insignificant. But we will learn." It was a sad prediction, but it would come true.

Pakistan (1980)

Two years after Varna, on a park bench in London's Hyde Park, I asked Jacob, "Do you remember Nikolai Orlov?"

He paused and thought about it. "No. Who is he and why should I remember him?"

"The prelude to the SALT II meetings... You asked me to tell you what I thought of three Russian economists that I was meeting with. Orlov was one of them."

He still looked at me blankly, so I said, "Varna. Three years ago."

He closed his eyes and pursed his lips. It was a fairly good impersonation of somebody trying to remember a distant experience. "OK. As I recall, there wasn't much there. I know we never did anything with the SALT II project. It was a waste of time for everybody involved."

"Orlov was particul –"

He cut me off abruptly. "Your brother ... Robert, isn't it? ... He's in the army still?"

So he doesn't want to talk about Nikolai Orlov. But why Robert?

Jacob persisted. "He's advancing real fast, isn't he? Robert?"

"He's a lifer. Drank the whole pitcher of Kool-aid. Presently a major in an armored unit. Been through a couple of Pentagon rotations. Or maybe it's something to do with intelligence. Somewhere in Europe right now, I think."

What is it now? Approaching fifteen years. A poster boy for the warrior class. Helped along by the three rotations through our dirty little war called Vietnam, of course. Not so little, really. And they put him through college and then posted him on three continents.

We saw each other at odd intervals, but each of us was traveling most of the time and it was difficult to find a time when our schedules meshed. We tried to coordinate trips to see Kristi, who was still in Minnesota. And he would sometimes stop off at Princeton when he was on one of his frequent postings to the Pentagon. Once he brought a woman along, a beautiful incredibly fragile-looking Thai woman named Chinda. But they didn't last and he never spoke of her after the one visit.

The visits were awkward. There was too much of the unresolved past hovering in the background, particularly when Deborah was with us. Conversation was halting, taking on the characteristics of a high school reunion. Which it was, in a way. It got better when Melanie was around, as though bearing a child finally, once and for all, settled the question of which twin had prevailed.

I'd forgotten about Jacob. Until he spoke. "And your sister? Still living in Minnesota isn't she?"

Where the hell is this going? I didn't bother to respond, realizing belatedly that Jacob probably had identified and vetted every twig on my family tree. But then the thought of him rooting around in my past made me angry.

"And don't forget Deborah. She's chair of our local PTA. And Melanie, my seven-year-old daughter? She's on the –"

"Brian."

"OK, OK. But why are we sitting here on this park bench? Other than to attract germ-infested pigeons who are hoping for bread and peanuts?"

"Leonid Brezhnev is done pretending to negotiate. The Russian 40th Army will cross into Afghanistan tomorrow at dawn."

Another jump-shift. I was beginning to get used to them. But this was a dandy. I sat up straight. I'd been following the deteriorating situation in Afghanistan for the last year, with its coups, counter-coups and heavy-handed interference by the Russians as they propped up their succession of stooges. One of the reasons I was in London was to work with a think tank that was – with far more optimism than was justified – working on planning a symposium to be titled "Economic Development in a Post-Cold War World."

Jacob became unimportant for the moment as the implications of his casual disclosure sank in.

So the Russians didn't take away the lesson from our experience in Vietnam after all. They'll say 'Afghanistan is different' and then recite the same rationalizations we did. Their generals will downplay the mujahedeen as poorly trained and badly armed rebels without a chance against a real army and the politicians will recite slogans about the will of the people and the Russian manifest destiny. They'll lose, but it'll take ten years and a million lives, including far too many women and children.

I asked Jacob the same question I had asked him the first time we met. "What exactly is it you want from me?"

Jacob didn't answer my question until we had left our bench and were standing watching a turbaned Sikh shouting at a small group of camera-toting onlookers – mostly Japanese tourists – at Speaker's Corner. It was one of those bizarre gatherings that tended to form at this historical spot.

"We're taking the lead to establish an Afghan-government-in-exile, probably in Peshawar, Pakistan or maybe London. The idea is to create a shadow administration, complete with cabinet ministers. I want you to spend a few days with some of the candidates for high-level ministerial posts. Help them think through some of the big picture economic policy stuff."

"And tell you what I think of them, I suppose?"

"Of course. I need your opinion. And Brian? These people you're meeting with … they're pretty … tribal. Don't expect a lot of sophistication."

"Why is the CIA involved in this? I would think this would be basic out-in-the-open statecraft."

"Two reasons. First, we don't want to antagonize the Russians any more than we have to at the moment, so this has to be out of the public view. The SALT talks are a political zombie, but they are still going. Second, there are different Afghan rebel factions and we don't want to be seen as favoring any particular one ... until we're sure they're the keepers."

It turned out that there was a third reason, but I would learn about that one the hard way.

Three days later, I was in Islamabad, Pakistan, sitting in a dingy office with two fierce-looking Afghans. Jacob had introduced them as Akmal and Qasim ... 'with a Q' ... and left us, saying he'd be back in two hours.

Finally, I feel like a real secret agent!

Previously, the two or three 'favors' that I had done for Jacob required nothing more than me doing what I usually did and then reporting back to him with my observations on certain people I had met or discussions that I had been involved in. There was nothing clandestine about it except the fact that I didn't tell anyone what I was doing. It was about as exciting as watching paint dry.

This time was different. I had no reason to be in Pakistan; I'd been sent on a mission. And that mission put me squarely in that ambiguous cold war zone where the big powers played their secret games. This was a headline waiting to happen.

It helped that the setting was straight out of a Hollywood screenwriter's imagination; a dimly lit office that ran the length of a loft overlooking a warehouse floor littered with stacks of cardboard boxes, wooden crates and tires ranging in size from bicycles to tractors. Windows opened a chaotic Islamabad street scene and the shouts and traffic sounds provided an audible backdrop. The two men sitting with me, Akmal and Qasim, were straight from central casting. Both of them were bearded, wearing flat caps, and dressed in traditional Afghan dress, with long knives thrust through their belts. It was quite easy for me to picture them carrying Kalishnikov rifles along mountain trails. Qasim had a four-inch scar from his left eye down to his chin.

The sense of adventure receded quickly, but it did make me wonder whether I was playing along with Jacob's little games because of some inner Walter Mitty.

It took about three minutes for me to realize that I had nothing to contribute to the meeting; that I was there solely because Jacob needed to impress the Afghans with an American with some status and one that believed in their cause. Among other things, their English was barely understandable, with the approximate vocabulary of a six-year-old.

I started by asking about sources of revenue. They looked at me blankly long enough that I wondered whether they even understood what I was asking. Then Akmal said, "You can finance stingers? The helicopter killers?"

The meeting quickly flowed downhill from there. They knew nothing about economics, finance, trade, banking or government finance. They represented rival tribal factions within the mujahedeen forces and each of them wanted to be sure their side was represented in the government-in-exile ... and, even better, that the other side was shut out. They had been fighting the foreigners or each other for so long that whatever they had been in some past life was lost to them.

They were arguing vehemently between themselves – in Pashto, I think – and I was purely an observer wanting the whole charade to end. When I heard the footsteps approaching the door, I was quite ready to tell Jacob what I thought of him and his crazy ventures.

But it wasn't Jacob. It was another man in Afghan dress, but with the long woolen scarf wrapped around the lower half of his face. What happened next was so fast and devoid of drama that I have trouble recalling the details. The man took three or four quick steps, bringing him from the door to the table where the three of us sat side by side. At the same time, be brought his right arm up and extended it toward us. His hand held what seemed to me to be a very large gun, further exaggerated by the silencer screwed onto the end of the barrel. He fired twice, first at Qasim, who had started to rise, and then at Akmal, who was opening his mouth to say something. The shots were surprisingly loud and I remember my surprise that the silencer was so ineffective.

I was half out my chair, frozen midway between sitting and standing, as though the absence of motion would somehow protect me from the next bullet. Qasim had toppled sideways and his head was resting against my right hand that was pressed against the tabletop. I could feel blood soaking into my shirt cuff and filling the gaps between my spread fingers.

The shooter was staring at me, the gun extended so that the tip of the silencer was only a few inches from my nose.

They say that your life flashes before your eyes, but all I can remember thinking was, *I hope that Robert and Deborah will get together.*

I don't know how long we stayed like that. It could have been five seconds or five minutes. But finally the man lowered the gun and unwound the scarf from around his face. He said, "Sit down, Brian."

It was Valentin Aslanov.

Hostage

"You should wash the blood off."

Those were the first words since he had said, "Sit down, Brian." The shaking had almost stopped, but the sense of unreality persisted, heightened by the way that everything around me seemed to be happening in slow motion.

Valentin had moved decisively. He used a small camera with a flash to take pictures of Akmal and Qasim, posing them in their chairs with their heads back against the headrest so that the gunshot wounds were clearly visible. Then we left, with him pulling me along with him like a mother with a dawdling two year old.

I was not processing very well, but I remember a car with a driver and what seemed to be a long time in start-stop Islamabad traffic. Somehow, I wound up sitting in a room that reminded me of an early college dorm with its sagging couches, cigarette-scarred tables and a mustiness that seemed to ooze out of the walls. The driver was sitting on a simple wooden stool near the only door into the room.

Valentin sat on the ragged couch opposite me. He placed the handgun and camera on the cushion next to him, making me wonder if that was for my benefit, and whether the two objects were placed there as a threat or reassurance.

I looked at my right hand. Qasim's blood was still damp on my shirt cuff and my fingers were sticky with the stuff. Valentin pointed at a curtain covering a doorway.

"There's a sink in there."

When I went through the curtain, I could hear Valentin and the driver speaking in rapid Russian but softly enough that I couldn't make out the words. When I came back into the room, Valentin had taken two bottles from a small refrigerator. The logo belonged to Coke, but the writing was Arabic. He handed me one of them.

"How's Deborah?"

The question was so out-of-place, so *ordinary*, that everything snapped back into place. Voices no longer had echoes and the nearby world resumed moving at normal speeds.

It was 1974. Almost seven years ago. I'd brought Valentin home with me after the last Abbott and Costello class. His one-year program to study capitalism was about up and he wanted to soak up as much American culture as he could. And Deborah had wanted to meet him.

"A Cossack! Horse people ... fighters ... They're very –"

"Not Cossack, Deborah. They were from southern Russia, Ukraine. Valentin is a Kazakh ... from Kazakhstan. That's more like Central Asia."

She was unfazed. "I don't care if he's from the moon. Wherever he's from, I know there was no one like him in our little town. I want to meet him."

They'd gotten along instantly, seeming to find some common core element in one another that I had not noticed and could not evoke. He came around almost every day during the last two weeks we were at Stanford and spent most of that time talking with Deborah even though we went everywhere as a threesome.

I asked her rather than him. "Does he have a wife? Girl friend?"

She looked sad. "No. And I doubt if he ever will."

When I looked at her, she said, "Valentin is missing something that other people have. Something happened to him ... I don't know what ... but he doesn't think of a future ... I don't think he expects anything good to happen to him."

He sat looking at me in that dingy room as if he understood the memories and emotions that he had triggered with his simple question.

"Deborah's fine," I said. And you remember Melanie? She's almost seven."

For the first time, I looked at him closely. He was seemingly unchanged, still of indeterminate age and ethnicity. But there was something ....

It was in the eyes. They had no curiosity, taking in images and processing them as coldly as a video camera. *They would be the same whether he was looking at a beautiful woman or his own firing squad.*

"Valentin. Why? Why did you kill those two men? And what do you want with me? Who are you?"

"Brian! So many questions! But I have only one for you. And you need to be very careful about how you answer my one question."

Suddenly the gun resting on the cushion became prominent and the indifference in his eyes became something much more ominous.

"Why were you in that room with those two men?"

Damn Connolly! What am I supposed to say?

"Our State Department set up the meeting. I was told that they were looking for advice on economic development."

Stop there. A simple lie, close to the truth. But then I made the mistake that amateur liars always make: I embellished.

"The meeting was set up before you ... before the Russian Army invaded Afghanistan. I was surprised that it went forward."

When Valentin just continued to stare at me, I dug myself in even deeper. "Those two men that you ... the men in the room with me ... they weren't what I'd been expecting. They didn't know anything about any branch of economics. And I don't even think they were officially in the Afghan administration."

He just watched me sputter. Then he asked, "Are you sure it wasn't Jacob Connolly who set up the meeting? Or your brother?"

The question was so outright ludicrous – the 'brother' part of it anyway – that I stopped worrying about whether my lies were convincing and responded completely naturally.

"Robert?" I actually laughed. "I haven't seen him for six months. And he's not connected to anything that I do. He's in the –"

I stopped because I didn't know anything about Robert's unit or assignments. Valentin, however, did.

"He's in the U.S. Army Military Intelligence Corps. For the last three months, he's been an 'unofficial' advisor to mujahedeen commanders in Afghanistan. One of the more effective ones. He's probably within a hundred miles of where we're sitting."

I started to protest, but he stopped me again. "And Jacob Connolly?"

A much more difficult question for me. "I've never heard of –"

"Stop. You insult my intelligence." He waved his right hand dismissively. And then rested it on the handgun. To this day, I do not know – nor want to know – how close he was to using it.

He sighed and looked at me with an expression of disappointment. Then he stood up and headed for the door. Just before closing it, he turned to the driver and said, "Keep Dr. Norquist in this room until you hear from me. If he objects too loudly or tries to leave, shoot him."

I stayed in that room for four more days. The driver and two other men who looked like they were brothers took turns babysitting me. There was always one of them in the room with me. At first, I tried the usual protests, several variations of the "I'm an American citizen and I know my rights!" that we've learned from television shows. They ignored me. I don't think they spoke more than ten words between them in the entire time.

In the afternoon of the fourth day, the driver left and no one came to replace him. After an hour of imagining gunmen outside the door, I tried to leave, but the door was locked. While I stood in the middle of the room looking for an alternative, the door opened and Valentin came in.

We stood ten feet apart, considering one another. He spoke first. "You can go. And be very glad that you have good friends in high places."

So Jacob has been working on my behalf.

"But there's a condition."

I waited, knowing that he would tell me the rules and that I would follow them. The four days in that room with the images of Akmal and Qasim were more than enough to keep me compliant.

"You are to tell no one about what's happened, what you've seen or what you've been doing in Islamabad. If asked, you've been cooped up in a hotel conference room in Cairo reviewing trade statistics or demographic trends or banking regulations. Nothing about mujahedeen or CIA or KGB or even Afghanistan."

"OK, and what –" But he simply turned and walked out. I would not see him again for more than ten years.

When I got to my hotel and asked for my key, the clerk said, "One moment, please?" and turned away to dial a call that lasted no more then ten seconds. I was not surprised when Jacob appeared at my door fifteen minutes later.

He said, "I'm glad that you're alive," making it sound about as dramatic as the clerk at the front desk saying, "Welcome back, Dr. Norquist."

I'd had four days in that stinking room to think about what I would say to him – if I ever had the chance. But when he was standing in front of me, all I could manage was a "Fuck you, Jacob.

And your Afghan government-in-exile." It lacked vehemence or indignation or any of the other emotions that I felt entitled to.

He took a step toward me and started to say something, but I spoke first.

"Akmal and Qasim? They're –"

"Dead," he finished the sentence for me.

"They were shot in the head, at close range, by –"

Again, he interrupted. "By Valentin Aslanov. Our friend from Palo Alto, now a KGB specialist."

Now I was getting mad. "If you know so goddam much, why didn't you get me out of that goddamned room?"

"I didn't know where you were until the desk clerk phoned me fifteen minutes ago. I thought you were dead, somewhere in a shallow grave."

That stopped me. "So you didn't organize my release? They just let me go? Why would they do that?"

He shook his head. "I don't know. It makes no sense. But I'm glad they did."

We flew back to the U.S. together, just the two of us on a Boeing 707 modified as a military transport. I slept most of the way, but with about two hours left in the flight, Jacob restarted the conversation that, one way or another, we'd been having since that first meeting in 1974, at the Stanford workshop.

"I'm really sorry about what happened, Brian. We did not anticipate that the Russians would move so aggressively, so quickly, against the mujahedeen leadership, especially outside of Afghan territory."

It was very clever of him. An apology and my sudden inclusion into the highest levels of CIA tactical thinking. That single inclusive word 'we' was the most effective sales pitch Jacob could have used. So much so that when the car stopped outside my front door, I had forgotten the fiery resignation speech that I had perfected during those four days of captivity. Instead, I said, "No more front line stuff. I'm an analyst. A good one. But no more assassination scenarios. Ever."

He set the hook even deeper. "Of course. But you did really well. As well as we would expect of a highly trained field agent."

I went into my house thinking I was James Bond, wishing I could somehow share my story with Deborah. But she wasn't home. The sitter said that Robert had been in town and had taken her out to dinner.

She came home late, long after I was asleep, but she was up at six, leaving me thrashing through a nightmare involving Qasim chasing me with a long knife. I heard her and Melanie downstairs, going back and forth about getting ready for school. It sounded much like a contest of wills, with the classic "Oh, yeah!" and "Because I said so!" kind of exchanges and I waited until I heard the door close behind Melanie before I went downstairs. Deborah was sitting at the table with both hands wrapped around her coffee mug, staring at it as if waiting for it to tell her what to do.

"Did I miss Melanie? I wanted to see her before she took off." *A lie so transparent that she didn't even pretend to answer my question.*

"If you'd tell us when you're planning to be at home, we could schedule a meeting. But I guess the telephones in Cairo aren't really set up for international calling." No raised voice or sarcastic tone. She projected an absolutely passive *acceptance* of my derelictions. It was an attitude that should have frightened me with its implications, but I was still reliving the Islamabad venture.

"How's Robert? Will I get to see him?"

She got up, took her mug to the sink, poured the coffee into the drain and walked out of the kitchen.

Helsinki (1988)

The eighties were easy to write about. I spent three weeks, writing eight to ten hours a day, and had an impressive number of first-draft pages of my memoir to show for it. For an economist like myself, the decade had all of the plot lines – massive deregulation, the rise of the Japanese economy, inflation rates at all time highs, disruptive Wall Street innovations, and the beginnings of the technology revolution.

And I was in the middle of much of it. My books and other published research coincided nicely with another new phenomenon – the professor as pundit. I was spending as much time on television, testifying at Senate sub-committees and speaking at various conferences as I was in the Princeton classroom.

I followed as well as I could the bloody Afghan War and wondered if Valentin was still trying to assassinate the tribal leaders. There actually was an Afghan government-in-exile and it was generally assumed that the CIA was providing significant assistance to the mujahedeen. The current *Economist Magazine* on my desk featured a long article about the Russian's claim to have intercepted a shipment of two hundred Stinger missiles, including *Izvestia* photos of Russian commandos posing with crates of rockets, including closeups of serial numbers.

From where I sat, it looked like a replay of our Vietnamese experience. By 1985, Russia's euphemistically named 'Limited Contingent of Soviet Forces' numbered well over a hundred thousand Russian soldiers, but the mujahedeen still controlled eighty percent of the country.

Jacob occasionally wandered into my office, wanting my opinion on various issues or, less frequently, wanting to know what I thought of some particular person's views. I had always gone along with the rationale that my role was to backstop him if technical language or data issues came up when the agenda got into economic policy. But I also knew that he expected me to provide him with a second opinion as to the personality and key qualities of the individuals on the other side. Since Islamabad, however, he had asked nothing of me that made me rethink my complicity in his clandestine enterprises.

Until a rainy day in June, 1988. He appeared without any advance notice, as always.

"I need you to go to Helsinki with me."

It was the usual pitch. "I need you there. I'm working on the commercial attaché at the East German consulate in Helsinki and he thinks he knows really valuable stuff. Our people there think he's willing to share his knowledge ... for a price. I told him I'm bringing somebody along that will understand what it is that he's selling. I've been working him for a year. I think he's ready to listen to specific propositions. By the way, how's your German?"

The Berlin Wall was still standing and no one, not even Reagan, thought it was coming down anytime soon. The Wall had become a hugely important symbol, a grim and foreboding reminder that communism was not a voluntary choice for many of the East's citizens. However, what they called 'the wall' was only a small segment of the so-called Iron Curtain that divided East and West. Eight-hundred and thirty-three miles of that barrier ran along Finland's border with Russia, often close to the Baltic shore. Helsinki was 188 miles from St. Petersburg and only a short ferry ride from Tallin. Because of that proximity and their occasionally bloody history with one another, Finland maintained a cautious neutrality with Russia throughout the Cold War. Inevitably, that same proximity and neutrality made Helsinki a natural watering hole for spies.

I needed to schedule a few days in Europe, so it was easy for me to agree. I was in Helsinki for a day before Jacob. He called me at my hotel.

"There's a bar called Finlandia, one block from your hotel. Our man will be there in an hour. I'll meet you there."

I had nothing to do so I went looking for the meeting place, thinking that a bar named after a piece of Finnish classical music might be more interesting than most. Once there, a plaque near the front door told me that this was the favorite drinking spot for Sibelius on his frequent visits to Helsinki and that he 'may have' much of composed his Fifth Symphony at the long mahogany bar that ran the length of the room. I could hear the strains of Finlandia coming from the interior.

Jacob was already there, at a corner table and in close conversation with another man. His companion was a little younger than Jacob, who looked like a lot of the other working-class patrons. He was stocky with closely cropped hair, dressed like a laborer, indistinguishable from the crowd at the bar. He was doing most of the talking, leaning close to Jacob with his hand clenched on his forearm as though needing to keep him attentive. As soon as I entered, Jacob said something to him and the man got up abruptly and walked toward the rear entrance of the bar, keeping his back to me.

"I don't think your friend wanted to meet me after all."

"That's not our subject for the evening. He's due in forty minutes. " He said nothing about the man who had made the hasty departure.

We sat in silence until the attaché arrived. He was obviously very nervous about me being there. Jacob introduced me as "a specialist in resettlement finance." I had no idea what that meant, but my role was purely as an observer in any case.

But the conversation did not even touch on technical or policy areas. The man was entirely illiterate when it came to economics. He was a thug who, as far as I could tell with my limited German, was a specialist in surveillance of foreign diplomats, concentrated on the Balkans. Their talk was entirely about what Jacob could offer him in money and protection if he shared his audio and videotapes with him.

Part of the enticement strategy involved alcohol, and both Jacob and his target were more than slightly drunk by the time the man accepted the notion that he could be a traitor. Aside from that, I couldn't quite keep up with their rapid-fire German language, so I focused on other things – body language, voice tones, frowns and such. It was easy to chart the man's changing moods, a progression that began with hostility and ended with active listening.

The two of them seemed to reach some kind of agreement. The man stood up and put out his hand. Jacob shook it and then handed him a few bills. We both watched him weave his way back to the bar.

I said what I'd been waiting to say for the last forty minutes. "You're wasting my time! You could have replaced me with your pet dachshund. That goon can't even spell 'economics,' let alone talk about it."

Jacob was unruffled. "Yes, I know. But what did you think about him as a double agent? Can I trust him not to betray me the way I'm asking him to betray others?"

God! The question actually makes sense to me!

"The man has no core. He's a drunk with no apparent conscience. Cares only about himself as far as I can tell." As I listened to my list of criticisms, I realized that I didn't know if these were strengths or weaknesses in Jacob's world.

I summed it up. "He'll belong to whoever pays him the most."

"Or to the one who he's most afraid of," Jacob said, half to himself.

As he spoke, Jacob seemed to become instantly sober, making the statement far more sinister. I wondered how much playacting had been going on.

"Anyway, he's not the main reason I wanted you with me. Think of him as the minor act at a rock music concert. The one that comes on to warm up the crowd for the really big name band."

So there's more to do tonight. As usual, Jacob has plans within plans.

He sat unmoving, pushing his half-full glass of aquavit in circles on the tabletop. So I asked him about what had been bothering me as I watched the two of them.

"How do you do that? Get people – your prospects -- who are suspicious of you and your intentions to do what you want them to do?"

He waved the question away, but I persisted. "He didn't trust you, didn't like you. At first, but not at the end. How do you do that?"

He turned to face me and saw that I was serious. Then he smiled mischievously. "You mean, like how do I to get a self-absorbed, arrogant young American doctoral student in economics to pay attention to me? One who doesn't like me or trust me?"

The question startled me, as it was meant to. It was also an answer to my question, in a way.

He didn't wait for my answer. "It's simple. Alcohol helps, of course. Especially with Russians. But what I am most interested in is sorting them – my prospects, as you call them – into three categories. They're either stupid, intelligent or in-between. Step Two depends on which cell I think they're in."

"The stupid ones?"

"I walk away. The dumb ones are both ineffective and dangerous. And, anyway, they wouldn't have the kind of access I need them to have."

"And the intelligent ones?" *Like the arrogant economics PhD student? At Stanford, in 1974.*

"I provoke them."

"Why not flattery?" I asked, thinking of my preferred approach for dealing with those all-too-frequent encounters with pompous academic types whose self-esteem was as fragile as the theories that they espoused. "My experience is that smart people like to be told how smart they are."

He shook his head. "If flattery works, it means they're insecure. And that's the kiss of death in this business. Trust me, you need a lot of self-esteem to betray your country."

"But provoking –"

He held up a hand. "Gets me to Step Two. If the provokee reacts with disdain, snobbery or a kind of 'I'm smarter than you are' attitude, they're no good for my purposes. They'll get caught before they steal their first secret file."

Both of us know where this conversation is going. What is unclear is why it's so important for me to hear his reasoning. Do I need his approval?

I prodded, "But if the target is intelligent and reacts ...?"

Jacob smiled, far more aware of my Freudian needs than I was. "If he tries to explain to me why I'm wrong, to *educate* me, then there are some ... possibilities."

"You started with three categories. What about the average ones? Those who are somewhere between smart and stupid?"

He sat back and watched me closely. "They're the best of all. They're dumb enough to do what I ask them to do ... and smart enough to be afraid of me."

Twenty-five years later, while writing a memoir and thinking about his answer, I think that single sentence was the most revealing fact that Jacob Connolly ever shared about himself. And I am ashamed that I failed to see its implications for me ... why I was sitting in that bar in Helsinki aiding and abetting him.

I felt like I was on the verge of learning something important about myself, but a man came to the table, whispered something to Jacob and promptly walked off. It was the same person that Jacob had been talking with when I came in. It was a brief encounter, lasting only a second or two. But this time, I got a clear look at him. He was around thirty, with a receding hairline and Slavic features. His eyes were cold, a washed-out color.

"Secret agent stuff?" I asked Jacob.

"There's somebody I have to meet. Come with me. I'll show you a whole new side of the game. And the real reason for your being here."

We walked for about thirty minutes; side streets, alleys, parks, through a mall. As far as I could tell, our path was randomly chosen. We passed a small park with a grassy amphitheater where a string quartet was playing for a couple of hundred spectators, mostly couples drinking wine and holding hands. I think it was Bach.

Tonight's my night for classical music.

It was late, around ten. But it was not yet fully dark at Helsinki's northern latitude and there were still a lot of people on the street. The second time we passed the amphitheater and the string quartet, Jacob sat down on a bench on the sidewalk bordering the park. "Let's sit down a bit." He patted the bench alongside him. "There's a couple of things you need to know."

He began, "You know of Dieterick Schreiber, of course."

Dieterick Schreiber. One of the best East German applied mathematicians. Nominated for the Nobel Prize in Economics. Five years ago, but the regime would not allow him to accept it. Rumor had it that they feared he would defect once in Stockholm.

"Yes. Actually, I corresponded with him several times about some of his work that I thought had some econometric applications. Until the censors cut us off. He's one of the two or three top mathematicians in the Soviet world."

Jacob nodded absently. *He already knows about our correspondence!* "He wants to live in the West. He's been in East Germany but the Russians are moving him to central Russia. There's a network of dissidents that's working to get him from Moscow to St. Petersburg and then onto a boat into the Baltic."

"Schreiber! That's the scientific equivalent of Mikhail Baryshnikov defecting from the Bolshoi ... what, ten years ago? They'll never let him out of the Soviet bloc!"

"He's already out. I just got word. We're meeting him in thirty minutes."

Suddenly, the dark seemed more intense, the shadows more threatening.

I stood up. "Jacob, I didn't sign on for this kind of thing. You almost got me killed in Pakistan and we agreed, 'No more.' I'll sit in on your meetings and advise you on import-export quotas, or the impact of inflation on arms productions, but I'm not going to get into on-the-ground CIA operations!"

I turned to leave, but Jacob grabbed my sleeve. Still sitting and without looking at me, he said, "Schreiber asked for you. By name. That was his condition for coming out – that you would be the one to meet him."

Me? "I've never met the man, for god's sake! We exchanged a few letters. I don't even know what he looks like. Why would he pick me?"

"I don't know. But he did pick you. He said to tell you that you were recommended by a friend."

A friend? I don't have any friends in that part of the world!

Jacob stood up. "Brian, if you don't show up, Schreiber won't get off the boat. And he can't go back or he'll put the entire dissident network at risk. Like it or not, you *are* involved."

He set me up. That's why he wanted me in Helsinki. For Schreiber. All that bullshit with the so-called commercial attaché was playacting. I said it out loud. "You set me up. You knew I wouldn't come if I knew what I was getting into."

Jacob shook his head. "The guy in the bar was real. But I didn't need you for that. I need you for Schreiber."

He took a step closer and put his hand on my arm. "And this is not another Islamabad fiasco. We meet him, he sees it's you, we take him to a safe house. You go back to your hotel. Schreiber will be on a special State Department plane tomorrow morning. Your name never comes up."

What was it he said about identifying prospects? 'They're dumb enough to do what I ask them to do ... and smart enough to be afraid of me.' Am I afraid of him? No, but maybe I should be.

Not for the first or last time, I regretted ever having met Jacob Connolly.

"OK," I sighed. "Let's go meet Schreiber."

A Late Night Meeting

You're never very far from the waterfront in Helsinki. It took twenty minutes of brisk walking, this time without any apparently random changes of direction. Our destination turned out to be one of the many public marinas that are so numerous in or around Helsinki's harbor area. By now, it was late enough that very few people were around. We walked to the end of the floating dock, past an infinite variety of craft ranging in size from rowboats to three-masted schooners. At the end of the dock, a battered wooden boat was nosing up against the rubber-tire lined stanchions with its engine turning over just enough to keep it in place. It was about forty feet long, with a single low cabin very near the bow ... the kind of all-purpose workboat common to harbors all over the world.

Jacob didn't pause, just stepped onto the deck of the boat and gestured for me to follow him. He led the way around the cabin to the rear deck, a space about twenty feet square. Four men were standing there watching us approach. Three of them looked like boat crew, tough-looking, unshaven middle-aged men wearing an assortment of foul-weather gear. The fourth was older, sixty to seventy, and was dressed in a suit and overcoat. A small black valise was at his feet. He was as out-of-place as a chimney sweep at a black-tie gala.

He stepped forward and came within a foot of me. He spoke in heavily accented English. "Dr. Norquist. You look exactly like the picture on your book jacket. Thank you for coming. My friend said that I could trust you, that if you were there, all would be well."

He turned to Jacob. "So, you are my escort? We go to America?"

"My name is Jacob. And yes, we go to America. Tomorrow morning. Many people are anxious to see you."

One of the men growled something in Russian. Jacob took a package about the size of an ordinary brick from his coat pocket and handed it to the man. Then he pushed Schreiber and me in front of him, nudging us along until we were off the boat and standing on the dock. The boat reversed as soon as we stepped off and accelerated rapidly away into the dark.

Schreiber watched it go. "I thought they might leave me in the middle of the Gulf of Finland. They are hard men."

"They come from a hard place," Jacob said. "But they are professionals of a sort. And they deserved to get paid."

"The people that made it possible for me to get to their boat? They do not get paid. And they take much risk for me."

Jacob spoke with some urgency. "We need to go. Now. We have a short walk, then we can talk."

We walked for forty minutes, staying close to the waterfront and then directly away from the water up a hill to a small square with a large fountain in the middle and with restaurants, shops and apartment buildings on all sides. It was dark and quiet except for a brightly lit tavern on the side facing us.

Jacob stopped at the entrance to the square and pointed to a three-story apartment building alongside the bar. "That is where you'll be tonight, Dr. Schreiber." He turned to me. "Brian, thank you for your help. Obviously, you can't tell anyone about any of this." He made it apparent that my part in the evening was over.

Schreiber put his hand on my arm. "I will see you in America and we will resume our discussion of dynamic econometric models. Without the Stasi censors."

I turned away to start back down the hill and the two of them started across the square. But within five minutes and halfway down the hill to the harbor, I stopped. *I haven't said a single word to Schreiber. He asked for me ... said that I was recommended by a friend. Who?*

It became of overwhelming importance to me to know who had recommended me as the go-between for one of the most important defections since the Cold War began. I headed back up the hill, hoping to catch him before he was out of sight.

Jacob and Schreiber were sitting at an outdoor table at the tavern across the square. They had been joined by two other men. Their backs were to me, and from my angle, the light spilling from the interior left them in deep shadow, more like silhouettes than three-dimensional figures. But when I was halfway across the square with a different angle of view, I realized that one of them was the one who had whispered in Jacob's ear just before we started out to meet Schreiber. The other was a tall thin man with white hair. He was well dressed, in a suit that – even in the poor light – looked expensive and tailored.

Everything happened in about a five-second period. The tall man stood up abruptly and pointed at Jacob and Schreiber sitting opposite him. At the same time, a black van with its side door fully open came out of the adjacent alley and stopped in front of them, blocking my view. It stood there for no more than a few seconds and when it pulled away, all four of them were gone.

The Lost Years (1991)

I was trying to work on the memoir from nine to five. Most of the 'advice to memoir writers' that I'd checked out recommended 'a disciplined approach,' although I was discovering that my most productive periods came at random intervals, often late at night. So I was spending lots of idle time staring out the window thinking.

Daniel was staying with us quite a lot this summer. Melanie was finding the FBI to be the kind of workplace where, although not actively hostile to single mothers, clearly expected them to spend a lot of time on airplanes. So he would wander into my study frequently, often just to browse through the photo albums that were strewn around the floor. Both of us liked the encounters.

"Papa, my teacher called me a Gen Z. Is that something bad?"

He's ten years old. Probably too soon to lecture him on the perils of stereotyping or the science of demography.

"No. It's just a handy label that we give to different age groups. All it really means is that you're a kid."

"So what are you then?"

"Me? I'm a baby boomer. Sounds kind of silly doesn't it?"

I think he felt better about himself. I suspect that 'Gen Z' sounded a lot more sophisticated than 'baby boomer.'

"Mommy says she's a Capricorn. I guess that's somewhere between you and me, huh?"

I wonder if it's OK to tell him that astrology is just codified superstition. Right up there with Santa Claus, equal opportunity and leprechauns.

Happily he got distracted by a sound from somewhere in the house and wandered back out before I could respond, leaving me with the view out the window and thoughts of demography.

Demography is the study of the changing structure of human populations. In my world – that of highly specialized economists doing research and publishing highly obscure papers – such study is done using highly sophisticated surveys, mathematics and statistics. The easy labeling of generations with catchy phrases is scoffed at as unscientific; 'the unfounded speculations of profit-seeking marketing consultants,' as one of my colleagues put it.

I was born in 1946, a classic 'boomer,' part of the spike in the birth rate as the GI's came home from the war. As the largest single cluster of consumers and armed with massive purchasing power, we were the engine of materialism in the American twentieth century. So I was sitting in a four-thousand square foot house, surrounded by what Caroline called *stuff*, meaning things that I no longer needed.

A lot of it was what an archivist would label 'memorabilia.' The very word implies that it is worth keeping. And, in fact, I had discovered that one of the more pleasant disciplines associated with writing one's memoir is the dredging up and poring over old documents and photographs, all that effluvia that piles up through time, of no interest to anyone except for the way it can trigger memories so intense and vivid that the intervening years drop away.

The lower half of one wall in my office was made up of built-in filing cabinets, containing the source material for the 'professional' half of my memoir. When I began, I vowed to myself that I would sort through every one of those cabinets. Two hours and six file drawers after starting this morning, I pulled a manila folder labeled 'Dieter Bauer Dissertation.' I grimaced, irritated at myself for storing such minutiae, and tossed the file into the 'discard' pile that had been steadily growing for the past two hours. The adjacent stack of papers – the ones to keep – was very small and I was beginning to think about just dumping the entire filing system, another dozen drawers of files just as irrelevant as the

Bauer file, and thereby feeling good about my time management skills.

But the file fluttered open in midair and a badly faded photograph fell out, a picture of an ornate granite building with a few German language phrases in black ink on the margin, and suddenly Nadia was in the room with me, along with the ghosts of Hans, Richter, Gunter and others whose names I couldn't remember.

The photograph was from late summer in 1993. Deborah had been dead for two years and I hadn't seen or heard from Jacob during that time. It was probably a calculated absence on his part. He had kept me incommunicado in Plovdiv for four days after Deborah had been murdered and I think he knew that I would have tried to throttle him if he showed up.

It had been a bad two years in every way – emotionally, professionally, morally; an acting out of every clichéd dysfunctional scene from a mid-life crisis fueled by a vague and unceasing grieving process that somehow, by some strange alchemy, made my behavior forgivable among friends and colleagues.

I canceled the one seminar that I was teaching and stopped showing up at the university. In the real world, I would have been fired, but this was academe. And I had tenure. The Dean called me three times in the first six months, timidly asking, "When do you think you'll be able to resume teaching?" He always added hastily, before I could respond, "Of course, not until you're absolutely ready."

I started drinking heavily, usually at home and always alone, but every few weeks taking off for a resort in the mountains or at the beach and twice in Hawaii. The trips were a sham, designed to fool hovering friends that I was 'taking some time for myself.' The sordid reality was that all I did was sit in my expensive room, watch mindless daytime TV and drink.

I developed an obsession about getting rid of things. It started with Deborah's clothes and books. Any physical object that would trigger her image. But it morphed into an anti-materialism that drove me to give away furniture, dishes, artwork, golf clubs, suits I hadn't worn for years, including all but three pairs of shoes. I invited Robert and Kristi to come and take anything that they wanted. The house began to look barren, the kind of place rented out to transient executives.

My worst lapse, however, was what I did – or didn't do – for Melanie. She was seventeen years old, had lost her mother and was left with a father that was a workaholic and absent much of her life. We spent an awkward month together after Deborah's funeral, each of us working from a script patched together from old movies and advice from well-meaning friends. It all fell apart in an inevitable and probably cathartic screaming session, with all the stock accusations.

"You don't love me! You didn't care about mom! You were never there for us! All you care about is work! You don't know anything about me! I hate you!"

I was enough of a basket case myself and there was enough truth in her screaming that neither consolation nor reconciliation was possible. Somehow we worked out an arrangement where she would enroll in a small liberal arts college in Minnesota, near Deborah's parents who favored the arrangement as a poor substitute for having their daughter alive. Kristi lived nearby and spent time with her when she could. During the next two years, I saw her every couple of months. The reunions were stilted, formal affairs; infrequent enough that I was always struck by the changes in her. She became serious, more co-equal – transitioning from a girl into a woman and ever more distant.

It took two years. Maybe I worked through all five of the Kubler-Ross phases of grieving or maybe I 'hit bottom,' as the AA fanatics liked to say, but I think I just got bored with myself and the self-pity that had engulfed me. At any rate, I was ready for a tipping point, and Kristi provided it.

She made a serious attempt to reach out to me right after Deborah's murder, but I repelled it. I hadn't seen much of her for several months, although we kept up an intermittent email traffic. She stayed close to home in Minnesota, supporting herself in a series of careers.

I found her sitting in my living room when I came back from a weekend of drinking in a dreary seaside hotel in southern New Jersey. By that time, I was so used to living in a fog that I wasn't even curious about how she got in.

"You're pathetic." She said it calmly, as dispassionately as if she was commenting on an untied shoelace. It was her tone as much as the criticism itself that conveyed the truth of what she said.

Have I gotten so bad that my younger sister is offended by me and finds me so far gone that she can't even get mad at me?

"Hi, Kristi. Long time, no see. Is this an intervention?"

"You don't have enough friends left to stage an intervention. And I'm the only family that you haven't driven away. I asked Robert to come along and he just laughed at me.... the way someone laughs when you get invited to a time-share pitch."

So far, we were operating in our email mode. Other than her opening comment, 'You're pathetic,' it was all big brother vs. kid sister stuff. Some carefully veiled emotions imbedded in a stream of sophisticated chatter. A little darker than usual.

But then it all changed. Just as she intended.

"You remind me of *him*."

Surely, lives can be altered with a single phrase -- 'I hate you,' 'You have inoperable cancer,' 'I want a divorce' – but those five simple words from Kristi – *you remind me of him* -- were the most damning indictment imaginable. They evoked images and feelings that I had pushed so far down into subterranean recesses that I thought they were irretrievable.

He would stumble into the room and stand there swaying, mumbling about how sorry he was about everything, cycling through the same phrases over and over. We would push him out but he would always come back, standing over the bed and apologizing to us for all of his failures. They were very long, often sleepless, nights.

She stood facing me, knowing the effect of her words on me. Years later when we talked about her visit, she said that she thought of it as 'the nuclear option,' a verbal bomb that could be used once and only once. It was not until then that I understood how difficult it must have been for her to bring up the subject of *him*. I remember how she had looked that night in her pajamas with teddy bear figures.

I was left with an overwhelming feeling of disgust. For what I had become in her eyes. But, even then, I had a flash of anger.

"Is that why you're here, trying to feed this two-year-old nightmare that I can't stop having? Because I'm so pathetic I need to be reminded?"

She stood up and looked at me searchingly, as though trying to decide if I was worth the effort of one more try.

"No. Because I owe you." She paused, clearly debating with herself, and finally said in a voice so soft that it was barely audible, "And because nobody deserves to be murdered and then deserted by those who were close to her. Nobody. You owe it to Deborah."

She walked out, and the sound of the door closing marked the end of my self-destructive need to feel sorry for myself.

Dresden (1993)

A very wise and cynical person once said that 'coincidence is the word we use when we can't see the levers and pulleys.' It could be that the Dresden offer only three days after Kristi left was a coincidence, and I certainly accepted that at the time. It was much later – more than a decade – before I began to look for the levers and pulleys.

Dieter Bauer called. I'd been his thesis chair and helped him get his initial faculty position at Berkeley. He was one of the brightest doctoral candidates I'd encountered and we continued to correspond and had coauthored a pair of papers that caused a mild stir among the thirty or forty economists able to appreciate the subtleties. Five years before the Soviet Empire collapsed and the (East) German Democratic Republic reunited with its West German counterpart, Dieter went home to Dresden and the local university. It was a move that dismayed me and everyone that knew him.

"How's it going?" I asked as soon as the pleasantries were over. Both of us understood that the simple question had multiple layers.

"About like you said it would. I feel like I've been teleported into an earlier century."

"If you're homesick, I'm sure Berkeley would be delighted to have you back. The Stanford economics department just hired another Nobel Prize winner and Berkeley's Dean needs a small win."

"I'm German, Brian. How can I be homesick if I'm in Germany? Especially now that the Russians are gone."

But Bauer was calling with a specific objective. We agreed that I would be a Guest Lecturer at Dresden University for three months. There would be ample time for the two of us to frame a first draft of a paper that we had talked about when he was in the U.S.

It was an inflection point. Now, fourteen years later, I find myself sitting on the floor of my office surrounded by the paper trail of my professional life and staring at a perfectly ordinary color photograph of a building, a relic of a past that had fluttered loose from a file on its flight to the wastebasket.

William Faulkner said it best. "The past is never dead. It's not even past."

The building in the photograph was the family home of Dieter Bauer's grandfather, who had been a prominent contributor to the development of the German railway system late in the nineteenth century. Both he and the building survived the war, but the communists that came in its place executed Herr Bauer and declared the home to be state property. They could not magically require its exterior to conform to the bleak and tasteless architectural standards of Soviet construction, but over the next forty-five years, they converted the interior into a graceless rabbit warren of offices and apartments.

Once the Wall came down and Germany began the reunification process, Dieter's father began the laborious legal process of reclaiming the home for the family and then restoring it to its prewar grandeur.

I lived on the top floor for the three months I was in Dresden, the sole resident until Nadia appeared. I stopped drinking and focused on the lectures that I was giving. As a western and, even better, an *American* professor, my lectures were standing room only. All those ex-communists wanting to be capitalists, many of them believing that there was a formula or a secret elixir that would make them rich. And others who believed that I could be their entry point into IBM or GE or Citibank.

And I was, for a few. The most memorable was the mathematician. He was, quite literally, a rocket scientist. His bio included a dozen or more papers with incomprehensible titles, but

– when deciphered – were about calculating trajectories of ballistic missiles. It turned out that a hedge fund in Greenwich, Connecticut wanted to develop program trading strategies based on the view that turning points in the stock market could be predicted using ICBMs as metaphors. He still sends me a birthday card every year and my hedge fund friends tell me that he's worth several hundred million dollars today.

Jacob was sitting on the low stone wall that bordered the sidewalk, next to one of the grime-encrusted columns flanking the front door. He looked exactly as he did when he put me on the plane at the Varna airport, even down to the baggy grey suit and the 'you can't surprise me' expression that never varied. He was holding a bundle of papers on his lap, tied together with twine.

"Hello Jacob."

"Brian."

There was a brief period of mutual assessment, a wary scanning for clues as to intention. I think each of us was surprised by the lack of animation on either of our parts.

I broke the silence. "It's been a while."

He nodded. "Two years."

"Centuries, not years. Time expands. Didn't you know that?"

Again, he nodded, watchful acceptance of what he thought he had heard.

He's nervous. He still doesn't trust me to stay calm. Doesn't want to risk setting me off.

But I was wrong, like every other time I thought that I understood Jacob Connolly.

"Those two years? You tried hard to become somebody else. I thought you might succeed."

So you've been watching. But that's what you do, isn't it? Watch people. I shrugged. "I didn't like who I was, so I tried another version. He wasn't any better."

Jacob stood up, and when he did, I noticed a stiffness that was new, as though certain motions required special thought. And perhaps he was slightly stooped.

I think that maybe it's been a difficult two years for him as well.

"A different world, huh Jacob? Here we are on the wrong side of the once-upon-a-time Iron Curtain, but it's now all one Germany. A scary prospect for you and your people, maybe?"

"We have some new enemies. But Germany isn't one of them." He waved his arm at the brightly lit café across the street. "How about some coffee? We need to talk."

Thinking about it fourteen years later while sitting at my desk in my office, I do not recall that I protested in any way. There was no expression of outrage, no heated recriminations about what he had done to me in Bulgaria, no outburst of righteousness about CIA exploitation, no perception that this was my chance to get out of the game. What I remember is that we walked across the street together, ordered coffee and then sat at a small table in the corner while he explained to me what he wanted from me.

"What do you think about the prospects for German reunification?"

That's not like the Jacob I know ... to ask about something where he already knew the answer.

I gave him what I thought of as my cocktail party response. After all, the question was on the minds of everyone in those days. "They're doing it. One of the greatest socio/political efforts ever undertaken, certainly in modern times. It will take ten years and will require a huge transfer of wealth from west to east, but it's going to happen. Germany will be the great power in Europe once more.

"And your lot – the CIA – should love it. Germany will be the counterweight to Russia. Makes NATO look a lot better with eighty-one million Germans on our side."

Then he asked his second surprising question. "But do we *need* a counterweight? Isn't Russia becoming a part of the westernized world, a market-based economy that will require peace and stability for the sake of trade?"

Enough of this stagecraft! "Quit the bullshit! We both know that isn't going to happen. Maybe some lip service, a little bit of structural reform, some bilateral agreements, but – sooner or later, and I think it's sooner -- they'll revert to authoritarianism and their grandiose notions of being a world power. One with nuclear weapons. The CIA can recall all those laid-off excess cold-war agents hanging out in Trieste and Riga and Varna."

As I spoke, a certainty emerged in my mind. "That's why you're here. To recruit agents! Isn't it?"

He didn't answer directly. "You know of the Stasi, of course?"

"Hard not to. Erich Mielke was sentenced last week, and the papers have been full of it. Six years. Some say he's senile and doesn't care." I went on, wondering about my need to prove myself to this dumpy little man sitting on the stone wall. But I recited, as though a sixth grader in a social studies class: "Erich Mielke was the head of GDR's Ministry for State Security, better known as the Stasi. Under his leadership, it became the single most vicious agency in the entire Soviet satellite system."

Jacob nodded. "It was also one of the most effective. We had a cell, but the Stasi had an informer. We lost some really good people." He paused and looked far away for four or five seconds. *Recalling some of those 'really good people' perhaps.*

"So you're looking to start over?"

Jacob smiled. "An American football coach would call it 'a rebuilding year.'"

"But why? Communist East Germany is no more. Part of the western bloc now. Calling for some genteel form of spying ... political and commercial espionage maybe, but surely not running some vast underground ring to snoop on a key ally?"

He looked at me with the expression one would use for a slow but earnest student.

I thought about it for a couple of seconds. "It's not the Germans. You want sources in Russia."

"Almost. What I want are the identities of three particular Germans, ones who hate Russians but love Americans. The ones in our cell that the Stasi never found."

"Just names? That's all?"

"We know the names... sort of. We even know what they do. What we need are their identities."

"You know the names? But – "

"Wynken, Blynken & Nod ... spies with a sense of humor."

I remember reciting it to Melanie. She was two and would not allow Deborah or me to leave her room until we would chant the entire Eugene Field lullaby.

I recited in a sing-song cadence.

> Wynken, Blynken, and Nod one night
> Sailed off in a wooden shoe —
> Sailed on a river of crystal light,
> Into a sea of dew.....

He stopped me. "Wonderful. But it doesn't tell us who they are."

"Wynken, Blynken & Nod ... I like them already. So much better than 'Boris and Natasha.'"

Jacob frowned at me, and then switched to a puzzled look. *Maybe he doesn't know everything after all. Probably didn't have a childhood that included Rocky and Bullwinkle cartoons on Saturday morning.*

He shrugged and went on. "East Germany was a Russian satellite for forty years plus, but there's always been an active underground resistance movement. Aside from the brutal repression, you've got to remember what the Soviet Army did to them in the last days of the war."

"So they spied for us? This Wynken, Blynken & Nod crowd?"

"Yes, but with two conditions. First, they would only provide intel about Russian operations in the GDR, nothing about Germany, ever."

"That's a pretty fine line to walk. What's the second condition?"

"We were not to know their real identities. No CIA contact whatsoever. Their stuff came through the mail, believe it or not. Postmarked out of West Berlin to my home address."

"Sounds like a frustrating arrangement. Strictly one way."

"It was. But their stuff on Russia's East German operations was very good. And unlike our other sources, the Stasi never found them. No people's bullet in the back of the head for them."

"But you said that you know what they do... Wynken, Blynken & Nod?"

"They're economists and they have a Dresden connection."

"And just how do you know that?"

Jacob winced. "*Know* is too strong a word; we *suspect* these things. To put it in bureaucrat-speak, 'Linguistic analysis and source-tracing algorithms strongly suggest that Wynken, Blynken & Nod are trained economists, are fluent in English and at some point have resided in Dresden."

"And what do I have to do with any of this?"

"Pretty obvious, I would think. You're here, in Dresden for three months. You're an economist, working with local economists. American, therefore to be trusted, maybe even approached. And, bloody hell, you can probably recite all forty stanzas of the goddam nursery rhyme!"

He sighed. "You may be able to identify them."

I shook my head. "Not a chance, given how little you know. Unless they walk up to me and say 'I was a spy for the CIA.' You don't even know if Wynken, Blynken & Nod are a single person or a trio."

"Nope, we don't. But they've left a trail." He handed me the bundle of papers that he was holding on his lap. "Here's what we've gotten from them for the last three years. It's redacted, of course. But I've left in anything that our in-house analysts flagged insofar as it indicated their economics backgrounds. I'm hoping you'll see something we've missed."

He pointed at the package. "Treat it carefully. No copies. And I want the whole thing back on Monday morning."

I stood up. "I'll take a look. And if I don't think I can help, I'll tell you so."

That weekend, I probably spent twenty hours on that stack of paper. Despite the redactions, which were extensive, it was pretty clear that the raw intelligence dealt with the negative impact of Russian-imposed trade agreements on the East German economy. The accompanying comments by Wynken, Blynken & Nod were even more compelling.

They conveyed a deep hatred of the German leadership. "Honecker is Gorbychev's whore!" was scrawled across one of the pages, "Mielke sucks!" on another. But they also demonstrated an impressive understanding of basic economics, maybe with an emphasis on labor markets.

Despite Jacob's admonition, I did copy one quote that I thought was representative of the stream of material. "We estimate that the policy of favoring Russian imports over German-manufactured durable goods leads to underemployment of GDR workers by several million man-hours each month and to related social problems. Note: See 'Mielke's public drunkenness statistics' in prior shipment."

Jacob was sitting outside my door on Monday morning, in the same spot as before. I handed him back the package of papers. He looked at me with a raised eyebrow as I recited the last verse from Wynken, Blynken & Nod.

> So shut your eyes while Mother sings,
> Of wonderful sights that be,
> And you see the beautiful things
> As you rock in the misty sea.

He stood up. "I take it that –"

"Your analysts are right about your nursery rhyme trio. They – or he, she, him or her – have some significant training in economics. Beyond that, I can't help you."

"You'll pay attention, though?"

"Sure. I'll especially watch for beautiful things on misty seas."

Office Mates

In 1993, I was forty-seven years old, recently widowed, just coming out of a self-imposed depression, living temporarily in a near-castle in an exotic old-world city and giving daily lectures to groups of intelligent young people who thought I was either a philosopher-king or a benevolent magician with a magic potion. And a goodly number of them were attractive women looking for a launchpad into what they thought was a capitalist paradise.

Given all of that, Nadia was as inevitable as the sunrise.

We met during my first day on campus. Dieter picked me up at the airport and drove me to the university. It was a short drive, but long enough to make it apparent that he was nervous about something. He seemed relieved when I asked him what was bothering him.

"You are a Distinguished Guest Lecturer." He said it in a way that made the capital letters quite apparent. "But there is little office space. My Department Chair has asked me .... that is, I'm wondering if you would ... if you don't mind, of course –"

I cut him off. "Dieter, I'll be glad to share an office. All I need is a desk, a telephone and access to a computer."

He was immediately relieved and spent the rest of the trip apologizing for the lack of a decent copying machine. Apparently, the East German authorities had kept them quite scarce, fearing them as a means for mass communication, the way Gutenberg's printing press altered the structure of pre-renaissance society and challenged the elite of the day.

The economics faculty and staff were officed in one of the older buildings on the campus. The core of the building dated back to the seventeenth century and the rooms were more like monastic cells than anything resembling functional offices. 'My' office was at the end of a second-story corridor.

"A little different than what you're accustomed to, I think," said Dieter as he knocked lightly on the door and pushed it open. A woman was sitting at one of the two desks, marking up a paper that she was reading.

She stood when we entered and held out her hand. "I'm Nadia Iska. Thank you for sharing your office with me." Her English was near-perfect, only the slightest accent. But despite the words and her extended hand, she radiated a suppressed hostility and I wondered if it was aimed at Dieter or me. The aura was amplified by the woman's severity. Her dark hair was pulled back and wound into a tight bun at the nape of her neck. She wore a grey wool skirt, quite long, and a shapeless grey sweater buttoned to her chin. Her shoes were lace up black oxfords. Her eyes were brown and huge, made even more prominent by the rimless glasses she was wearing. She radiated disapproval. All in all, she looked like a caricature, something that you might see on one of those early Soviet propaganda posters entitled 'Hero of the Office Worker's Union.' I guessed her age at mid-thirties, but allowed for a big margin of error, given her overall severity.

We went the first several days without speaking, other than 'Guten Morgen' and 'Guten Abend.' She was always there when I arrived, still there after I left, always taking papers from the left side of her desk, making notes on them and placing them in a stack on the right side. When all of the papers were transferred from one side to another, she would take the stack and leave the office, always coming back with a new batch that she would carefully align on the left side of her desk.

Her wardrobe was uniformly grey, although the sweater was sometimes a cardigan, sometimes a pullover. Several times, I saw her in the cafeteria, always eating alone and reading a book. She also attended each of my twice-a-week lectures, sitting in the back of the room and seeming to take continuous notes.

Shortly after the fourth lecture, she was in our shared office and working at her desk when I came in. As soon as I sat down, she looked up and said, "You made a mistake today."

The remark was so startling and free of context that I just stared at her.

"In your lecture. This morning. You said Heilbroner."

The lecture was the last in a series of four dealing with the underlying causes of the Soviet collapse, mostly a synthesis of works from various economic historians who were beginning to publish sweeping analyses of the forces at work. Robert Heilbroner was one of the most influential economists in that sphere and I cited his work several times during the lecture.

"I said 'Heilbroner?' A mistake?"

She spoke very fast, as though she feared interruption. "Your quote about how economics could never succeed as a predictive science ... that people in groups were too complex ... too subject to forces that could not be captured with mathematical models ... That was from Adolph Lowe, not Robert Heilbroner."

She turned away from me, back to her stack of papers. And Dieter came in just as she did so, looking for a lunch companion and wanting to talk about our joint paper.

It took me two hours in the University library to prove that she was right, during which time I learned a great deal about an economist that I should have known better than I did. Adolph Lowe was the first German professor of social sciences to be dismissed by the Nazi government. He was able to leave Germany and wound up at the New School for Social Research in New York, where among other things he acted as a strong influence on Heilbroner.

The next morning I stopped at the kiosk on the corner and bought a bouquet of assorted wildflowers. She was at her corner desk and I handed her the bouquet. "I should give them to Adolph Lowe as an apology, but you'll have to accept them on his behalf."

She smiled and stood up, reaching out for the flowers and executing a small curtsy, like a schoolgirl being praised for her first piano recital.

The smile was transformative. That and the splash of color added by the bouquet of flowers made the severe hairdo and grey wardrobe seem mere backdrop, a means of accentuating the smile. And, somehow, it made the curtsy seem incredibly flirtatious.

"And what shall I do with the flowers? Hold them while I work?"

I brought Deborah flowers once, very early in our marriage. "Nice gesture," she said, "but so typically male. Now I have to trim them, find a vase, arrange them prettily, water them and tend to them through their life cycle. And do all of this while letting you think that you've given me a special gift."

Not only had Nadia evoked the memory, but she was unknowingly acting out Deborah's part, standing with the flowers, looking mischievous and clearly expecting me to finish what I had started.

I looked around. It was the kind of dismal space where one expects to see scratches on the wall from previous inmates, marking the passage of days. There were two metal desks, a bank of grey filing cabinets, a wall filled with bookshelves but without books, a chalkboard on casters, and a single window so grimy that it was opaque. The only ornamental feature in the entire scene was a single pathetic orchid that had long since died but was valiantly standing, held up by a thin bamboo rod.

"Let's liberate some state-owned property." I yanked the orchid out of its simple ceramic mug and threw it into the metal wastebasket. I took the flowers from her, stuck them in the mug and placed the arrangement on top of the nearest filing cabinet.

But the flowers were much too tall and the whole affair simply fell over.

Nadia's smile was still there, but she had her arms crossed and her entire demeanor translated as, 'Let's see if you can deal with this!'

I took a scissors from my desk drawer, cut off the stems and tried again. This time, the bouquet stood and the flowers even seemed to distribute themselves fairly evenly, with gravity as their only guide. I made a show of standing back and looking critically at the display, nudging a couple of the blossoms into a slightly altered position. Finally, I took the plastic bottle of water from my briefcase and poured half of it into the mug.

I stood looking at the bouquet, feeling silly about the small surge of pride that I was experiencing at having done all that. Nadia walked past me, picked up the mug and placed it on the corner of her desk.

"Thank you for the flowers, Dr. Norquist. On behalf of Adolph Lowe, of course. They're very nice."

"How do you know about Adolph Lowe? Are you an economist?"

"Nothing so glamorous as that. I took some graduate courses, but got bored with the mathematics ..."

An interesting phrasing. Was she bored because she didn't understand the math or because it didn't pose enough of a challenge?

We talked for the next ten minutes. I learned that she was a researcher for the Centre for Teacher Training and School Research, one of several special purpose 'institutes' at the University. She was thirty-one, divorced and living with her two sisters in a one room apartment in the center of Dresden.

I asked Dieter about her that evening, but didn't learn very much.

"Iska? She's only been here a week or so before you came. She's working on one of the Chairman's special projects dealing with vocational education. Seems smart enough, but she keeps to herself."

"Would you call her an economist?" I asked the question because somewhere in my back brain I was thinking of Wynken, Blynken & Nod. But Dieter interpreted my interest differently.

He grinned at me. "She's a woman, Brian. And you're a man who's been without a woman for two years. Why does it matter what her title is? I see happy endings all around."

He turned out to be right. And horribly wrong at the same time.

The Other Nadia

The next morning, Nadia was wearing a red sweater and she had arranged her hair differently, still pulled back but with tendrils of black hair trailing down her behind her ears. It was disconcerting, as if she was deliberately confirming Dieter's view of the age-old relationship between men and women. But the day passed exactly like the previous ones: she transferred papers from the left stack to the right stack and ate lunch alone in the cafeteria.

The next day was the same. Until she stood up to leave the office at five. Without the slightest bit of forethought, I blurted out, "Would you like to have dinner with me?" It surprised both of us. I rushed on. "After all, I've taken half of your office space, thrown away your orchid ..."

"And substituted these." She gestured at the wildflowers on her desk. They were beginning to droop, but the colors were still the most vivid element in the room other than her red sweater.

I stood there trying to think of what to say next. The silence began to sound awkward. *My social skills are non-existent, especially with women. Twenty-plus years with one woman and then two years of self-imposed celibacy enforced by heavy drinking. You really don't know what you're doing.*

But Nadia rescued me, a harbinger of what she would do many times over in the next three months. "Dinner would be very nice. But I have to go home first and you have to let me choose the restaurant."

I recovered enough to hold the door open for her. She stopped immediately outside and said, "Why don't you come with me? It won't take me long and I can give you a mini-tour of Dresden on the way."

The mini-tour was the streetcar trip from the University to her home, with a thirty-minute stop to walk around the Dresden

Cathedral. Nadia spent most of the time there describing the life and times of Augustus the Strong, whose heart was interred in the central crypt.

I teased her. "You seem much more interested in current events and politics rather than architecture or religion or music. Didn't Bach hold recitals here?"

She said, "I'm sorry," without seeming at all contrite. "I promise that we'll come back and I'll do it properly." Halfway down the steps into the plaza, she turned and said, "And the Bach recitals were in Leipzig, not Dresden."

On the way out of the church, a boy, maybe seventeen or so, took our picture with a Poloroid camera and sold the photo to us for five deutschemarks. In the photo, we were both smiling and she was pointing at something in the square. We looked happy.

She lived in one of those incredibly dreary concrete warrens that blighted the Soviet world, on the third floor with a single hallway that seemed to stretch for miles. The sounds of domestic quarrels and the odor of sauerkraut were constant as we passed doorway after doorway, distinguished only by the number on the peeling paint. When we reached Number 367, she hesitated and I thought that she looked faintly apprehensive.

"Would you mind waiting outside? They ... the apartment is really not suitable for company. And I'll only be a minute."

I said, "Of course not," but I was wondering why she had brought me this far only to stop short at this point.

She slipped in, but I had a quick glimpse of a single room with two women in shapeless dresses sitting at a table with teacups in front of them. They seemed significantly older than Nadia, perhaps because of the way they sat, with their slumped shoulders and downturned eyes.

I could hear an animated outburst in German, sounding like all three women were attempting to talk at the same time. She was out within three minutes but as an entirely new person. The rimless glasses were gone, along with the baggy wardrobe. She wore a blue sleeveless dress with a long silk scarf looped around her neck, which she had accented with a simple gold necklace. And there was a trailing scent of perfume.

The transformation reminded me again of how little I knew about women. She had gone into the room as a slightly frumpy, spinsterish and asexual creature and emerged three minutes later as an alluring modern woman exuding subtle hints of possibility.

She smiled in a way that reminded me of that ambiguous curtsy when we first met. We did not talk until we were outside. She took my hand and said only, "My favorite restaurant is close by."

It was one of those late summer evenings that travel agents conjure up when they're trying to sell the idea of a Mediterranean cruise to a middle aged Midwestern couple looking for a romantic venue to celebrate their twentieth anniversary. We even had the cobblestone streets and sidewalk cafes. She intertwined her arm with mine and pulled me along, clearly with a destination in mind. It turned out to be a very small restaurant – only eight or nine tables – facing onto the central plaza. The proprietor greeted us at the door.

"Nadia! Es ist schon so lange! Ich habe dich vermisst!"

"Danke, Gunter. Sie sind sehr freundlich."

She nudged me forward very gently. "Gunter, this is Doctor Brian Norquist. He is a Distinguished Guest Lecturer at the University."

Gunter switched to fluent English without losing a syllable. "It is my pleasure, Dr. Norquist, to meet a friend of our Nadia. There is no one better in all of Dresden. You are an American, no?"

Nadia responded for me. "An American *economist*, working with Dieter Bauer at the University."

It was so slight that I first thought I imagined it, but Gunter flinched. What seemed to be genuine pleasure at Nadia's introduction changed into a definite wariness. The smile became less real, the held-out hand less spontaneous.

Is he bothered by Americans? Or economists? Or Dieter?

I reached out and shook his hand. "Please, it's Brian, not Dr. Norquist. Nadia tells me that this is the best restaurant in Dresden. Or was it in all of Germany?"

Nadia poked me. "No, all I said was that it is my favorite restaurant. And that is because of Gunter."

Gunter was the genial host once more, the wariness tamped down and out-of-sight, something that I had imagined. "Come and sit down. After a little wine, the restaurant ratings will not matter so much."

He was right.

Nadia came home with me that night, to my rooms on the fourth floor of the Bauer ancestral home, and she stayed there for the rest of the time that I was in Dresden.

It was a strange existence, the time neatly divided between work and non-work, with their respective rules and structure. During the day, we shared the office but behaved exactly as we had before she came to work that day in the red sweater. She continued to process papers, shifting them from the left side to the right side of her desk. We exchanged polite remarks, exactly what one would expect between a visiting professor and an imposed-upon office mate who speak different languages.

After the office day and on weekends, we spent our time together, much of it in bed, as chatty and intimate as a pair of coming-of-age teenagers. For me, she was at first a reincarnation of Deborah in a new form and then something much more than that; a completely different woman whose history and habits had to be learned through the osmosis of daily living. We walked all over

Dresden, visited museums, churches, parks, war memorials and even the train station. We watched rented DVD's on an ancient TV we found in one of the downstairs rooms in the house, but any scene that involved sex would send us scrambling up the stairs to the bedroom, often leaving articles of clothing strewn on the staircase. It was as if the emotional austerity that we practiced during the daylight hours required an equal and offsetting degree of wantonness when we were at home and behind closed doors.

We ate at Gunter's restaurant two or three nights every week and I met some of her friends that also frequented the place. Most of them were like her, civil servants and researchers who were uniformly curious about me and what I did. All but one of the half dozen that I met were men and, at first, I wondered if any of them had been her lovers; but Nadia was so focused on me that such jealousies came to seem petty and then irrelevant.

But there were parts of her that were inaccessible to me.

"Where are you from? Before Dresden?"

She became exceptionally still, but she answered quickly. "Why? Do I not seem sufficiently German?"

"That first night, when I waited outside your door. Your sisters were speaking to you in German, but with a definite accent. Definitely not from here."

She hesitated. "They lived for a while in a small town on the border with Poland. Many of the residents spoke Yiddish. Anyway, German accents change from village to village."

"You said *they*.... That *they* lived there. Where were you? And they seem much older than you."

"Why do you care? They are not the ones naked in bed with you ... the ones who do this for you..." and she pressed the entire length of her body against me and changed the course of our dialogue.

I tried a couple of other times to ask about her family; where she was from, her parents, the usual biographical data that lovers would share.   But she always found ways to divert the conversation to other topics.

The same way that I do if someone asks me about my childhood! I've found my match.

Wynken, Blynken & Nod

Philosophers advocate living in the present moment. And so we did. Who we were or what we had done before we met was irrelevant. The future extended no further than our plans for the next weekend. It could not last.

We had staged a candlelight dinner to celebrate our seven-week anniversary. Just the two of us in the vast dining room in the Bauer mansion. The phone rang in the middle of the dinner, a rare enough event that I felt compelled to answer it. It was Melanie, calling, an equally rare event. Nadia listened to my end of the conversation, becoming visibly sadder as it went on.

When the call ended, she said, "So you have a daughter."

"Melanie. She's nineteen. In college." *I wonder why I'm speaking in sentence fragments, without using any adjectives? Why does this topic seem so dangerous for us?*

"Do you have other family?"

"A brother ... twin ... and a younger sister."

"Dieter told me about your wife. Deborah? That was very sad. It made you seem ... heroic ... to me, someone that I should be respectful of." She leaned over and kissed me on the corner of my mouth. "Not someone that I should do such things with."

"I'm glad that you do ... Such things."

And then she asked, "What about your parents?"

I will not go there. Not yet. Maybe not ever. "They died a long time ago. But enough about me and my family. Tell me about yours."

The story came out in bits and pieces. It was not a happy one. She had no family. The two women in her shared apartment were not her sisters, just people that she lived with. She was abandoned by her father when she was fifteen and the state placed her in the Soviet equivalent of a foster home, but she didn't stay.

She said, "I was lonely and thought I was ugly. I hung out with a bunch of misfits ... rebels ... some of them political, others just sad. We thought we could change the world with rock-and-roll music and slogans painted on walls. The Stasi taught us otherwise."

Another time, we were at a wine bar with two of her friends – she introduced them as Richter and Hans. It was late and all four of us had taken on too much wine. Hans and Richter got into a heated argument about the theories of Ronald Coase, the prior year's recipient of the Nobel Prize in economics. It quickly became apparent that Nadia had no idea who he was or why he was important in the field.

I tried for a casual tone. "Where did you study economics?"

"Here and there. But in East Germany, the theories of *western* economists were scoffed at. We were not permitted to study many topics."

I have studied Marxist economics. Hell! I taught it once. Ronald Coase's theories were an important part, precisely because they explicitly identified market failures and how they could be exploited if capitalism was dominant.

I began, "The University here, in Dresden, the faculty –"

Richter was watching us closely and stood up. He was more than slightly drunk and steadied himself by using the edge of the table for leverage. In doing so, he tipped the entire table along with the several glasses of wine and half-full bottles on its surface. It was a colossal crash and it effectively got us kicked out of the wine bar.

Our ejection didn't dampen the discussion. Once out on the sidewalk, we were still laughing and talking loudly, much of it directed at Richter and his wine-soaked trousers. But then Hans said something that sobered me instantaneously.

"Shh! Mielke's ghost is still out there. He'll have us in his public drunkenness statistics tomorrow morning!"

Nadia and Richter laughed even harder, but all I could do was remember that exact language in Jacob's file, the quote from Wynken, Blynken & Nod.

"Herr Professor. You look happier and healthier than when I saw you last. German food and hospitality agrees with you."

I peered into Jacob's eyes and reran his greeting in my mind, searching for the slightest hint of irony. Then I laughed at my naivete. There was no chance of Jacob revealing his mood or real intentions. He was far too skilled and habituated to dissembling. It also occurred to me that he probably knew every detail of my torrid nightlife with Nadia.

We were meeting at the train station, probably the single most public place in all of Dresden and therefore a place where two people could meet in that strange form of privacy that crowds afford to their members. We were drinking espresso, a habit that Nadia brought about.

"Your lectures? They are going well?"

I shrugged. "The students are intelligent and highly motivated. But the communists seemed to assume that the self-interest that is at the heart of economic theory should not be taught. I seem to be doing a lot of remedial microeconomics."

"Ah, yes. The one-for-all and all-for-one bullshit. A slogan in place of a theory."

It was the first time I recall Jacob using profanity. It startled me.

The waitress stopped to clear our cups, but Jacob asked for refills and a dessert menu. He and the waitress engaged in a spirited argument about the merits of German vs. French pastries. Jacob's German seemed completely natural, but I could not keep up.

When she left, I said, "Your German is quite fluent."

The compliment seemed to bother him. He looked away from me and pursed his lips. "Yes, I spend a lot of time here. It rubs off after a while."

I asked him, "Have you thought about Wynken, Blynken & Nod, maybe whether their choice of that as their group pseudonym is meaningful in some way?"

He laughed. "Our back room people at Langley had a couple of crackpot ideas. The Director has been pushing a fad called 'Think Outside of the Box' and I think they're trying to demonstrate compliance. The reality is that all of the agencies now assign project names using random word generators."

The thought clearly amused him. "They had one called 'Titanic.' It was intended to cut down on the consumption of paper by widening the margins for all CIA-generated documents by two-tenths of an inch."

He changed the subject abruptly. "Speaking of Wynken, Blynken & Nod, have you had any insights as to their possible identities?"

I knew he would ask and had thought about how to respond. In keeping with that strategy, I began cautiously. "It's hard. First, I have almost nothing to go on. Second, and what I didn't anticipate, everybody I've met in the Soviet Bloc – beginning in Varna in 1978 – is so paranoid about informers that they won't even tell the truth to themselves. Those habits don't go away when the regime changes. I think it's so ingrained by now that we could view it as genetically transferrable to the next generation."

Jacob sat patiently, recognizing my lengthy prologue as the equivalent of the "I have some ideas, but ..." disclaimer that most academics use when actual policy makers ask for their opinion.

When I paused, he said, "Why don't you tell me about the people you've met without trying to sort them into likely or unlikely? Then we'll circle back and dive a little deeper." He took a small notebook and a ballpoint pen with the logo of the local soccer team from the bulging inside pocket of his jacket, opened the notebook to a blank page and sat looking at me expectantly.

I began talking, beginning with Dieter picking me up at the Dresden airport and ending with the graduate student that I had spent two hours with just before leaving to meet Jacob. I was surprised by the number of people that I had interacted with enough to have strong opinions about.

Jacob did not interrupt me. He jotted down occasional notes, never more than a word or phrase. When I was done, he began asking questions about several of the individuals I had talked about. It quickly became clear that he had paid close attention and that he had other sources of information about those same individuals.

"Dieter Bauer. A good friend?"

I thought about it. "Yes. He's been invaluable to me here in Dresden."

"He's pretty rare, isn't he? A very fast-track academic career in the U.S., but then he leaves to make less money and get treated worse in East Germany, long before the wall came down."

I said, "Yes, it was a surprising move," and left it at that.

"And Hans and Richter, your occasional drinking buddies ... they spoke that phrase about public drunkenness ... the same as the language in those reports I showed you?"

"It was Hans who said it. And there were three or four others that were part of the beer hall crowd after work. They all had something to do with economics. Students, I think. But I didn't get their names."

"And this man Gunter ..."

"He owns a small restaurant on the central square. Not an economist. There's nothing about him to connect him to Wynken, Blynken & Nod."

He held up the notebook and waggled it in the air. "Out of this whole lot, are there any of them that seem to dislike Russians more than the average East German?"

I laughed. "I have no way to measure that. Everybody I've met seems to hate the Russians, more or less at the maximum possible. And the Stasi, maybe even more."

He asked a few more questions, but they were perfunctory. He took no more notes and clearly was preoccupied with whatever was next on his agenda. He stood up abruptly. "Thanks for meeting me and for sharing. I think this moves us a little bit closer to the Wynken, Blynken & Nod crowd."

He turned to leave, but stopped and said, "You really do look happier than three months ago. Perhaps you should think about staying longer in Dresden."

After he left, I sat for twenty minutes, thinking about what I had told him. And hadn't told him. *I left out much of my life with Nadia, made her sound like a minor character, telling myself that all that detail wasn't really relevant and that Jacob had no need to know.*

It bothered me that I had this unacknowledged need to protect Nadia. But from what? Or who? I worried about that until a much more ominous thought pushed its way into my consciousness.

He didn't ask me about Nadia. Not a single question. He knows.

End of an Interlude

My university appointment ended in a week. Neither Nadia or I talked about it or the obvious "what next" question that went with it. We talked less and made love more, as if in recognition of a mutual need that would be diminished if it were to be acknowledged.

Dieter came to the office. "I want to host a small going away dinner for you. At Gunter's restaurant this Saturday. Just a few friends, the faculty and students that you've worked closely with while you've been here. Including Nadia, of course."

When he left, I looked over at Nadia. The bouquet of wildflowers was still standing on the corner of her desk, its blossoms as vibrant as the first day I brought it to her. *She must be replenishing the flowers.* I know nothing about flowers, but I could not help but see it as a sign. And she had propped the Poloroid photo of the two of us at The Dresden Cathedral against the mug.

"Nadia, I ..."

I stopped, not knowing how to complete the sentence.

"I know," she said. "Me too."

"Come to the United States with me."

She did not seem to react for a long time, but a glint of wetness emerged in the corner of her eye and she turned her head away from me.

"I can't."

"But – "

"I have no passport. I cannot leave Germany."

There was a very faint note of hopelessness in her voice, like a young girl feeling sorry for herself because she believed that all of her friends were prettier than she was. It was the first time I experienced Nadia as vulnerable. When we first met, she was forbidding and sexless. Then, without going through any transitional state, she became open and alluring. This was a new incarnation.

No passport. Not so uncommon in the chaos of converting a communist dictatorship into a democratic society. If citizens are not permitted to leave a country, why should they have a passport? A short-term problem, one that requires only patience in dealing with bureaucratic obstinacy.

"Then perhaps I might stay in Dresden a little longer. Until we work out the passport problem."

I said it without thinking, but having said it, it became an obvious solution. Nothing that required discussion or analysis. A perfectly natural and cowardly substitute for the words that I should have used.

I love you and want to be with you. It does not matter where.

I worked out the details with Dieter. The university would provide office space and a title. I would be an unpaid and (very occasional) lecturer. The much more important and informal agreement was that I could continue – with Nadia – as the resident of the Bauer family home.

I pressed Nadia about the eventual need for a passport, but she pleaded that the process was underway, snarled in red tape, and that a restart would only delay the outcome even further into the future.

In the flurry of details, we forgot about the going-away party until Saturday morning, when Gunter called me to ask me my menu preferences. We quickly agreed to keep the arrangements, but change the theme from parting to reuniting. We relabeled it a 'continuation party.'

"I have the guest list," Gunter said. "A half-dozen of your friends. We should have assigned seats."

"Gunter. It's just the usual bunch. I do not think –"

"Ach! There are protocols to be observed. There will be flowers on the table and embarrassing toasts will be offered. And certain people should not be seated next to certain other people. Especially when wine is involved. Please?"

Nadia left early that Saturday afternoon. She said that she needed to spend a few hours with her roommates, but had promised to be at Gunter's restaurant on time. She had on a new dress, one that we had picked out together from an expensive boutique.

I spent the day reading through the backlog of working papers that the departmental secretary at Princeton had forwarded to me. Some of them were intended as submissions to refereed journals, so I spent extra time marking them up. It was a pleasurable activity, although it reminded me how much work was required to stay on the academic fast track, and how much momentum I'd lost in those two years after Deborah died.

She called at the same instant that the doorbell rang, three floors below. "I'm at the restaurant. A couple of the others are here already."

I looked at my watch, thinking about the doorbell. *Probably a student. Still ten minutes to spare, and the Bauer house is only a short walk from the restaurant.*

"I'm on the way. Ten minutes."

It was not a student. It was Valentin Aslanov. He stood motionless, simply looking at me with his hands in his pockets, as though waiting his turn in a slow-moving queue.

Thirteen years ago, in Islamabad. Akmal and Qasim. Me locked up in a room for four days expecting to be executed.

Other than the clothes, he looks the same. Somehow no older, but seeming even more cynical and emotionless than he was before. He looks like he hasn't slept for a week.

He was dressed in working man's clothes, with a cloth bag slung over his shoulder. A white name tag sewn on the front of his shirt said that his name was "Fritz." He stood in the doorway, saying nothing.

"Well," I said.

"Yes."

The two words, each a complete sentence, seemed to work for each of us; serving as an introduction, an acknowledgement of all that we had shared, and an apology for wrongs inflicted.

"Come in," I said. "But I have to leave in –"

"I know. I only need a few minutes."

I gestured to the room on my right. Originally it had been an elegant reception room for guests entering the Bauer home. The communists had subdivided it into half-a-dozen plywood-sided cubicles for minor functionaries to process long lines of petitioners. The restoration was ongoing, but at the moment it was a giant empty room, barren of furniture except for two folding chairs in the middle of the room with a telephone sitting between them on the floor, as if to emphasize the room's emptiness. We sat facing one another in the fading light from the windows facing onto the street. It felt like a stage, with an unseen audience beyond the windows, and seemed to require something more than ordinary conversation.

"So, Valentin, Afghanistan did not go well for the Russians. And your glorious Soviet empire has imploded of its own weight. And yet here you are on my doorstep once more. But I think our debate about the merits of our two economic systems is no longer very interesting. So what do you want? Are you looking for work?"

He looked at the pair of leather gloves in his left hand and at the scuffed boots on his feet, and then up at me with a weary smile. "I am working. My ... firm ... has reorganized itself, but it continues."

"To where? For what purpose? Your world vision is obsolete. All those ex-Soviet satellites? They're all converting to democracy and capitalism! You and your KGB colleagues need job retraining strategies, rather than secret codes."

He paused and sat up straight. "Everything under heaven is in utter chaos; the situation is excellent."

A quote from Chairman Mao's little red book. He was sitting in the Stanford Student Union reading ... memorizing ... "Valentin, Mao is dead. His cultural revolution set China back a hundred years. But even the Chinese are becoming capitalists, slowly and surely, just as your country is. You don't need spies and assassins; you need lawyers and accountants and bankers and advertising executives."

He nodded, as if in agreement, and then changed the subject. "And you shall teach us how to do that. I hear that your classes are very popular and that you've decided to extend your stay in Dresden. A form of geographic therapy, perhaps? After Deborah?"

His words brought back Deborah with a rush, accompanied by a sense of guilt because I realized that Nadia had driven thoughts of Deborah back into a part of memory that was harder to access, no longer triggered by ordinary sights and sounds.

"You know about Deborah? What happened?"

He nodded. "I'm sorry." He clearly thought about saying more, but stopped.

I looked at my watch. It was past time to go. I thought about calling Gunter about being late, but it would be only a few minutes, so I let it slide. I remember hearing the dull 'thud' in the distance, but only to the extent of mild curiosity. It was not until later that I appreciated its significance. But the sound seemed to register with Valentin. He stood up, looking at me with an unreadable expression.

"You go ahead. What I have to talk about can wait."

We walked out together and went separate ways once into the street. I would not see him again for another seven years.

It was not until I was three blocks from the square and I could hear the sirens and see the smoke in the fading daylight that I began to run.

I was stopped by a solid line of polizei. They formed a human barrier between a rapidly growing crowd and what had been Gunter's restaurant. Glass, bricks and unidentifiable types of debris were scattered a hundred feet into the square. There was no longer a building. In its place was an inferno, a solid wall of flame.

The CIA and Me

I need a ghostwriter!

I went a full week without adding a page to the stack of paper. The memoir was stalled by my disinterest in myself. I had started the project after asking myself "Am I famous?" thinking that a positive answer to that question was sufficient to motivate me. But I found myself boring, except for those parts of my past that I could not write about. It was not enough that I had lived during remarkable times and been close to the people and events that shaped the world.

Women meeting for the first time will engage in conversation where the central question, posed in a variety of ways, is *"What are you like"?* Men in that same social context will focus on *"What do you do?"* as the most efficient route to deciding whether this person is interesting. Inevitably and sadly, we define ourselves and others by what we do, rightly or wrongly.

It's a sensible heuristic. Since we spend fifty or sixty years working at a career or two, our characters inevitably are shaped by the demands of our work world. Even allowing for the self-selection factor, a mortician will be substantially different than a nuclear physicist than a kindergarten teacher. Certain edges are rubbed off, while other facets are polished to a high gloss. We acquire trained disabilities, blind spots as well as insights.

Flashback to age ten or so and the lame question that adults would ask the children of their friends -- *What do you want to be when you grow up?* Surely, given my limited knowledge of what was possible, my response was equally lame. I do know that – like all boys of that time – I thought that forest rangers and airplane pilots were exotic. The post-war images of the successful male were from *The Man in the Grey Flannel Suit* (think 30 years rising through the ranks at IBM) or the TV sitcom *"Ozzie & Harriet."*

Any career preferences I would have had would have been trite, driven by role models of the moment. And they most certainly would not have included 'secret agent!'

Today's Sunday morning news program had a twenty-minute segment with the theme "where are they now?" It was devoted to one-time VIPs that were flying high and then caught up in a scandal. I was reading through the Times and only halfway paying attention, but my attention was caught when one of the panelists said something about 'the accidental spy.'

They were talking about an ex-Navy officer, a rear admiral who had command of one of our carrier task forces that circulated through the Middle East on a regular basis. He was a superstar, out of Annapolis, young and moving upward through the ranks at a record pace. He was viewed as a sure thing for the Joint Chiefs of Staff. Then it was discovered that he was sharing certain classified information with the Israelis. Nothing very dramatic and it was even agreed that his leakage actually furthered American interests in the region. But he was court martialed and summarily discharged from the service.

The TV newswoman was an earnest, perfectly constructed young woman. She had flawless skin and perfect diction. It was hard to imagine her confronting a serious moral choice. But the camera zoomed in and she looked directly at me and asked, "Why would this person, among the best and the brightest our society produced, risk everything for so little reason?"

The music came up and the screen was filled with an ad that featured galloping horses and large pickup trucks. But the question stayed with me.

What would she say about me if my history with the CIA became public knowledge? I didn't give away state secrets, but there would be serious conflict of interest issues. Given who I was and what I had done, it would blow up into a significant scandal.

I played with the idea for a while, but got bored with imagining the possible defenses that I would throw up to TV interviewers. I had been around enough political scandals to appreciate that the media steamroller would go where it wanted no matter what the central character had to say. So I began to think about another question.

Why did I get involved with Jacob Connolly?

I quickly ruled out the classic reasons – money, revenge, sex or power. And I wasn't entrapped or forced; it was a knowing and completely voluntary decision. Perhaps patriotism was a small contributor to my decision, but one that was so encrusted with cynicism that any of its effects were entirely subconscious.

I was to learn that it wasn't just me trying to understand what I did. And my secret agent career was not nearly as secret as I imagined. It seems that Robert, Kristi and Melanie were equally puzzled and concerned.

"Do any of you appreciate what a rare event this is?"

Melanie, Kristi, and Robert were sitting with me on the deck in lounge chairs facing the fire pit in the center. Each of us had our legs outstretched with our feet resting on the stone rim, with a glass of wine resting on the broad arm of the chair. The sun was just settling into the fog bank that was creeping over the tops of the coastal hills. An observer would have thought we were posing for one of those 'life style' ads aimed at the baby boomer generation.

All three of us looked at Kristi inquiringly, but Robert asked the question first. "Surely you're not referring to Daniel's birthday party?"

"No, stupid. I mean that the four of us are sitting in the same place at the same time. Alone. And none of us have a plane to catch or a pressing deadline to meet."

Robert looked around the deck as if to verify that there was no one else there. "You're right. It's kind of spooky."

What's spooky is the geneology. Three siblings, only one of us married. And one lone child and grandchild between the three of us. Kind of bleak. But it explains why Kristi and Robert go out of their way for Daniel's birthday parties.

"The nuclear family at play," said Melanie with a heavy overlay of sarcasm.

"We aren't exactly a model of the modern extended family, are we?" I thought it was a rhetorical question, but Melanie took it further. She said, "We won't know until we can read your memoir. It looks like you're going to be the one to explain us to ourselves."

All three of them were looking at me in a way that signaled that Melanie's statement was something more than a throwaway line.

"How's the writing coming?" This from Kristi, and I had the first inkling that perhaps this was a planned session, with me as the subject.

I was being asked that question quite a lot since word had gotten out that 'he's writing a memoir.' At first, I found it curious. I'd authored three books, all of them quite notable, and no one other than Deborah had ever asked me 'how's the writing coming?' It was something about the word 'memoir,' with its hints of soul baring and possible scandal. Or perhaps the implication that I myself was somebody important.

I never really answered the question. Oh, I would say 'fine,' or 'it's more work than I thought,' or – if the asker was a good friend – 'the more I write, the less I like myself.' But I never told them the truth.

But these three are different. They deserve the truth. At least part of it.

"They should outlaw autobiography as a literary form. Or put it in the 'fantasy/fiction' section of the bookstore. And require the author to undergo deep psychoanalysis as a precondition for publication."

Robert was listening closely. "I thought you economists knew all about moral hazard. At least you're the people that throw the phrase around all the time."

Moral hazard. Self-serving behavior enabled by incomplete information, in this case an author who makes himself look better than he is. And he can, because he knows more about his subject than the reader. Maximum temptation combined with maximum opportunity, as Shaw said about sex in marriage.

"We can define it and even study it," I shrugged. "But we are as susceptible to it as any other person with an ego."

Melanie jumped in. "So, why not just stick with the facts. Dull, but not very hazardous."

"So called 'facts' are cryptic things," I said. And hearing myself say it out loud, I realized that the statement was true, and that it was why writing was so hard for me.

The task for the memoirist is to gather the so-called facts, arrange them in a sort of literary Rubik's Cube, to be manipulated in order to speculate about invisible and internal forces that answer "why" rather than just "who, what, where and when," while avoiding both hindsight and the temptation to fudge the context.

They say that dreams are merely the brain's attempt to impose a pattern, a coherent story, on the random firing of neurons as we sleep. It is human nature to look for narratives in a stream of perhaps disconnected events. More likely, we begin with the stories, and then select the events that seem to make sense in the welter of people, events and twists that make up a life. Any such story will be untrue, partly because of the randomness, partly because memory is imperfect, partly because perception is so personal, but most of all because self-understanding is so misguided.

Robert picked up the conversation as though he was reading my mind. "Facts are not your problem. I took a philosophy class a long time ago. The only thing I remember from it is that we exist in four guises – who we think we are, who others think we are, who we think others think we are, and who we really are. It sounded right to me and I remember thinking that these four views should converge through time. But I'm not sure that's so."

Kristi said, "The bible says 'Know thyself.' That's about as far as I go."

I think all of us were startled at the way the conversation had been diverted into dangerous territory, and a silence settled over us. I was still thinking about what Robert had said, trying to decide whether he was right, when I realized that Melanie was saying something, and the three of them were looking at me with a curious intensity.

Is this a planned conversation? Is this 'rare event' some kind of family intervention? Some kind of back-door attempt to stop me from writing about them?

"Uh, I'm sorry, Melanie. I was thinking about something else and –"

She wasn't interested in my excuse. "How are you going to tell the world about your work for the CIA? That won't go over very well with your various publics."

I looked at Robert and Kristi. They were not shocked or even surprised by the question and were clearly waiting for my response.

I waved my hand dismissively, knocking Kristi's wine glass over. It didn't break and the little bit of wine splashed onto the deck at her feet.

Dresden in 1993. I was pushing Nadia, asking difficult questions for which she didn't have answers. Richter stood up and knocked over all the wine glasses.

"I never worked for ... "

I stopped. I heard the lack of outrage in my own voice, and I saw their unchanging expressions, like a cop listening to a falling-down drunk saying he'd only had two beers.

"Brian, please," Robert said gently. "Melanie is an FBI agent involved in counter-intelligence. I've spent thirty years in military intelligence, half of that fighting with spooks who supposedly were on my side. We know you're not on their payroll and that you don't view yourself as one of them, but – even if we hadn't looked – it's pretty clear you've been involved."

Even if we hadn't looked? "You've been checking on me? Officially? With your sources?"

Melanie said, "Your name has come up occasionally."

As if scripted, Kristi chimed in. "It wouldn't look good, would it? Eminent professor, distinguished author, unofficial back-channel ambassador. Carrying out grubby little errands for intelligence agencies."

Then she asked the really hard question.

"Why did you do it?"

My first reaction is to say 'I didn't do all that much.' Passed on a lot of impressions about people that Jacob was interested in. Provided some informed opinions about the merits of some of the economic policies in certain small third world countries. Held hands with a few defectors. I would like to be able to say that nothing that I did changed the world or upset the moral order of things.

But then there was Islamabad, Dresden, Nadia, Orlov ... real people, real harm. And I was a part of what happened to them. Maybe not the sole agent of harm, or even aware of it, but I was a necessary part of what happened.

And those are only the ones that I know of.

When I started ... that first 'Jacob project' in Varna with the three Russian economists ... the 'what harm can it do' question was a persuasive argument. But it was hopelessly naïve and self-serving and became obviously so once I saw the real people involved.

Then there was patriotism. Not the jingoistic, flag-waving 'my country right or wrong' sort, but the belief – still with me today – that the United States is different ... better ... exceptional in ways that confer both privilege and responsibility. The reality that it is highly imperfect, often wrong and sometimes truly evil does not outweigh the need to preserve and nurture the good.

For that attitude, I am a product of my times. Later generations – the Gen X's, Z's and Millennials – can and will judge us through various moral prisms, but they didn't grow up during the Cold War with the very real belief in the possibility of nuclear holocaust, reinforced by Russian intransigence and an insane arms race.

Then there's the reason that I don't like to think about. Maybe it was just ego ... Jacob playing on my little boy need for heroic deeds. But that would be true only at the beginning, before I saw the wizard behind the curtain with all the levers and pulleys ... before Qasim was dead and his blood was soaking into the cuff of my shirt. Before Nadia.

And Deborah.

Toronto (1988)

"I want to go with you," Deborah announced.

The G7 meeting was in Toronto in 1988. Ronald Reagan's last summit meeting. I was going there to meet with the primary advisors to the Finance Minister of West Germany. It was at their request, probably because I had just published a major article in *Foreign Affairs* dealing with the role of markets in transitioning economies. It had attracted a lot of attention.

I was surprised by her interest in going along. When I had suggested that she come along to a particularly interesting venue during the last few years, she always said 'no,' saying that she enjoyed the time by herself.

I recited the lines that I always used. "It'll be pretty dull stuff. Meetings with boring people, rubber chicken dinners ... all those things you don't like."

She arched her eyebrows. "So you don't want me to come? Maybe there's some other woman you've invited?"

It was a standing joke between us, 'my astonishing puritanism,' as she labeled it. We both knew that there was not and never had been, any other woman.

It was not for lack of opportunity. Given the time and circumstances, I've had lots of chances for infidelity. I was usually a reasonably important presence in exotic locales. This included most of what I did – lecturing in universities, advising policy makers on banking crises, testifying in billion-dollar trials; most of this far from home and in pressurized situations. The women that I worked with were smart and often beautiful. Many of the cultures, particularly in the Westernizing markets, had far more liberal – and enlightened -- attitudes about sex and episodic relationships. Other males around me frequently took advantage of what was on offer, sometimes with disastrous consequences.

One took home a Thai bar girl who turned out not to be neither Thai nor girl.

I was honorable throughout. I'm not sure why, although I think it was as simple as that I loved Deborah and found her to be all that I needed.

She smiled at me in a way that I had been missing. "Toronto is a wonderful city, and I have some college friends there that I'd like to see. Book a suite and leave your pajamas at home. You won't need them."

We went three days early, slept late, wandered aimlessly, made love, and talked and talked and talked. We did not know it then, of course, but those three days would be the high point of the remainder of our marriage.

I came down to the lobby early on the morning of the fourth day. Jacob was in the lobby reading the New York Times. He was seated on a sofa between two huge potted plants, ferns of some sort. There was a coffee carafe on the table in front of him, with two cups.

"Hello, Brian. Coffee?"

I sat down and watched him pour, thinking about the last time I'd seen him, sitting in that square in Helsinki with the defecting German mathematician.

"How's Dieterick Schreiber?" I asked.

It was an important question for me. I'd been watching the news for any mention and had quietly asked around among my university network. But his name was not in the news and nobody knew where he was. The most important defector in a dozen years and no mention …

He reacted sharply, sitting up straight and looking around as though for eavesdroppers. I think it was the first time I saw any demonstration of alarm on his part.

"That's classified, Brian. *Really* classified."

"Bullshit! I was there. I met the man. He got off the boat because of me. What are you going to do? Give me a pill to erase my memory banks? Stamp 'top secret' on my forehead?"

Jacob made soothing gestures, patting the air in front of him with both hands. "I'm not asking you to forget about it. Just don't talk about it. Not even to me. It didn't happen."

"Jacob, I want to know."

"Forget Schreiber. Let's talk about your meeting with the West Germans. I'd like you to –"

I stood up. "No. Let's forget about the West Germans. At least until you tell me what happened to Schreiber." I was surprised by my own defiance. I think it was the first time that I actually resisted his influence.

He stalled, sipping his coffee and then pouring another cup. I stood waiting.

"All right. He's here. That is, in the U.S. He's been given a complete new identity and is working for us. The Russians know he's missing, but they have no idea we have him. Word is they think he's holed up somewhere in Russia, part of a dissident group. And we want to keep it that way, hence the gag order."

"Who were the two men that joined you in the plaza in Helsinki? And why did the four of you take off in that van when his hotel was thirty feet away?"

Jacob's whole demeanor changed in the blink of an eye. He went instantly from defensive to suspicious, staring at me in a way that – for the first time in our strange relationship – made me feel threatened.

"You were supposed to be gone, headed downhill to your hotel. Why were you watching? You're not playing games with me, are you Brian? Do you have loyalties that I don't know about? Maybe some other patrons?"

I sat back down. "I wasn't *watching* you. I went back to that square because I wanted to ask Schreiber a simple question. And as to my *loyalties*, I'm a professor of economics who does occasional favors for the CIA. That's all. But I can stop doing that, so cram all that paranoia back where it came from and tell me who the other two men were and where you went from that tavern."

Jacob looked at me long and hard, then shrugged and said, "The *other two men* work for me. A driver and gofer. Schreiber got nervous when you left and we changed the safe house location. It made him – Schreiber – feel better about the arrangement. We got it worked out."

"Where's Schreiber now?"

Jacob sighed. "Living in New Mexico, working at Los Alamos National Laboratory with a brand new identity. And Brian, I meant it when I said this stuff is classified. I've only told you because I owe you that. It stops here."

I thought about it. "OK, now we can talk about your West Germans. What is it that –"

I broke off because Deborah was suddenly in front of us, appearing without warning from around one of the huge ferns.

"Brian, let's get some break –"

She was startled to see Jacob sitting alongside me, but recovered quickly. "I'm sorry. I didn't mean to interrupt. Brian, I'll meet you –"

Jacob was standing, holding out his hand. "Hello, Mrs. Norquist. Deborah, isn't it? How nice to see you again. You probably don't remember, but we met at Stanford a few years ago ... a dinner with Professor Griggs. I'm Jacob Connolly. If I'd known you were here with Brian, I would have included you in our meeting."

She smiled sweetly. "Thanks, but no thanks. Brian's meetings are terribly boring. You two go ahead. Brian, I'll see you at your lunch break, OK?"

Jacob watched her walk away toward the lobby coffee shop. And then asked the same question that was bothering me.

"I wonder how much she heard."

Oligarchs in Moscow (2000)

The writer's block went away as mysteriously as it had appeared. Perhaps it was my realization that those people closest to me, the ones whose opinions really mattered to me, knew of my 'other' career. More likely, it was that I was down to the last of the file cabinets, and therefore dealing with more recent memories.

I thought back to that long-ago dinner with Grayson Griggs, when he predicted the collapse of the USSR and the subsequent need for a blueprint for what came next. By the end of the century, it was clear that he had been right: The Soviet Union did in fact collapse and all those new heads of newly market-oriented states were seeking an instruction manual to help them navigate from a totalitarian system to the mysterious workings of capitalism. And, just as he predicted, I was the go-to resource.

I was in Moscow on a consulting project with the European Bank for Reconstruction and Development. The Bank was created with a good bit of haste in 1991 to help restore financial order in the post-communist world, mainly by fostering market-based financial practices in the old command-and-control economies and encouraging the development of efficient banking institutions. Russia was by far the biggest and most important target for them, and billions of dollars and Euros had been invested, much of it wasted.

It was January 1, 2000, an easy date to remember because that was the infamous 'Y2K', the day when doomsayers predicted that planes would fall out of the sky and banks would fail because ancient computer programs would not recognize the arrival of a new millennium. It turned out to be an utterly ordinary day.

But it was not an ordinary day in Moscow. Yesterday, on the last day of the twentieth century, Boris Yeltsin had appointed

Vladimir Putin to be the Acting President of the Russian Federation. It was a long step up for an ex-KGB officer.

Jacob was waiting for me in the lobby of the Moscow five-star hotel with its view of the Kremlin, sitting in an armchair reading through a thick document. I watched him flick through the pages, pausing every fourth or fifth page to read more carefully. He looked exactly as he always had, rumpled and unenthusiastic about who, what or where he was at the moment. He could have been any sixty-five-year-old Russian or American or Swedish business executive after a hard day of meetings or a transatlantic flight. Most of all, he looked harmless.

When he looked up and saw me watching him, he showed no surprise. He just smiled and waved me over. I wondered if he'd known that I was studying him and had arranged himself accordingly, and I thought again about how little I knew about this man who wandered in and out of my life.

"Hello, Brian. You look tired."

"It's been a very long day," I said, and emphasized it by flopping down on the massive sofa opposite him, with a big sigh.

"Yes. I can imagine that dealing with thuggish ex-communist bosses who wound up owning a few Russian banks might be difficult. Especially when they crack open the vodka cabinet at ten in the morning. And when they keep on asking the Americans for so many freebies to … how do they say … 'help us with this difficult transition.'"

It was a fairly accurate characterization of my day, a reality that depressed me even more. I tried to respond in kind. "How's life at the CIA? Must be pretty dull now that capitalism and democracy have won the day … nobody to spy on. North Koreans, maybe? Or Cuba? I hear that Venezuela is threatening to invade Miami Beach."

"There's a big push to learn Arabic, actually. And there's always China, of course."

"Must be hard for you to recruit in Damascus or Beijing. You don't exactly fit in."

I said it teasingly, but he apparently took me seriously.

"I'm the closer. By the time I'm brought in, cultural fit doesn't matter very much."

A tall blonde woman in a very low cut blouse and a very tight and short skirt stopped in front of us and, in perfect English, asked if we would like to order a drink. "With the compliments of the manager, of course."

A James Bond moment if there ever was one. I'm sitting in a thousand dollar a night Moscow hotel, talking with a CIA operative who recruits double agents while beautiful Russian women ply us with drinks.

Jacob did not order a vodka martini, shaken, not stirred. "A glass of white wine. Thank you." I shook my head and she left us, walking like a model on a runway. I wondered how she imagined her future.

"A hopeful sign," Jacob said. "The last time I was here, their idea of customer service was to change the sheets once a week."

"Give it time. Consumerism has to be learned. Lots of cultural barriers to overcome."

"Actually, that's what I'd like your help with." He showed me the cover of the thick document in his lap. The title was "Nine Years of Shock Therapy: An Assessment of Russia's Conversion to a Market Economy," just above the prominent logo of the World Bank.

"I've read it. Twice." To prove it, I quoted from the Executive Summary.

"The transition strategy relies on three main policies: liberalization, stabilization and privatization. The two major threats to its success are, first, overreliance on the extraction and sale of natural resources; and, second, the political power of the oligarchs and new rich."

"You have excellent recall," Jacob said drily. "But do you think it's correct?"

I thought about it. "Yes and no. 'Yes' insofar as it's describing what's happened since Gorby dissolved the Soviet Union; 'no' as to the inferences about what comes next."

"Too optimistic?"

"The World Bank has a vested interest in optimism. It tends to slant their forecasting toward a rosy tint."

"But the data –"

I waved my hand. "The data will tell any story you like. Their economy has been in the tank, so the pessimists will extrapolate and say the sky is falling. The optimists will conclude that we've reached a bottom and it's upward and onward from here."

The blonde brought Jacob's wine, placing it on the table between us in such a way that each of us had an unobstructed view of her breasts. She smiled and said, "If I can do anything else, my name is Tanya."

When she turned to leave, I was surprised to see Jacob watching her with an incredibly sad expression. Not with lust, but with an intense wistfulness. I thought I knew the reason. She reminded me of many other women like her in Russia. Eager to get to the west and, especially if they were smart, capable and attractive, discovered that the fastest and easiest escape route was through the bedroom. A surprising number of them were named Tanya.

After she walked away, I said, "If the World Bank wanted confirmation of Russia's so-called conversion to a market-based economy, Tanya would be a good case study of an export market that's developing very fast."

Jacob said nothing, still processing images that I couldn't see. *I know nothing about this man ... Where he's from, what he wants, who he loves ...* So I asked him, "Do you have a wife? A family?" It was not a subtle question, but it brought him back to the present.

"No. But I did. A long time ago." To my surprise, he reached into the pocket of his coat for his wallet. It was overflowing with papers, but he extracted a black and white photograph of an infant, a girl posed against a plain white background that accentuated her large dark eyes and black hair.

"She's beautiful. Why did –"

"She died, a long time ago," he snapped as if he was offended by questions about her. He then said quite forcefully. "Brian, on this matter of the Russian outlook, I would like your help."

One more time, a chance to say 'No.' I wonder what he would do if I exercised that right? But I asked the same question I always asked. "What is it you want from me?"

"When you were showing off, quoting from this report" – he held up the World Bank document – "you cited – and I quote – 'the political power of the oligarchs and the new rich.'"

"Yes. So what?"

"So I would like to know what you think of the motivations, abilities and plans of the various constituencies that you are meeting with during the next ten days. We're particularly interested in the nature of their relationship – if any – to our newly appointed President Vladimir Putin."

Same old stuff. Nothing like Islamabad or Helsinki.

"OK. Same disclaimers as always. And most of the people I'm meeting with are government officials or bureaucrats, maybe the occasional academic. Pretty skimpy on oligarchs."

But there is one.

Jacob said, "I'll rely on your ingenuity, as always."

He stood up, moving stiffly, like an arthritic old man.

I said, "Jacob, don't take this the wrong way, but you should retire. You're old and Russia's a second-rate nation, more interested in its balance of payments than in the balance of power. They're more interested in knowing Apple's product strategies than they are in getting our nuclear launch codes."

With hindsight, my assessment of Russia's aspirations was as wrong as it could be. And Jacob knew it. He always had the advantage of me when it came to cynicism.

He smiled, the kindly old uncle smile. "I appreciate your concern. And I am working on a retirement plan. Just a few more troublesome details to work out."

I would not see Jacob Connolly for seven more years, until the day he walked into my office and placed the pistol on top of my manuscript and said, "You can use it, or I will." I left him in the lobby with his glass of white wine and strange wistfulness, so that I could visit another nemesis from a past that I could neither change nor forget.

"So, Brian, we seem to meet every few years. It's like a college reunion, no?"

Stanford in 1974, Islamabad in 1980, Dresden in 1993, ... now Moscow. Not the usual venues for reunions.

Valentin looked no older than we first met as graduate students, thirty years ago. That impression was helped by the setting – a corner office on the twentieth floor of one of the modernistic office buildings that had sprouted in the Presnensky District of the new Moscow. And Valentin was a match for the office, dressed in a pinstriped and tailored suit. He looked like what he purported to be: a prosperous banker in the modern Russia.

For a second or two, I envied him; but then the images from Islamabad began to play. I had come to accept them as a conditioned response to any recalled memory of Valentin. First came the five seconds of him raising his arm and shooting Akmal and Qasim in the head. Then the even briefer one of him on that ratty sofa asking that question. "Why were you in that room with those men?"

I shook off the visions. "You seem to have done well in the new Russia, Valentin."

He smiled and said, "Once all struggle is grasped, miracles are possible."

I remembered our first meeting in the student union at Stanford. "Chairman Mao. The Little Red Book."

He nodded. "Mao was a peasant. But *his* system of communism still exists, while the rest of us have become capitalists."

"You sound resentful. Yet here you are." I made a sweeping gesture, indicating the view through the floor-to-ceiling windows and the expensive contemporary furniture around us. "Surprising to find a Goldman Sachs banker reciting quotes from Mao."

"No more surprising than finding American professors in Pakistan in 1980, meeting with jihadist fanatics. And Goldman Sachs is only a minority partner."

We looked at each other for a long ten seconds. And came to an unspoken détente, an acknowledgment of our shared history. It reminded me of the way that we had surveyed each other from opposite sides of the Abbott and Costello classroom and detected something in common with one another.

"How are you, Valentin?" It was a serious question, and both of us knew it. Even as I said the words, I realized that I really wanted to know and I remembered Deborah's characterization: *I don't think he expects anything good to happen to him.*

"How am I? Such a complex question ... I would say ... *adaptable.* A most Russian personality trait."

"Prosperous, apparently."

"Oh, that too. There's nothing like a tripling of crude oil prices to make a Russian banker well off. Poor Boris Yeltsin … he resigned a little bit too soon."

I was misled by Valentin's ironies and decided to take a risk. "I imagine that the ex-KGB associates of Mr. Putin will do very well in the new economy, now that he is your democratically chosen leader."

It was one liberty too many. Valentin swiveled in his high-backed executive chair, turning to look out the window. When he turned back to me, his demeanor had shifted. He was now an important Russian banker engaged in conversation with a slightly annoying visiting dignitary.

"I was sorry to hear about your wife. Deborah. She was a good person."

Nine years was not long enough. I looked away for a few seconds, hoping to disguise the sharp reaction to her name. "That was a long time ago. In another world. Ancient history. But thanks for the thought."

His expression softened. "And your daughter Melanie? She has a career? A husband? Children?"

She was a year old. She sat on his lap and he sang Russian lullabies to her.

"Career? An FBI agent of all things. Husband? Long gone and divorced, not a success story. Children? A son Daniel, four years old and looking more and more like his mother."

Valentin had a faraway look, and I imagined him seeing the same long ago scenes from our Palo Alto kitchen. But then his voice and expression shifted once more, this time to the sort of indirect and calculating look of a distant relative asking for a loan.

"And your brother Robert? How is he?"

"Beginning to talk about retirement. It's been thirty-six years."

"Quite a story. From private to general. I'm surprised he's thinking of retiring. He's only fifty-five years old and still has some room for promotion."

What's going on? He hasn't seen these people or had anything to do with them for most of his life! And he's not the type for small talk. What am I missing? "I suppose. But I think he's tired of the whole thing. Too much time fighting wars for too little gain." *What was it that Robert said? Too many ambiguous moral choices. Too much time doing nasty things for people that he didn't like.*

"Look, Valentin, I appreciate your interest in my family, but that's not why I'm here. I wanted to get your impressions about the change program. Nothing on-the-record or for publication. Entirely unofficial."

He held his hands outspread before him.... *Tell me what you need.* The gesture was, however, at odds with his closed and cold expression.

Jacob said, "Try to get him to talk about Putin." That looks like it may be difficult to do. "So, how do you like being an executive in a newly privatized Russian bank?"

"As opposed to what? Being a high-ranking KGB officer in the last days of the Soviet empire?"

What the hell? He's the one who brought it up! All he can do is throw me out.

"You and Vladimir Putin have that in common." I rushed on before he could say anything. "You're about the same age, you were both senior officers in the intelligence service. You must have had some interactions with each other."

He sat absolutely still, his hands folded on the desktop. "Putin is Russian, from St. Petersburg, I'm Kazakh, from a village that no longer exists. He spent the 1980's in East Germany; I was in Afghanistan and other places. He went into politics, me into business. He's the President, I'm a banker. We don't move in the same circles. Never have, never will."

Lots of words, but he didn't answer the question.

I started, "What do you think –"

Valentin abruptly stood and then recited with a deadpan expression and the intonation of a bored street cop reciting the Miranda warning to a multiple offender. "What I think is that Acting President Putin will immediately undertake multiple initiatives to address the needs of the Russian people. It is the beginning of a new era for a new Russia, an era in which Russia will assume its rightful place among the nations of the world."

He moved to the door. "Is there anything else? If not, enjoy your time in Moscow."

I was halfway down the hallway when he called out, "Please tell Melanie and Robert 'Hi' from Valentin."

The Hoover Institution (2007)

From my office window looking down on the sidewalks of University Avenue, the pedestrian looked familiar for a few seconds. But he was half-a-block away, foreshortened by being three stories below me, and I spent only a few seconds trying for the connection that would not click into place.

Then he was standing in my office door, waiting for me to notice him. It was Valentin.

"Hello Brian."

I was startled to realize that I was pleased to see him. *I have to think about that. Maybe it's just longevity. I've known him longer than anybody except my family members. And we've had some intense times together, not all of them good.*

"Hello Valentin. Come in. Would you like some coffee?"

"Of course. And one of your American cigarettes, if you have one."

"Can't help you with that. And you need to be careful about asking for cigarettes, at least in this town. You can be sentenced to the American equivalent of a Siberian gulag, for reeducation."

"Capitalist propaganda! There were no gulags. Those were voluntary settlements. Heroic workers and their families committed to the fullest development of the people's resources."

"Sure. Patriotic selfless Russians, such as Mikhail Khodorkovsky, who signed over his billions of dollars to Vladimir Putin and now works in a mitten factory in the Siberian outback. One of your fellow oligarchs, isn't he?"

Valentin smiled in a way that reminded me of the all the times he had sat at our kitchen table, entertaining Deborah by telling stories of Communist blunders.

"And Hamid Karzai is not the American stooge in Kabul," he said. The first general election in the history of Afghanistan had happened the week before.

I stood up and held out my hand. "It's good to see you again, Valentin. Can we declare a truce as to the debate of our respective political systems? At least until we get to a bar?"

He took my hand and said, "Better than a truce – a peace treaty. And I declare you to be the winner."

I thought of the implications. "So you have finally become a capitalist? A true convert, not just an oligarch taking advantage of market imperfections?"

"Even better than that. I am a Visiting Scholar at your Hoover Institution."

The image of Valentin at the Institution was hard for me to bring into focus. The Hoover was one of the more conservative think tanks and research institutes in the U.S. I'd run into Henry Kissinger, Milton Friedman, and more ex-generals, admirals and DOD types than I could keep track of. But it was surprisingly open to alternative points of view and I seem to recall some coffee room discussions about some 'new directions.' Still, I didn't realize that we had taken in ex-KGB officers.

He was as perceptive as ever, apparently able to hear me thinking. "The Director said I was 'an experiment,' to be watched closely. He emphasized that I can be terminated 'at-will," an expression I am not familiar with."

"Think of it as like a red card in a soccer match, but one that is played according to unknown rules."

"Ah! Like the game in Alice in Wonderland, with the Red Queen –"

"That was croquet. But why *are* you here?"

"There are two reasons. The first one is the official one, which is also true, even though it is official."

When I just looked at him without answering, he said, "I am writing a book. About Soviet intelligence operations during the Cold War. The Hoover Institution has a wonderful library and a large number of Fellows and Visiting Scholars interested in that particular topic, so I shall be a resource to them, and them to me."

I think I know the second reason.

Again, he was ahead of me. "Yes. Such a project cannot be done – safely – in today's Russia. So your ivory tower shall be a sanctuary of sorts. Very medieval."

"But, your KGB position –"

"Is long gone. And the KGB, as you know, is now the Federal Security Service. And its mission has shifted. It now acts as the business development division for Putin Enterprises. Alas, I am no longer an oligarch."

"No Swiss bank accounts?"

He smiled. "Switzerland is passé. There are so many other more congenial places for discreet foreign investments, many of them tropical islands. But, of course, I do not frequent such places."

I tried for as much seriousness as I could put into my voice. "Are you in serious danger?" The question sounded ridiculous, melodramatic even as I voiced it.

But he paused before responding, and then spoke thoughtfully. "I don't think so. I know enough about Putin and his associates to be a threat to them. But that knowledge is also a shield."

"But the book? Won't that –"

"My book is like your book. Your memoir. It shall be informative, entertaining, provocative … all those adjectives one finds on book jackets. But it shall be like the bikini."

When I looked at him with a quizzical expression, he said. "What it reveals is interesting, but what it conceals is vital."

Nikolai Orlov Redux

It was my habit to print out what I had written at the end of every writing session and my draft of the memoir was growing by two or three sheets of paper every day. Single-spaced, Times New Roman font, size 12. It was – to me – an impressive stack of paper, maybe two inches thick by now.

Caroline, Robert, Melanie and Kristi had all volunteered, several times, to read and comment on the draft, arguing that they could fact-check, copyedit and suggest alternative phrasing. But I said no, that I would show them a complete first draft only.

In any case, the stack of paper was more like a diary whose pages had fallen out and been reassembled in random order than it was a coherent, linear story of a life. That was because my method was to go through Deborah's plastic boxes in the order I found them and, on alternate days, pick one of my 'professional life' file cabinets and proceed from back to front, stopping to write or do focused research when I found something that I thought might be of interest to Daniel thirty years from now.

The first file in the drawer labeled 'V-W' was titled 'Varna, Bulgaria – SALT II – 1978' and it triggered cascading memories.

My first 'job' for Jacob and first time behind the Iron Curtain. Three Russian economists, one of whom was quite interesting – Nikolai Orlov from a Moscow research institute.

Then I realized that my time in Varna with Orlov was legitimate, part of a perfectly transparent government panel, that the only clandestine part of it was the post-meeting briefing with Jacob. I could include the entire experience in my memoir, excepting only the Jacob piece.

I wonder where our Nikolai is today?

I accessed the website for the Russian Academy of Sciences and flicked through the list of academic members. No Nikolai Orlov was listed. That surprised me. Full membership in the Academy is reserved for the very elite, and my impressions of Orlov were such that I assumed he would to be one of those.

The obvious next step was The Plekhanov Russian University of Economics. It had been in existence for over a hundred years and seemed the most likely place to continue the search. There was no Orlov listed as faculty or staff, but the name 'Nikolai Orlov' appeared in a list of past graduates. From the class of 1965, which would make him about six or seven years older than me. There were no pictures, but the graduation year was consistent with him being the person I met in Varna.

I called Ivana Vorskaya in Moscow. She was a demographer that I had met at a UN conference on labor mobility in developing markets and subsequently co-authored a relatively influential paper with. She had been a long time member of the Russian Academy of Sciences and a faculty member at the Plekhanov school. Just before she picked up the receiver, I realized that she must be well into her seventies by now.

After the pleasantries, I asked, "Do you recall a student named Nikolai Orlov? It would have been a long time –"

"Orlov? My God, yes. He was brilliant!"

"Ivana, I'm looking –"

"It must have been somewhere in the sixties. I was a new professor. But I remember him. He transferred into Plekhanov from somewhere else, one of the satellites, I think."

"Do you know what happened to him? Where he is today?"

"No, I don't. And that's odd, because I assumed he would be quite prominent."

"Could you ask around for me?"

"Sure. I'm curious myself."

"Thanks, I really do appreciate your help."

"I'll get back to you in a day or so. But Brian ... the most likely result is that he's dead. He was too interested in *western* economics for his own wellbeing. And even if there's nothing sinister, remember that the average life span for a Russian male in the time frame we're talking about is fifty-five years! And even economists are not immune to vodka."

Ivana Vorskaya had said to expect a response within 'a day or so,' but it was only six hours. And she was much more subdued, like someone making a phone call that they really didn't want to make.

"Brian, I have good news and I have bad news. The good news is that I found Nikolai Orlov. And he's alive. I just got off the phone with him. I was right: he transferred into Plekenhov in 1964. From Martin Luther University in Wittenberg, Germany."

"That was fast, Ivana. But what's the bad news?"

"He doesn't want to talk to you."

"Did he say why?"

A very slight hesitation. "No."

"Can you tell me how to reach him?"

A longer hesitation. "No." The discomfort in her voice was painfully obvious.

"Ivana, I'm sorry to put you in the middle of this. Just one question: Did he know who I was ... how we met?"

"Yes. He said to tell you Bulgarians brew even better beer now than in 1978, probably because they are all capitalists now."

So he exists, won't talk to me, but sends whimsical messages ...

"Brian? Are you there?"

"Yes."

"Don't pursue this. Forget about Orlov. He's dangerous."

Dangerous? For whom? "Ivana. It's 2007. The KGB, the informers, the gulags, the bad old days ... they're all gone. You've got McDonald's in Moscow and we have American astronauts in your space station. Hell! We're even –"

She wasn't listening. "They're not gone. Google Litvinenko." And she broke the connection.

I sat staring at the phone. I didn't need to Google Litvinenko. I already knew who he was ... an ex-KGB officer who died in London three months ago. Rumor had it that he was assassinated based on the personal orders of President Vladimir Putin.

The phone rang again, just two hours later.

"Hello Brian. This is Nikolai Orlov."

The voice sounds about right. Older, of course, with a very strong undercurrent of something ... depression, resignation, hopelessness? And tentative, definitely tentative.

I felt melodramatic, but Ivana had said, 'Forget about Orlov. He's dangerous.' So I asked, "Do you remember the names of your two colleagues when we first met in Sofia?"

"Their names were Lena and Vasily. She smoked too much – unfiltered Russian cigarettes -- and he drank too much. And it was Varna, not Sofia."

Enough of this paranoia! "Nikolai. I've thought of you many times since we met."

"Me too. I viewed our meeting and talking together as a turning point for me. And I was right ... but for the wrong reasons."

"Are you safe? Professor ... our mutual friend ... seemed to think you were in some kind of trouble."

"I've been in trouble for a long time. But I'm in a safe place at the moment. They won't know I'm talking to you."

They? "Are you calling from Moscow?"

"No. Can you come to Russia? To Smolensk?"

A medium-sized Russian city on their western border, close to Belarus. Should be easy to get to if you're starting from Europe. But does it make sense to fly ten thousand miles to be able to draft a few paragraphs in a memoir that probably will never be completed? But Nikolai Orlov was my first venture into the shadowy world of Jacob Connolly. And he had just said that meeting me was a turning point for him.

"I can be in Smolensk. Say in two days?"

"Book a room at the Hotel Rus. In the city center. I'll find you there."

Two days was just barely enough. I learned that scheduled air service was intermittent and even then unreliable. The Hotel Rus turned out to be only ten rooms; the sort of accommodations that travel agents describe as 'a boutique, authentic and centrally located' without mentioning the closet-sized rooms or showers that are either scalding or freezing but never in-between. I checked in for three nights, not knowing exactly when to expect Orlov.

Smolensk is one of the oldest cities in Russia, with some of the buildings in the old city dating back to the twelfth century. First Napoleon and then Hitler turned much of it into rubble on their way to Moscow, and the city was probably best known because Tolstoy featured it in *War and Peace*.

Nikolai Orlov approached me while I was walking around on the grounds of the Smolensk Fortress. There were a fair number of tourists ambling around, so I didn't see him until he touched me on the arm.

"Good morning, Brian. You've aged well."

Not so for you, Nikolai. He was gaunt and stooped, with thinning hair and a missing tooth. He kept his hand on my sleeve and it was easy to see a significant tremor in his fingers. And he moved as though in pain. His clothes were worn, even shabby, and didn't really fit him. But the most alarming change was the furtiveness, the way his eyes constantly jumped from side-to-side and gave one the impression of someone who would flee at the slightest excuse. It was hard to believe this was the exuberant, alive Nikolai that I had met in Bulgaria so long ago.

He was watching me, probably reading the shock that I was trying hard to conceal. Then he smiled, and it was suddenly easy to remember him in the sunlit square decades ago, drinking beer and spouting subversion.

"Yes, I know," he said. "To quote a very wise person: 'And meanwhile time goes about its immemorial work of making everyone look and feel like shit.'"

"I *am* glad to see you, Nikolai. But you do look awful. Are you alright?"

"Side effects from too many years at Perm-36. And I'm one of the healthier alumni."

Perm-36. The main forced labor camp – gulag – for political dissidents during the seventies and eighties. Reserved for those who persisted in 'anti-Soviet propaganda.' A logging camp in the Urals near the Siberian border.

"I am sorry. I know that it was a brutal place."

He took my arm, saying, "Let's get away from the tourists. Where we can talk freely." He led the way to an alcove in the wall. There was a stone bench built into the wall and we were shielded from the strolling tourists and occasional gaggles of Russian schoolchildren.

Once seated, he went right to the point. "It's your fault that I was put there… in Perm-36. You know that, don't you?" His smile did not change as he spoke, and the incongruity between his expression and his words was as startling as the indictment itself.

Ivana Vorskaya as much as told me outright that he had a grudge, that he didn't want to see me. Yet here he is, telling me I've ruined his life. But there must be more. "I don't know what to say, Nikolai. I cannot think of anything that I have said or done that would cause you harm. What makes you think that I am the cause of you being an inmate in a gulag?"

"Post hoc, ergo propter hoc … a notable logical fallacy … 'After this, because of this'. In my case, all was well, then I met you, and all was not well. Therefore, it follows that you must be the cause of the change in my welloffness."

His voice hardened and his eyes narrowed. "Before Varna, I had a wife and daughter, a promising career, a future … After Varna, I was labeled a dissident and everything was taken from me."

He took a single black and white photograph from his pocket. It was in a plastic sleeve, but even then faded and ragged. "Do you remember this?" It was the same photo he had shown me in 1978, the one of his wife and daughter. His wife still looked like Deborah and I even thought his daughter looked familiar to me. *Melanie had that same sullen expression when we tried to pose for a formal family portrait*

Could this be about revenge? Payback for what he thinks I did? I looked around, cursing myself for not paying more attention to his possible motivations for setting up this meeting.

Once more he immediately understood what I was thinking. I suspect that one does not survive very long in a Soviet labor camp without a finely honed ability to read non-verbal cues.

"Relax, Brian. I don't want to get even. I want to understand what happened to me."

"So do I."

"Why? To you, I was one of many. A week-long beer-drinking companion. You went home to your four-bedroom house and distinguished university. Your life did not change. You lost nothing. Why should you care about my story?"

How do I explain? Because a defecting mathematician said 'Nikolai said I could trust you' late one night at the end of a pier in Helsinki harbor? Because you knew more about economic theory than I did but pretended not to during that one week? Because I am writing a memoir and I want to understand why I did what I did in Varna? Because I know – without understanding how I know this – that your story is important to my own.

Instead of answering his question, I asked, "Did you tell Dieterick Schreiber that he could trust me?"

The question visibly shook him. He closed his eyes and I had the impression of someone who is trying to absorb unexpected bad news.

He answered, "Yes, but ..." and then stopped, obviously thinking about how to continue.

When he remained silent, I said, "Nikolai, I did nothing to harm you."

"I believe that you believe that. But –"

"*Post hoc, ergo propter hoc* is a fallacy," I said with an emphasis on the word 'is.' "There must be another factor, something in that time or place that explains what happened. I was just a coincidence. Maybe it's just that the KGB finally got tired of your dissent –"

"But I was *not* a dissident then. Perm-36 made me one, but in 1978 I was a believer in the system."

I smiled and shook my head, remembering how passionate he was about the failures of communism. "You didn't sound that way to me. I remember looking over my shoulder for listening KGB agents when you were recounting all the problems with *the system."*

He was shaking his head. "Brian, Brian ... That was exactly what I was told to do. I was following the wishes of the KGB. They wanted you and the SALT negotiators to view us – the Soviets – as open to Western ideas. They thought it would give them an edge."

It was my turn to be shocked. *So he was being played by the Russian intelligence services. The same as me with the CIA. I wonder what his 'Jacob Connolly' was like?*

His smile turned bitter. "And I did a good job, didn't I?" He waited for my nod before continuing. "But then they arrested me for 'anti-Soviet agitation' and played the recordings of our conversations – I was wearing a wire at those beer drinking sessions – as evidence of my treasonous behavior."

"Why?"

"That's my question. The one we started with. And it has something to do with you."

"How can you know that?"

"Everything was fine when I got back to Moscow. The KGB was even congratulating me on how well I had played the game. Then somebody higher up the ladder saw the transcripts and panicked. They locked me up and interrogated me for five days. And it was all about you. *What did Norquist say? Did he ask you a lot of personal questions? Did he talk about his own friends or colleagues? Did he seem nervous around you? What did you tell him about your childhood, growing up?* At the end, they arrested me, gave me a one-day trial in a closed courtroom and sent me to Perm-36 for five years."

It makes no sense. "Who was it that saw the transcripts and panicked?"

"I don't know. But it was somebody in the East German Stasi. I heard them talking about 'somebody close to Marcus Wolf.'"

Markus Wolf was the head of counterintelligence for the Stasi for most of the Cold War period. But why in hell would the East Germans be concerned about a loyal Russian economist talking to American academics in Bulgaria? Stasi was all about domestic surveillance, managing a huge pool of informers within the GDR borders.

I asked Nikolai. "Any idea why the East Germans would care about what a Russian economist was doing under the auspices of the KGB?"

But he wasn't listening. He sat very still, his eyes unfocused, clearly bothered by something. Then he repeated, just barely audibly, "Markus Wolf."

I wasn't paying much attention, trying to think through the puzzle. *We met in 1978, then he spent five years in Perm-36. That leaves the last twenty-five years.* I tried again, hoping to keep him talking. "And you, Nikolai? What have you been doing since 1983?" *Judging by your appearance, I would guess that you have not resumed a career as a promising economist.*

He laughed. A very sardonic laugh. "I became what they accused me of being. A dissident. A chronic complainer who organizes protests and makes long futile speeches about the need for the rule of law. A person who is watched and tolerated."

We sat in silence, each of us trying to absorb too much information. Finally, Nikolai shook himself and said something strange.

"It's not over, you know?"

I said nothing, knowing that he would go on.

"The Union of Soviet Socialist Republics and its Berlin Wall and its Iron Curtain are gone, but they're all still there. The communist bosses and secret police ... with new titles and repurposed gulags. They can arrest you, torture you, kill you and quote 'the rule of law' that authorizes such atrocities. And they still have the same goals and plots ... the same secrets that must be kept."

He paused, adding emphasis to what he said next.

"My name is not Nikolai Orlov. I do not know who Nikolai Orlov is, but I have his name and I have become him."

It was a dramatic U-turn in our conversation and my first reaction was to wonder if he was completely sane. I tried to look and sound as reasonable as I could, and I asked him, "What is your name? Your real name?"

"It is not important."

"How did you acquire the name Nikolai Orlov? And what does that have to do with me?"

"It was 1961. I was a student at Martin Luther University in Wittenburg, Germany. A very good student, in the Law and Economics department. One day ... it was winter ... a man named Markus Wolf came to my room ..."

He stopped, "Markus Wolf was –"

I said, "I know who he was."

He shrugged and went on. "Markus Wolf told me that from then on my name was to be Nikolai Orlov, that I would be transferring to Plekhanov University in Moscow, and that a one-year-old would be going with me as my daughter."

"Did he say why?"

He laughed. "You do not ask the number two man in the Stasi 'why.' He said that all I had to do was to be Orlov and to raise my 'daughter' to be a proper Russian woman; that I was free to live where I chose and work where I wanted once I finished the Plekhanov curriculum."

"Do you know who the *real* Orlov is?"

"All that I know is that he was also a student of economics in Wittenburg. I did not know him but I found his name on a roster. He disappeared when I became him."

The real Orlov disappears and Markus Wolf has a personal interest in making sure that the world is unaware of that disappearance, that Orlov is seen as alive and well and living in the Soviet Union. He doesn't care where he lives or what he does. Saddles him with a daughter. Then, fifteen years later, he doesn't mind exiling him to a Siberian gulag.

I spoke aloud. "So Orlov disappears and the number two man in Stasi goes to great lengths to hide his disappearance. Why would he do that?"

"Maybe he killed him?"

"He could do that with impunity in those days. No need to hide the fact."

"Perhaps Orlov defected, using some other name?"

"Tens of thousands of East Germans and Russians defected every year. Again, why would Wolf care so much about this one person?"

"Maybe he would have been embarrassed by the defection ... the person was closely identified with him?'"

Nikolai was watching me carefully, knowing that I was gnawing at the same questions that he'd been wrestling with for forty-three years.

I asked, "Is Wolf still alive?"

"He died last year. November, 2006. At home in Germany."

A dead end. Unless the Stasi or KGB – back in 1978 -- thought that my meeting with Nikolai – the avatar – would threaten the real Nikolai in some way.

"Nikolai, why did Wolf pick you as the impersonator? Did you look like the real Orlov?"

"I don't know. I never saw him or any pictures. But I can think of a couple of reasons why I was chosen. I was the same age, enrolled in the same school ... and we were both very, very smart. I could easily pass for him among those who didn't know what he looked like, especially if I was transferring from Wittenburg to Plekhanov."

He was thinking hard. "And ..."

"And what?"

"The last thing Markus Wolf said to me, that day in my room: 'By the way, congratulations. You are now my godson' and 'take very good care of your new daughter.'"

Wolf and his beloved Stasi became obsolete institutions almost two decades ago when the Wall came down. Files were opened up and everybody in the GDR was given access to the files that the Stasi maintained on them. But nothing changes for Nikolai. Maybe they just forgot about him after all that time?

"Why didn't you say something when the Stasi collapsed? You could have gone public and claimed your own identity?"

"Two reasons. As I said at the beginning, it's not over. Wolf came to see me in 1990. I was back in Perm-36, this time for twenty years. He was seeking asylum in Russia at the time, but that wasn't the reason for his visit. He told me nothing had changed, that I would continue as Orlov. He told me that he had personally given my file to his KGB liaison officer – a Russian -- to ensure that I behaved. And he promised to get me released from Perm-36 as an incentive for my compliance. That made it an easy choice for me. I would have done anything to be out of there. Besides, I had been Orlov so long that I don't think I could have shed him that easily."

"You said 'two reasons.' What's the other one?"

"My daughter. She does not know of the substitution. She was a teenager when they sent me to Siberia and I thought that I could find her again. She thinks that I am her real father. I like that."

So they still need a pseudo-Orlov alive and in Russia. To protect the original Nikolai for some reason. Who must still be doing whatever it is that they don't want to see in the open.

"Nikolai, brainstorm with me. What would happen if you were to go on CNN or BBC and tell your story?"

He grinned and I saw a glimpse of the Nikolai from 1978. "Two things. First, my daughter would be vindicated. She always said that I was too ugly to have been the father of such a beautiful girl as she was."

Then his features reverted to the dark and furtive look. "And, second, I would disappear again into the new gulag. Or worse. As Wolf promised."

"Where is your daughter now?"

The question saddened him instantly. "I have no idea. She was one of the casualties of Perm-36. I tried to find her, but ..." His expression darkened even more. "I worry that, even if I found her, she would be embarrassed by me. Ashamed of me."

He brightened again. "But your CNN hypothetical is interesting ... I think that others would begin to ask the same kinds of questions that you and I are posing to one another ..."

I broke in. "Such as various intelligence services that would be interested in whatever Markus Wolf sought to hide ..."

"And they would ask themselves, 'So who is the real Nikolai and why would the Stasi and KGB try so hard to keep us from asking these questions?"

My turn. "And they would know, thanks to your hypothetical CNN interview, that he was very smart, your age, from

Wittenburg, and that he left there in 1961. That's a lot of information for them to work with. They could find him."

Nikolai sat up straight. "Markus Wolf was called the greatest spymaster ever. He was particularly famous for his ability to plant deep cover agents into foreign intelligence services or government agencies. One of his agents actually became Chief of Staff for the West German chancellor Willy Brandt."

We sat looking at one another, thinking the same thing. He was first to ask the glaringly obvious question that each of us came to at the same instant. "Brian, why have they left me still alive?"

A very good question, I think. It's been forty-six years since the original name swap. Both the original Orlov and this man sitting in front of me are almost seventy years old. Surely, there's no need to maintain this elaborate pretense and risk that Nikolai will work out the scheme, whatever it is. It would be so much safer to arrange for him to go away, quietly and permanently.

And the other question? Why was I such a threat to them? Why was Nikolai's meeting with me in 1978 of so much concern that they sent him to Perm-36 for five years?

We sat in our little alcove in silence, each of us absorbed in our own thoughts. Then he abruptly asked, "Brian. You asked me earlier whether I told Dieterick Schreiber that he could trust you? Remember?"

"Yes, and you said that you did."

"I did. It was our last day at a mathematical conference in Moscow. Our little group was working to sneak him out of Russia, to the west. He wanted to know how he could be sure that he was really out, not just being used. He said, 'I need a sign.' He wanted someone who was a scientist or fellow professor to be there. He asked me for a name and I gave him yours. It turned out that he knew you as well, because of some correspondence."

"OK. So what?" Both of us heard the underlying exasperation.

He paused, creating an expectant silence. "But what I don't understand is how did *you* know that I told him that?"

I made no attempt to hide the exasperation. "He told me. When we met in Finland. It was the first thing he said."

Something's wrong.

Nikolai slumped back against the bench and closed his eyes for a second.

"Nikolai. Tell me."

"Dieterick Schreiber died in the Lubyanka prison basement. Six months after I told him that he could trust you. It was never announced, but one of our group saw him there. The word is that he tried to defect but was caught."

He was in Helsinki – out of the Soviet Union. Schreiber and Jacob Connolly were sitting in the outdoor bar with those two other men, the one who had whispered to Jacob about the rendezvous and the tall very dignified one. Then the van came and they left. A few months later, Jacob told me that Schreiber was in the U.S. with a new identity, working in Los Alamos.

I began, "It was Helsinki. June, 1988. He came in on a boat ..."

The setting sun was just touching the outer wall of the Smolensk Fortress when I finished the story of my meeting with Dieterick Schreiber. It was chilly in our little alcove.

Nikolai was skeptical when I began my story, but by the end he had accepted it. "So he never made it out. That van that picked up the four of them in the Helsinki square was KGB."

"Maybe. Or maybe he was picked up the next day, before he got to that State Department plane."

Nikolai was thinking hard, clearly worried about something. "It's curious that there were no other arrests. Several of us helped him to get from Moscow to St. Petersburg and from there onto that boat. The KGB would surely have worked their way back down the network. They're very good at that."

I thought about it. "But the whole thing – his escape, capture, even his death – was kept secret. A bunch of arrests would have exposed the whole story."

Nikolai nodded, clearly thinking about it. "But your side – this CIA agent, Connolly – why would he make up this story about him working in Los Alamos with another identity?"

That's a very good question. And I intend to find out.

I think it was at that point in time that I began to ask myself, "Who is this man named Jacob Connolly?"

First Person History

Robert was in the same booth at the 620 Club. No beer this time, a water glass half full of an amber colored liquid.

I slid into the space opposite him. "What are you drinking?"

"Cheap scotch. Want one?"

I shook my head. "The 'cheap' part sounds good, but scotch gives me a headache. Anyway, I just wanted to ask you a couple of questions."

"Fact checking for the memoir?"

I thought about it. "I guess so, but it's pretty indirect. Have you heard of something called the Association of Former Intelligence Officers?"

"Not only have I heard of it, I'm an actual member! I spent the last couple of deades of my army career in intelligence, so I'm sort of a second-class member."

"Is it an active organization?"

"Monthly meetings in DC, a newsletter, website, special research funding and – best of all – a lot of reminiscence about things that never happened. It gives real meaning to the term 'good ol' boy.' I get to meetings about once a year. Most of the regulars seem to be ex-analysts rather than field people. "

"What if I wanted to talk to someone that was involved in interviewing Soviet bloc defectors? Or at least knew how the process worked?"

"That's probably half the membership. The reason they're *former* intelligence officers is because the CIA and KGB – oops, the FSS -- no longer need elaborate schemes to move spies around. Now they pick up a tourist visa and walk across the border. Between that and the NSA satellites with their cameras, it's a pretty bleak world for the old fashioned spy."

"Would they talk about it? To me?"

Robert thought for a bit. "Sure. If it's not classified ... just stories about the good old days. You'd probably have to sort through a lot of chaff. A lot of what they remember probably didn't happen."

"And if I was interested in defectors, coming across from East Germany, in a particular time period, of a certain age ... Is there a particular person that I should be talking to?

He leaned back and stared at me for a long ten seconds. "Brian, what are you up to?"

So I told him about Nikolai. Not the names nor the precise details, but about the elaborate substitution scheme and Markus Wolf's strange behavior. By the time I finished, he was hooked.

"Sounds like an early LeCarre novel, before he got captured by the Save the Whales bunch. But I think I know a couple of people that might be able to help you, or – if they can't – would know someone that could. I'll make some calls."

"Great. And Robert ..."

He waved his hand. "Yeah, yeah, I know. Don't tell anybody what I'm doing or who I'm doing it for. I know how the game is played."

I spent the next two days on the internet and in the Hoover Library at Stanford. The amount of information was incredible and after a while I became obsessed with following the trail of information into narrower and narrower channels, like Alice down the rabbit hole.

I've done research all my life, but it's been dedicated to *proving* things, selecting or even creating data and facts to support a position. The destination was a given. This was about *finding out* things that would lead to other things that would ultimately lead me to a single consequential fact. I was trying to find a trail that was never intended to be found, winding through more than four decades.

The Woodrow Wilson School had launched *The Cold War International History Project* in 1991 and it became the entry point for my research. It led me to, among other things, *The Stasi Records Agency,* an official German government agency founded during the reunification to preserve the archives and investigate the past actions of the Stasi. With Teutonic thoroughness, the Stasi had maintained surveillance and other records for six million people, about one third of East Germany's citizens. During the regime's final days, Stasi officials began destroying documents by shredding and burning, but were unable to complete the process. In 1995, the Agency developed a computer system to reassemble an estimated 33 million shredded pages. All of this is now in the public domain.

Entire books had been written by historians and biographers, including biographies of Markus Wolf and Erich Mielke, two of the key players in the narrative developing in my head. The *Cold War History* project had a comprehensive dossier devoted to "KGB/Stasi Cooperation" and it was quite clear that the relationship was a close one but dominated by the Russians.

At the end of the two days, I had about thirty pages of handwritten notes and half-a-dozen heavily underlined sentences. I was staring at one of them when Robert called.

"I've got a name for you. An ex-European desk analyst. Specialized in Soviet defectors from the sixties until the Wall came down."

"What's his name and how do I find him?'

"*Her* name is Sheila. And she'll find you. I gave her your number."

She called the next day. "Dr. Norquist. This is Sheila Weiner. Your brother Robert told me a fascinating story and gave me your number. I'd like to talk with you."

She sounds like an eighty-year-old radio announcer. Very prim, precise diction. And a very faint accent ... maybe Bostonian?

"Thank you for calling. I think I need your help. Maybe a couple of hours of your time. Can we schedule an extended call for a time that's convenient for you?"

"How about tomorrow? Say at two in the afternoon? Will you be at home?"

"Yes, Ma'am. I'll be waiting for your call."

At precisely two PM, the bell rang. Not the phone, the front door.

She reminded me of my high school English teacher. "Elfin" came readily to mind. She was small – maybe five-four -- with twinkly eyes and short white hair that clung to her skull. A pair of half-glasses dangled from a chain around her neck. She was carrying one of those accordion envelopes used for legal documents.

"I'm Sheila. I hope you don't mind that I came to your home." She walked past me, saying, "Can I come in?"

"Please do. My study is straight ahead." But I was talking to an empty space in the doorway. She was already halfway down the hall.

The study was a mess. The Deborah Cube had been decomposed into scattered individual boxes and there were stacks of paper scattered around the floor, so that she had to weave her way to the chair near the window. Once there, she sat down and looked around. I think she approved of the clutter.

"I thought you were in the Washington area," I ventured.

"I am. But I was overdue for a visit with my grandchildren. They live in the Bay Area, so I thought .... You know, two stones, one bird?"

"Actually, I thought the proverb was the other way around, but –"

"Soviet defectors." Apparently, we had run through the thirty seconds of small talk that she had allotted for our meeting. She pulled one of the nearby lamp tables to a spot in front of her, took a sheaf of documents from her folder, placed them squarely on the table and sat looking at me over the tops of her half glasses. The whole sequence reminded me of my thesis oral examination.

"Sheila, I –"

"Your brother said you needed to know about how we handled Soviet defectors. I may be able to help you. What would you like to know? Specifically."

"OK. For starters, who were the really prominent ones?"

"What time frame? George Balanchine came across in 1924. And then –"

"The borders were pretty loose until 1961. Let's start with that."

"Stalin's daughter, Svetlana, in 1967. Shevchenko in 1978, the Russian UN Undersecretary. The best known ones were probably the arts types -- Barishnykov, Shostakovich and Nureyev –"

"Did you – the CIA – employ any of them? Convert them?"

She sat back and looked at me as if she was reconsidering the wisdom of her visit. "I can tell you about the ones that are declassified. There's a few of those over the years. Some settled in the U.S. and some went home again and became double – and sometimes – triple agents. Very mixed results. If you want names, I can't help you."

"Maybe later. How about mathematicians? Any of those?"

"A few, mostly from the satellite states. There was –"

"What about Dieterick Schreiber?"

She leaned forward, her elbows on the small table in front of her, very intent. "We would have been delighted. He was one of their best. And a known dissident who wanted out. There were rumors, but the Russians held on to him."

"Could he have gotten out and you wouldn't be aware of it? The old 'need to know' doctrine or some such thing?"

She smiled and shook her head. "Schreiber was German. I would have known."

"How can you be so sure?"

"Markus Wolf." The words seemed to hover in the air around us, as though waiting for me to comprehend their meaning.

"Dr. Norquist, Markus Wolf founded the foreign intelligence arm within Stasi in 1953. He was thirty-five years old. I joined the CIA that same year – I was eleven years younger than Wolf, fresh out of Smith College. Because I was fluent in German and a *woman*, they put me in a windowless basement room and told me to translate uncoded radio intercepts from Stasi facilities. I did the translations and sent them upstairs, but nobody read them. So I not only translated them, but I began to *analyze* them. I was able to show that Wolf was creating a significant network of deep cover agents in West Germany, France and Britain. For that, I was moved upstairs to a room with a window and told that my job was to find out more about Wolf and his operations. And I did just that. Within the European Division, I was referred to as WWDN."

I raised an eyebrow, and she said, "What's Wolf Doing Now?"

She continued. "So if an East German as prominent as Schreiber had gotten out, I would have known about it. Since I didn't know, he didn't get out." She spoke with an absolute assurance and I began to wonder how far up the ranks this woman had gotten within the Central Intelligence Agency.

I did the arithmetic. "So you're seventy-eight years old and have been involved with Markus Wolf for thirty-seven of those years?"

She smiled. "Phrased that way, it sounds like a marriage. And I suppose it was, in some twisted sort of way. He certainly fucked me enough times."

The vulgarity was so opposed to her prim appearance and precise language that I laughed. And immediately changed my assessment of her grandmotherliness. *Caroline would like this woman.*

"Not literally, of course. Although he was quite handsome, and a big hit with women. No, Herr Wolf rolled up our networks ... friends of mine died because of him ... and he was very good at putting his people into place in Western Europe ... you know of the Willy Brandt fiasco, yes? ... And maybe even here, in the U.S."

She said 'maybe.' I filed that away for now and asked, "So, what happened to you when the Stasi went out of business in 1989 and you and WWDN lost your professional reason for being?"

"I was one of many who were ... *rationalized.* Such a nice word! Stasi was gone. Wolf was gone. Hell! *Communism* was gone! I became part of *the peace dividend!*"

She was sitting on the very edge of her chair, ramrod straight and increasingly angry with every word.

"That was premature, wasn't it?" I said. "Stasi worked closely with the Russian KGB, didn't they? Wolf in particular? So if he infiltrated agents into NATO countries, especially the U.S., the Russians might still be working them? Most of what's in the recovered Stasi files is about domestic surveillance – Germans on Germans -- but clearly Wolf used defectors as Trojan horses in other countries –"

I stopped. Sheila was positively beaming at me. "Why, Dr. Norquist! You've been doing research, haven't you?"

I didn't answer directly. "I've been talking to a friend. Did Robert tell you about a Russian named Orlov?"

"Yes. A fascinating story. I would like very much to meet your Nikolai Orlov."

We talked for two hours. It seemed that no matter what the topic, she had some knowledge of details. But not once did she open or refer to sheaf of papers that she had extracted from the fat accordion file on the table in front of her.

"Sheila, help me with a puzzle. Markus Wolf retired in 1986 and the entire Stasi apparatus went away in 1989. What happened to Wolf's agents that he was running in the Western nations?"

"They were blown. Remember: all those Stasi files became public. Most of them came home to the new Germany once they were outed. There were some informal amnesty agreements. A few trials. A few went to Russia and retired with a medal and a small pension, but we knew who they were."

"Could he – Wolf -- have handed some of those agents off to the Russians without you knowing? Could they have been kept in place, just with different handlers?"

She sat very still, looking inward. "It's possible but unlikely. The Germans were very obsessive about documentation and we've seen most of it, even what they thought they had destroyed. But Wolf – and Mielke too – worked very closely with their KGB liaisons, so it's possible that some of the assets shifted before the whole thing fell apart. Wolf formally retired in 1986, but he was never very far away from Mielke."

I added, "And we know that Wolf tried for asylum in Russia. And neither Mielke nor Wolf -- the most powerful figures in the whole warped system – cooperated with the West Germans after the whole thing collapsed, did they?"

She was taking longer to answer my questions, clearly thinking about the story that I was trying out. "No. They were unrepentant to the end. They told us nothing."

"Do you know who the KGB liaisons were for Wolf and Mielke in the time leading up to the collapse of the Soviet Union?"

There was an extra-long pause before she answered. When she did, she sat up slightly and her voice was more formal. "Dr. Norquist. I've told you everything I can. I've really enjoyed talking with you and I'm impressed with all the work that you've done. But East Germany, Stasi, the Cold War ... that's all ancient history. It's an era that's best left to the historians and novelists."

The room was suddenly chilly. Her body language clearly signaled that she was done; that I'd asked one question too many. She punctuated that reality by standing up.

I held out my hand. "Thank you for your help. So, you're going to visit your grandchildren now?"

She smiled at me. "There are no grandchildren. I never married. I only told you that to make you feel more comfortable with me ... more likely to confide in me."

"Kind of sneaky, isn't it?"

She said, "It worked well for the defectors I interviewed. They expected bright lights and sleep deprivation. So, when this mousy little woman walked in speaking their language ... "

I began to wonder how many subterranean layers there were to this woman. "Those people ... men ... who put you in that windowless basement room when you joined the CIA out of Smith College ... what happened to them?"

She smiled sweetly. "Oh, they didn't last very long. They probably went to work for the post office or the Bureau of Indian Affairs, I think."

The Orlov Suicide

The ringing phone was a welcome interruption, giving me an excuse to stop working on the memoir.

I was going through a filing cabinet that was entirely devoted to PhD theses that I had supervised as Chairman. I was determined to include at least one chapter that would demonstrate what I thought of as my 'second-order impact' on economic policy through research done by others under my influence. But it was slow going, partly because I was losing interest in the 'professional' dimensions of my past. Even when writing about it, my back brain was worrying at the unresolved questions from the personal side – Nadia, Orlov, Wolf and – always – Deborah and Robert. Ashley had told me, "It has to be about you" and she was right in more ways than one.

It was Ivana Vorskaya calling from Moscow. Her voice was stilted, formal, as if she was reading a prepared text. "Brian, I thought that you'd like to know. Nikolai Orlov committed suicide two days ago. Hanging."

Shit!

I met him twice. Bulgaria in 1978 when he was young and arrogant, and Smolensk a month ago, as a broken down relic. He asked me, 'Brian, why am I still alive?'

"Are they sure it was a suicide?"

Ivana's voice became even more wooden. "There's no question whatsoever. The authorities carried out a thorough investigation and the case is closed."

That must have been lightning fast police work if he hung himself two days ago.

The last time we talked, she said, 'Remember Litvienko!'

"Thank you for calling, Ivana. He was a good man." And I hung up. Then I picked up the receiver again and pushed the speed-dial button.

"Melanie, this is your father. I have a big favor to ask. I'd like you to go to Moscow …"

"You owe me. Big time. I'll be famous forever … as the idiot who used up scarce vacation time to go to Moscow in January."

I was meeting Melanie in the Delta Lounge at the San Francisco Airport. She'd flown in from Moscow with an intermediate stop in New York. Now she had a two-hour layover before leaving for Honolulu with Daniel.

"How about if I dedicate the memoir to you? Sufficient compensation?"

She grimaced. "How about you don't write the bloody thing and we'll call it all square? Maybe I'll even pay you a little on the side."

"At the rate I'm going, it'll never be finished. Too many interesting detours down memory lane …"

"And I gather Nikolai Orlov is one?"

"So it seems. Were you able to find out anything about his death?"

She settled back into the armchair and took a black leather folio from the large handbag next to her. She didn't open it, just held it on her lap and looked at me intently.

She took a deep breath. "OK. First, all of this is unofficial and mostly hearsay. I went to Moscow as a private citizen for tourism purposes –"

I smiled at her. "Sure. A citizen who just happens to work in counterintelligence for the FBI."

"Which is why I told my boss where I was going and for whom. He didn't like it and we agreed on the ground rules. He thinks I'm helping you do research for your memoir."

"Which you are."

She shrugged. "One of those ground rules was that I couldn't make any official contact with the Russian police or the Federal Security Service. And I don't speak Russian and have zero background on this Nikolai Orlov character."

"It's beginning to sound like you're going to tell me that you've traveled twelve thousand miles for nothing."

She smiled. "Actually, I think I've got a skeleton plot for a mystery novel."

She opened the leather folio. "I talked with three people. One of them was your Ivana Vorskaya."

"And?"

"Three things. First, at one time, she must have been quite beautiful. And she thinks a lot of you for some reason. It made me wonder about the exact nature of your relationship."

Melanie paused, clearly expecting a response. Her expression was that of a juror expecting a defendant to plead the fifth amendment.

She thinks that I was unfaithful to her mother! Maybe even thinks that that's the reason why it took me so long to get home when Deborah was killed. No wonder she's opposed to this damned memoir.

I can't deal with this now.

"We co-authored a paper together. That's all. Our relationship was purely platonic, the meeting of great minds. And she's fifteen years older than I am. What are your other takeaways from Ivana?"

Melanie said "OK" in a way that meant the opposite, but went on. "Second, she completely rejects the idea that Orlov committed suicide. She called his death – and I quote – 'a farce, put on by the Federal Security Service.' Third, she thinks your phone is being tapped. Apparently, some agent came to call on her after she talked to you the first time. Asked some funny questions."

That's why Ivana spoke so formally when she called the last time.

"The second person I talked to ... *unofficially, of course* ... was .... never mind his name ... someone medium high up in the Moscow police, the equivalent of what we would call a senior homicide detective. I once spent some time with him in an Interpol-sponsored program in Warsaw designed to foster interagency cooperation."

Something about her intonation and the way she looked away from me made me wonder about the exact nature of her relationship with her Russian policeman, but I didn't say anything, thinking about how little I knew about my daughter's relationships with men. *This damnable memoir is exposing every one of my human flaws, including those that I never suspected until I started writing. I wonder if I'll be able to stand myself when I'm done?*

Melanie was talking while I was daydreaming. " ... took me to Orlov's room where he supposedly hanged himself. Was Orlov a midget, by the way?"

"Huh?"

"Because, the ceilings were just over six feet high. He would have had to bend his knees to activate the noose! And the ceiling was cheap plasterboard – gypsum – with no hooks, beams or anything else to anchor a rope."

"Didn't the police –"

"My friend said that the Moscow police were not involved, that a 'special investigative unit' of the FSS handled it."

"Isn't that unusual?"

"Extremely. The Moscow police force is quite professional and takes homicides seriously, including suspicious deaths like this. My friend said that they protested but were told to stay out of it … an edict from, and again I quote, 'from the highest level.' I assume that means the Kremlin."

"Sounds like Ivana was right. About the farce."

Melanie nodded. "The New Russia is not so new after all."

"Is that it?"

"Not quite, but I don't understand the rest of it. Vorskaya gave me the name and address of another person. She described him as 'part of Nikolai's network and one of his few good friends.' I went to see him. He was very nervous … insisted on no names, no attribution, denied he knew anything … the whole bit. Understandable under the circumstances."

"Did you get anything from him?"

"Not until I was leaving. He walked out to the sidewalk with me. I got the impression he was afraid of hidden microphones." She looked down at the open folio on her lap. "He said, 'Nikolai said, if I die suddenly, the name on my grave should be Horst Weber.'"

In Smolensk, I asked him 'What is your real name?' and he said, 'It is not important.' Unless he dies suddenly, then it is.

She was watching me. "Does that mean something to you?"

"No." *But I will find out what it does mean!*

"Anything else?"

"Yes. Nikolai's friend gave me something to give to you. He said that Nikolai told him that you would come, and to give you this." She reached into the folder and handed me the same pasteboard photograph that Nikolai had shown me in Varna thirty years earlier, and then again in Smolensk. It was creased and ragged, but his wife still smiled out at the world with a hopeful expression and the daughter still looked like a teenager that didn't like who she was.

"And when I was leaving Moscow ... going through all the security bureaucracy at the airport ... an official pulled me out of the line and took me into a screening room ... asked me a bunch of questions about what I was doing in Moscow, was I there officially on FBI business, did I buy anything, who did I visit, that sort of stuff."

"Routine pre-boarding check?"

"I don't think so. He was fixated on my name. It was like 'Norquist' was a key word for him. At the end, he asked me if I was related to a 'Dr. Brian Norquist, the famous economist.'"

Ivana thought my phone was tapped. And right after she called me about Orlov's suicide, I used that phone to call Melanie about going to Russia. Somebody's keeping tabs on me.

Writer's Block

The memoir is not progressing. I have not added a single page to the stack of paper on my desk for the past week.

The writing is stalled by a paradox and a fear.

I think the fear has always been there, lurking. Ashley warned me when I asked her whether she thought I should write a memoir. She said, "Be prepared for surprises, not all them good." But it has become a major inhibitor since I learned of Nikolai's death. It seems that I am responsible for what happened to him, even though I was unaware of that fact for decades.

Like Nadia. Did I cause her death? And now it seems that Dieterick Schreiber may be another casualty of my naivete.

And I fear that this memoir may add to the toll. All of my experience has taught me that the law of unintended consequences is both real and sinister in its possibilities. What if my writing harms or causes pain to others that I care about? What if I unknowingly say hurtful things; things that are untrue, or – more likely – things that are misinterpreted? The danger seems real: partly because autobiography can be and is employed as a form of literary vengeance, a working-out of grudges and long-suppressed hostilities ... a reading of the last will & testament of a cranky old uncle without the compensatory benefits of monetary legacies.

In quantum physics, the Heisenberg uncertainty principle states that the very act of measurement changes the thing being measured. If that is so for physical particles, then surely there must be a social equivalent, such that public introspection by one can stir repressed memories in another, or bring old animosities out of remission. And since I exist only in relation to others, I cannot write about myself without invoking the actions and motives of others that I bumped up against.

But what's the alternative -- To not write about my failures? To sugar coat the abuses of my childhood? Leave out the inner doubts? It would be like Moby Dick without the whale or Wuthering Heights without Heathcliff!

The paradox is that, with one exception, I find myself to be uninteresting and therefore am bored by the rendition of the ordinary stories that make up most of my past life. The exception is my secret life with Jacob Connolly. And I can't write about that. Because it's secret.

Or is it? I reached for the phone to call Valentin.

Valentin's Recollections

I found Valentin in a small office at the Hoover Institute. The only furnishings were a table, two chairs, and a wastebasket . The only other objects in the office were on the tabletop – a computer and a desk lamp. And when I looked closer, I realized that what I thought was a laptop computer was actually one of the early word-processors.

I stood in the doorway looking at the barren space. "I thought a distinguished visiting fellow would have a better office."

"Actually, it makes me feel at home. I've lived most of my life in rooms like this."

I gestured at the machine on the desk. "That's an antique. You should –"

"It suits me. Actually, I tried to get a typewriter, but they couldn't find one." He smiled. "They said, 'But it doesn't connect to the Internet!' They were horrified." The smile went away. "I should have told them about how their beloved Internet enables the government to read their mail."

"How's the writing coming?"

He grimaced. "It's typing, not writing. I seem to have forgotten all the adjectives that I once knew. It comes from lying for so long."

I got to the point. "You spent some time in East Germany, didn't you?"

Valentin nodded. "Yes, counterintelligence assignments. But I was a specialist, never there for very long. But I was there in 1989, when the whole bloody system was coming apart. Hoenecker and Mielke were intent on preserving what they could and they called in backup resources from the KGB."

"What do you know about Wynken, Blynken & Nod?"

He looked at me for a long time, and then began reciting.

> Wynken, Blynken, and Nod one night
> Sailed off in a wooden shoe —
> Sailed on a river of crystal light,
> Into a sea of dew.....

When I held up my hand to signal 'enough,' he stood up and walked over to the window. "I thought for a long time that the poem stood for something, that maybe they were stupid enough ... arrogant enough ... to taunt us with a riddle. Maybe the reference to a wooden shoe meant they were Dutch ... stuff like that.

"Why would a ring of traitorous Germans identify themselves with an American nursery rhyme? It drove us nuts. And they were very good. They really did hurt us with the East Germans. Misinformation, disinformation, leaks, state secrets ... But the worst was the intelligence they gave the Americans."

"You keep saying 'they.' Maybe it was just a single person?"

"No. What they took? It came from different sources, totally sealed off from one another. And it went on for a long time; four or five years at least. It had to be more than one person."

"You never found them, did you?"

The question seemed to amuse him. "We did. And we didn't."

I waited.

"Actually, the Stasi claimed to have arrested them. This was just a month before the Wall came down. Erich Mielke saw the proverbial handwriting on the wall –"

He grinned at me. "Sorry about that, a purely accidental pun. As you know, I don't have a sense or humor."

But I wasn't listening. *Erich Mielke and the Stasi were out of business in late 1989, after the wall came down. But Jacob called on me in*

Dresden in 1993, four years later, wanting me to help find Wynken, Blynken & Nod.

Valentin was still talking. "... was saying, by early 1989, Mielke saw the end coming and ordered Stasi agents to arrest anybody and everybody for any form of subversive behavior, no matter how trivial. They found a trio of graduate economics students who were working in state bureaus. They 'questioned' them ... with their special methods ... got confessions, shot them and declared the Wynken, Blynken & Nod case closed."

"But you don't think it was them, do you?"

"No, I don't. I think Mielke was just grabbing at straws, doing what you Americans call 'running up the score.' That late in the game, most of the Stasi hated us. Hated us because we were Russians ... because we were the arrogant KGB ... because the war hadn't been over long enough. In those latter days, they would tell us whatever we wanted to hear, just to make us go away and leave them alone. In a way, Wynken, Blynken & Nod were on their side."

"But maybe Mielke got it right after all. The Stasi was very good at what it did, right up to the last. Maybe he really did get the right spies."

"I saw the paperwork, read the interrogation transcripts. The three he arrested were kids who bragged too much to strangers in beer halls about the *important work* they were doing. They had zero contact with the West. They weren't spies, just naïve idealists who admired the materialistic west. About the equivalent of teenagers with cans of spray paint who write slogans on brick walls."

"Do you remember their names? Were they men or women? Were they from Dresden?"

Valentin looked at me with amusement. "Brian, I do not have superhuman memory powers. This was eighteen years ago. So, no, I do not remember their names, gender or street addresses. I was in Moscow, trying to find ways to keep my little section of the KGB functioning when the whole bloody house of cards finally collapsed."

It was my turn to grin. "KGB officers did pretty well for themselves in the brave new capitalist world. Like Vladimir Putin. From a minor KGB officer in St. Petersburg to President of Russia."

He stared at me in a way that told me I had missed something important. It was a combination of disappointment and anger.

"Valentin, what?"

"Do you know what Erich Mielke and I have in common?"

I shook my head, trying to read where this was going.

"In 1989, when everything fell apart, the two of us were among the longest-serving non-Russians in the entire Soviet intelligence apparatus – a German and a Kazakh. He headed the East German Stasi and I ran a major section of the KGB in the Second Directorate. Mielke was a pig, but he was a very good pig. And me? Well, let's just say I was very good at what I did. Both of us were high-up in the ranks, but we weren't going any higher. Because we weren't Russian, like Putin."

He has grievances about the way he was treated. Is that why he wants – needs – to write about them? Literary vengeance?

He changed the subject. "Why do you care so much about Wynken, Blynken & Nod?"

Because of Nadia, of course. Because I'm hoping that I didn't cause her to be incinerated in Gunter's restaurant in Dresden. That the information that I gave Jacob didn't somehow lead to a Russian operation to terminate her and her friends 'with prejudice.'

I was close to the truth, but I didn't know it at the time. As somebody once said, "It's not enough to ask the right questions. You've also got to ask the right person."

Russian Assassins

The memoir – that innocuous looking stack of paper on my desk – was a constant rebuke, a massive example of lying by omission. It covered my professional life and may have been a contribution to historical research and maybe even to literature, but it left out what was for me those parts of my past that were the only ones worth reliving.

More and more in the last few weeks, when the writing became so boring as to be disabling, I would divert myself by doing research on my clandestine life, as though I would include it in the narrative.

I asked Google, "Who is Jacob Connolly?" and got 5,347,000 'hits' in 0.73 seconds. I skimmed several pages of suggested references and gave up. I also tried the official CIA website and phone books of the Washington DC metropolitan area. I found four Jacob Connolly's in the official CIA phone directory and called each of them. None of them were 'my' Jacob Connolly.

Valentin was in counter-intelligence, fairly high up in the KGB. If Hollywood is telling the truth, they must have had files on agents from the other side.

I called Valentin and he agreed to meet me at a popular roadside bar on Skyline Drive that was popular with motorcyclists on weekends. It was well before lunchtime on a cool Tuesday morning, so we had the outside deck to ourselves. We were alone except for the occasional car or motorcycle entering or leaving the parking lot alongside the deck. The crest was still shrouded in fog, a surprisingly physical force – wet, gray and semi-solid – that we could feel and see sliding past us to cascade down the hillside to its usual position hovering off of the beach. It was a strange sensation.

"Do you know that an average cumulus cloud weighs about the same as one-hundred elephants?"

It was such a non sequitur, so unrelated to who we were or why we were there, that I stared at Valentin, trying to fit his crazy remark into some recognizable context. For some reason – probably having to do with Valentin sitting across from me – I remembered our first meeting at Stanford, in the class on Marxist economics.

The mismatched professors .... That's what Costello would do. Toss out an apparently unrelated story that would leave Abbott twisted in knots. Then, hours later, we would all recognize the obvious moral.

"No, I must admit that I never learned about the mass of cumulus clouds. Was that part of your KGB training? Meteorology?"

He just smiled at me.

I said, "I ordered us a carafe of coffee. Is that OK?"

"Of course. Too cold for beer and too early for vodka."

"How's your book coming?"

Valentin knew that I wasn't just making small talk, that this had something to do with why I wanted to meet.

"Slow. I've spent too long writing lies to my superiors to feel comfortable telling the truth. How's yours?"

"Too many memory gaps. I thought maybe you could help. I particularly wanted to ask you about Jacob –"

I stopped while a pair of motorcycles, the very loud retro Harley types, cruised slowly through the parking lot, alternating between distinct and blurred as they coasted through the moving fog bank. At the same time, a waitress brought the coffee. She was wearing a quilted down parka and a stocking hat.

Valentin looked at her and laughed. "It's summertime. You look like someone going ice fishing."

And then he tackled her.

At first, I thought it was the bikes, but the loud bangs were too discrete, not the rising and continuous *blat blat* that Harley owners coveted. The carafe exploded and I heard glass shatter somewhere behind me. Somebody screamed. I heard the bikes accelerate rapidly and by the time I looked, all I could see was fog.

I heard whimpering and turned to see the waitress lying facedown under the table with both hands pressed to her head. Coffee was dripping from the table onto her parka and spreading beneath her.

Valentin was getting to his feet, like an arthritic old man, with both arms tightly clasped across his chest. He fell backwards into the chair where he had been sitting, and then began rocking back and forth. When he did, I could see a neat line of four holes across the front of his windbreaker.

"I had three broken ribs once. The fuckers really hurt!"

The waitress's name was Becky. She'd already told us that she was divorced, had a restraining order served on her ex, and that – in her words – 'This is the most excitement I've had since I got stoned and naked with a biker gang."

Valentin pulled his shirt back on over his head. The four distinct bruises were beginning to merge into a single multi-colored blob spanning his chest. The paramedics had offered to tape his ribs, but he declined. "Thanks, but I know a good bit about orthopedics – learned the hard way – and I'll heal the old fashioned way."

"Yeah. As in, painfully and slowly," said the older paramedic. "You were really lucky." He picked up the Kevlar vest that Valentin had pulled off and shook his head. "A lot better than what they gave us in Iraq. Ours were OK for a paint ball fight, but that's about it."

Valentin looked at me as he said, "It's high quality gear. Good enough for the Israelis, anyway."

The fog was gone and the sun felt good. The cops were huddled in the far corner of the deck. We had the entire police force caste system. The local sheriff's deputies were first on the scene, followed closely by the state highway patrol, then by something called a 'major crimes task force', and finally by three FBI agents, one of whom was Melanie. There was a lot of discussion about jurisdiction going on.

Everybody agreed on two things. First, they weren't going to catch the shooters anytime soon. The western slope of the foothills was a spider web of back roads and logging trails that provided access to a dozen population centers. There was no description of the riders or their bikes. They had some shell casings, but that was about it.

They also agreed Valentin had indeed been lucky. The fog and his own hyper-awareness had limited both the number and the accuracy of the shots.

"A classic urban ambush," said Valentin.

"Except something went wrong. It failed."

"Something always goes wrong. The only issue is whether Plan B is any good."

I gestured at his chest. "This wasn't Plan A?"

"Nope. Plan A would have been two bikes, one shooter. The target is in a vehicle in traffic. Bike A cuts off and stops the vehicle. Bike B pulls alongside, shoots target in head from six feet away. Both bikes leave the scene at speed. Right out of the KGB procedures manual."

He picked me up in his car. We were in moderately heavy traffic until we headed up the hill. Were the bikes there then?

"So why did they wait until we were out of the car, thirty feet away from the parking lot and sitting in a fog bank?"

"No choice. Once they saw the vehicle."

"Huh?" I looked at his car sitting where he had parked it, an ordinary looking if somewhat large SUV.

"Armor plates on all doors, bulletproof glass, … a few other bells and whistles. It's popular with government officials and mafia bosses in Russia. "

He smiled. "The sort of people with Swiss bank accounts and lots of enemies."

Valentin was gone. Headed for a long session with somebody from the State Department and a half-dozen cops.

He'd tossed me the car keys. "Here. Would you bring our personal tank to your place? I'll pick it up there."

I realized that I hadn't moved for the last two hours. I think there was some delayed shock involved. One of the cops had worked out sightlines and trajectories and as I watched it was clear that some of the nine rounds fired must have come within a foot of my head. I heard one of the local and very young cops suggest that maybe they were shooting at me. That theory got him dismissed to doorman duty, told to keep the reporters at bay.

Melanie came over and sat in the chair opposite me, the one where Valentin had been sitting. She had on a blue windbreaker with 'FBI' on the back in huge yellow block letters, just like on TV.

"Your friend is an interesting fellow."

He is that. I watched him murder two Afghanis in Islamabad and I thought he was going to shoot me as well. He recites Mao, in Chinese, has offended Vladimir Putin, is somewhere between a billionaire and a pauper, drives an armored car and is writing an expose of the Russian secret service.

It was a perfectly innocent and natural comment, but something in her voice reminded me that she was a relatively senior FBI agent at a shooting scene, not just a concerned daughter.

"Uh, Melanie. This must be a little bit awkward for you. My involvement, I mean?"

"I can handle it," she said. And then looked at me intently. "Assuming Valentin Aslanov is just a casual friend?"

"I've seen him a few times in a third of a century ... maybe a few hours total."

She looked at some notes on a small pad she was carrying. "Stanford in 1973, Moscow in 2000, back here again in 2007. That's three times."

The intense look was there again. *So she doesn't know about Islamabad or Dresden. And I'm not going to tell her about that!*

"Right. Three times. Sorry to be so vague."

Then I surprised her. "You've met him too. When you were a year old, at Stanford. We were students together and he visited us several times. Deborah – your mom – liked him."

She sat still, unfocused. I assumed she was trying to bring back childhood memories. But I was wrong.

"Do you trust him?"

A strange question. And one that I don't know how to answer. I stalled, and lied. "I never thought about it. He's ... we've ... never been in a position where either of us was dependent on the other. The question of 'trust' never came up. Why are you asking?"

"You know what I'm doing in the Bureau?"

"Actually, I don't. I assumed it was general purpose stuff."

"Since 911, it's been all about counter-intelligence."

"I thought that was CIA territory?"

"The lines get kinda blurry, but if it's outside the country, it's CIA; inside, it's FBI. Comes under the label of homeland security."

I think I see where this is going. "So when an ex-KGB agent decides to spend a year or two in the U.S. ..."

"We get very interested. And we *really* get interested if he's an assassination target for what the press calls *foreign elements.*

Valentin walked into my office two days after the shooting incident. He didn't waste any time on small talk. Our brush with near-death had apparently changed the whole dynamic of our relationship, such as it was.

He said, "I did some follow-up research on the Wynken, Blynken & Nod case. You wanted to know more about the three subversives that the Stasi arrested and executed in 1989 ..."

I nodded, and suddenly felt nervous.

"Two men and a woman, all in their late twenties. Their names were Elena Schafer, Rainer Koch and Thomas Neumann. And they all were from the Dresden region."

So, no one that I knew. How could I? They were dead four years before I got to Dresden.

"I also found this." Valentin slid a single sheet of paper across the table, face down. He watched me very closely as he turned it over. It had three black-and-white, wallet-sized photos of very poor quality, head shots composed against the same background, very much like the booking photos from a police lineup.

Nadia Iska, Gunter and Richter – of unknown surnames -- from the wine bar.

Valentin nodded as if I had confirmed something, and I knew that I had given myself away. Seeing Nadia so unexpectedly was a shock that I could not disguise.

"So you know them. And you would have met them in Dresden, in 1993. Four years after they were supposedly executed by the Stasi." He leaned back in his chair and swiveled it to gaze out at the street. "So Mielke was playing games with us even that late in the game ..."

He turned back to me. "Who were they? You obviously know them."

I shook my head. "The order to release them had to come from Mielke. But why would he fake their executions ... give them new identities, particularly when the place is collapsing around them? Most of the Stasi were scrambling to save their own skins at that time."

It happened to Nikolai Orlov too. Markus Wolf gave him a new identity. And arranged for him to maintain it after the collapse of the USSR, even when Wolf knew that he himself was out of the game and that East Germany would be reuniting with West Germany.

Why would a rational man try so hard to maintain a fiction when he derives no benefit from it? Perhaps because he has another client, one that does benefit.

"Valentin, didn't Markus Wolf and Erich Mielke work closely with their Russian counterparts? Didn't the KGB influence them to run programs that did more for Russia than for the GDR?"

He nodded. "Absolutely. And it was much more than *influence*. We – the KGB – had a senior officer assigned to each of them. Officially, they were 'liaison' only; but the reality was that they were in control."

He sat up straighter, seeing the direction I was taking. "So our question is why would the Russians -- the KGB -- want Wynken, Blynken & Nod to be protected?"

Good question. But it makes no sense. According to both Jacob and Valentin, they were strongly anti-Russian. Provided intelligence to the Americans. And Nikolai Orlov was a highly troublesome dissident within Russia. The KGB should be delighted to be rid of the whole lot.

I'm missing something.

Robert – One Month Ago

Robert came by today. He was in pretty good shape and I felt the inevitable surge of hope that a corner had been turned, that the future would somehow be different than the past. It was a momentary feeling, because it had proven so illusory so many times. I was still trying to learn how to distinguish between a forecast and hope.

I made a pot of coffee and we talked for a while, maybe half an hour. Mostly about Daniel and Kristi and his real estate deals that were in the works. It was as comfortable as we've been with each other for a long time, but both of us felt the weight of other things that were not being said.

There was a pause and Robert shifted in his chair. I read it as a defensive move and knew that his real purpose for visiting was about to surface.

"I ran into a friend of yours."

"Who?"

"A Russian. Visiting at Hoover for a year."

Valentin? That seems unlikely. He's as close to a hermit as he can be.

"Valentin Aslanov? I'm surprised the two of you would happen onto one another. Where did you see him?"

Robert didn't answer. He smiled as though at a secret joke. "Your friend ... Aslanov ... I asked him if he wanted to buy a house. Figured a Russian in Palo Alto is probably looking for a place to park some of that flight capital."

Robert's voice had taken on an edge. It was pretty clear that he did not like Valentin. *But why?*

"He's not my friend. Just someone I've met a couple of times over the last twenty years." *Actually, five times in thirty-three years. In 1974 at Stanford, 1980 in Islamabad, 1993 in Dresden, 2000 in Moscow, and then a couple of weeks ago. Can you call someone a 'friend' if they've held you hostage for four days and threatened to shoot you?*

I tried to sound disinterested, but Robert was watching me intently and I doubt if it worked.

I asked, "Is he interested in real estate?"

Again, he didn't answer me. Or maybe he did. "Russians are difficult to deal with. Expect real value for what they're buying. The kind of people you can't negotiate with."

"Robert, why are we –"

"He'll be back. He didn't say so, but he'll be back. They always come back."

It was a strange rhythmic recital, almost an incantation. It made no sense. And then it got even weirder.

"You're an economist, Brian. You're used to valuing things and making rational tradeoffs, aren't you? What's the value of a single human life? Yours, for example?"

I looked closely at him, wondering if he was on some kind of hallucinogen. He was not making sense, jumping from point to point, apparently talking to himself. He looked OK, although he had a faraway look to him and I don't think he knew that I was in the room.

And then he made another leap. "Tomorrow is the sixteenth anniversary of Deborah's murder. Did you know that?"

I said, "Yes," although I hadn't been keeping track for the last few years.

"I loved her, you know."

Where is this going? "Yes, I do know. And she loved you too. She always said how lucky she was to have you as big brother."

He seemed to be depressed by what I said, or maybe he was envisioning those days in the woods, where the three of us were bound together in so many ways, before it became important whether she *belonged* to me or to him. Before she chose.

Maybe it was the ongoing silence, or the way Robert's visit had evoked all of the old, good feelings that we once had, or perhaps it was his odd behavior and quirky, strangely intimate comments that encouraged me to ask the question.

"Robert. Do you remember the day of your going-away party, in 1964? At the park near our house? Deborah was there with her quarterback, but then she walked up to you, said something and walked away. Do you remember?"

Maybe, for him, it was no big deal. What's to remember? Some casual comment from a high-school beer party forty years ago?

But he did remember. It showed in the slow way he turned his head to look at me, in the stillness that came over him, and in the sudden intensity in his eyes that – for the briefest of seconds – flashed something that could have been hatred.

"Oh, yes, little brother. I remember quite well." He hesitated very slightly, and I thought that he was done, that he had decided to keep it to himself. But he went on. "She said," – and here his voice changed to a higher pitch, infused with emotion – 'I can't do this any more, watching the two of you watching me and hating each other. I have to choose.'"

I pictured the scene, still incredibly clear in my mind after all this time. *She said that. Then she turned away, towards me. But she stopped, turned to face him, and said something else.*

Robert stood up to leave. "Then she said, 'And I choose Brian. He needs me more than you do. But I will always love you.'"

He was almost out the door when he stopped and turned to face me. "She was wrong, you know? I needed her more than you did."

Then he left. But his words echoed in my head long after he was gone.

At three in the morning, the sound of a ringing phone is memorable. First, because it yanks you back into the real world, disoriented and charged with adrenalin. Second, because once fully conscious, there is that one or two second hesitation before you say, very tentatively, 'hello.' Because you know that a three AM phone call cannot be good news.

It was Robert's caller ID on the tiny LCD screen. But there was no response. I said, "Robert, are you there?" three times, each time listening for the sound of breathing or even distress. Nothing. Then the screen read 'Call Ended.'

I sat on the edge of the bed for thirty or forty seconds, running through the options. I tried redialing his number, but it rolled immediately to voice mail. I looked on my cell phone for a text, a message or an email. Nothing.

It took twenty minutes to get to Robert's house. He lived halfway up the coastal foothills in a two-bedroom cottage nestled among giant redwood trees and overlooking the reservoir. I had been there only two or three times and found it to be a gloomy sort of place, kept perpetually damp and shaded by the giant trees. It was a habitat for banana slugs, lichens and deer. And morose alcoholics.

His car was there and a light was on inside the house. I knocked, but there was no answer and I heard no movement. The door was unlocked and I went in and called out, "Robert?" No answer. I pushed open the door of his office. The only light in the room came from his desk lamp. But it was sufficient.

Akmal and Qasim!

It wasn't them, of course. They were dead long ago, in Islamabad. But he looked like them – tipped back in his leather high-backed office chair with his arms hanging down on either side and his head turned away from the door as if to show off the bullet wound. Blood – black in the poor light – trailed from the headrest, down the side of the chair and dripped into the already large pool on the floor.

The gun, a large pistol, was on the floor immediately below his right hand.

The desk was bare except for a nearly empty quart-size bottle of gin, two glasses and an open laptop computer. When I touched the pad, the screen lit up, displaying a single-page Word document with a lone line of type centered at the top.

It read, "I'm sorry."

I sat in the semi-darkness of his office for what seemed like a long time, looking at Robert and thinking. Not yet grieving, but remembering. Mostly flashbacks to our adolescence together … the good times in the woods with Deborah as the third musketeer … the times before we made her choose between us. But the same two memories came back and forced out the good ones, as they always did. That awful night with Kristi and the black ice. And the image of Deborah and him at that last going away party … how he said something to her and then she chose.

I stood up and it was as if that simple motion caused the desktop to come into sharp focus.

Two glasses, not one. And gin. Robert always drank scotch.

———————————————————————————————

I don't remember much about the week after I found Robert. Melanie and Kristi were staying at the house, mostly for my benefit. But we didn't talk very much, each of us sunk in our own thoughts and memories. Until this morning.

"I can't believe Robert would commit suicide," I said.

Melanie leaned forward for emphasis. "I've seen the reports. Trust me: Robert committed suicide." Her eyes were red, but she spoke with the authority of a grizzled veteran street cop on his neighborhood beat.

"What did the reports say about fingerprints?"

She leaned back with a profound sigh, signaling her intention to deal with any questions I might want to ask, no matter how many or farfetched they might be. She knew that I was thinking about the 'suicide' of Nikolai Orlov and trying to apply the same logic to Robert's death.

"On both glasses, the gin bottle, the telephone, the laptop and the gun. Robert's and only Robert's prints."

"The laptop keyboard –"

"… had prints of all ten fingers. We know he was a very good touch typist. Eighty words per minute at one time."

"And on the keys for 'I'm sorry' …

She frowned slightly. "Only the right index finger."

"Why were there two glasses?"

"We don't know. But both had traces of gin and only his prints."

"Robert didn't like gin."

"He did that night. He had a blood alcohol level of 0.20 and the autopsy confirmed that it was mostly gin."

"Was there any scotch in the liquor cabinet?"

Again, that slight frown. "Yes, unopened."

"What about –"

Melanie's voice rose. "Forensics was solid. The gun was his. One shot fired, close to his temple. Angle consistent with self-inflicted. The casing was under the desk. Only his prints on gun and shell casing. Significant gunpowder residue on his right hand.'"

"But —"

"There were no witnesses, no phone calls in or out except the one to you, no neighbors hearing arguments in the night, no tire tracks, jilted lovers, looming scandals, … There was nothing. Except those two words on his laptop."

Something's wrong. She loved Robert. He was her uncle and more of a father to her than I was for long periods of time. But she's talking about him as if he's an unknown, an inconvenient and thoughtless imposition on her. I know that family, lovers and close friends experience anger at the suicide victim, but this is something more than that …

She sat back and looked at me, her case made. So I repeated the most compelling argument I had.

"I can't believe Robert would commit suicide."

"Why not?" Melanie shrugged. "He was depressed. Living alone and drinking far too much to cover up things he didn't want to remember. Really nasty stuff. Alcohol and bad memories are often fatal for people like Robert."

Bad memories. I looked at her, but I was visualizing Kristi when she was fourteen, huddled half naked in the corner and sniffling. Then Robert and I out on the ice, waiting. *Melanie can't know about that, can she? Would Kristi have told her? And if she did, would she have told her the rest of what happened that night?*

"Could some of that really nasty stuff have been related to his military career?" *That's what I want to believe!* "He was involved in some pretty dirty little operations in Vietnam, Afghanistan … probably even in Europe …."

She stood up, clearly tired of my questions. "No. That was behind him."

"Why would he call me and only me? And why didn't he say something instead of just hanging up?"

She became instantly still. Then she sat down again. She didn't answer for a long time, just sat and looked at me. For the first time since I had begun my litany of challenges, she seemed uncertain. As I watched, she visibly softened. All the tiny muscles in her face seemed to relax slowly and her expression changed from that of an offended policewoman, becoming that of a concerned mother with a hurt child. Sadness settled over her like a shroud.

Finally, she said, "I think he wanted to be sure that you were the one to find him."

"Why me?"

"Because of what he wrote? His last words? *I'm sorry.* They were meant for you."

Melanie was gone, leaving me to deal with the apparitions raised by her policewoman's instincts. In her world, Robert's last words were an apology to me. But she could not know what they were apologizing *for*.

What is the half-life of guilt? Apparently much more than forty-three years!

A Childhood Incident (1961)

We actually lived on an island, one of several that dotted a chain of connected lakes and bays. The shoreline was highly irregular and when I saw it from the air for the first time, I was amazed at its complexity and thought of it as a topological Rorschach test. Our house – a two bedroom cottage without enough room for a family of five or enough insulation for Minnesota winters -- was separated from the small town on the other bank by a channel that was only about a hundred yards across. It was the quarter-mile long linkage between two lakes. When I was a kid, our neighbor would run his aluminum fishing boat with a five-horse Evinrude outboard back and forth, charging fifty cents per trip. As families acquired cars, they switched to driving across the causeway that ran from a landing on the other side of the island to the main shore, where a road ran to that same small town.

On foot or by car, it was a three-mile circuitous trip and we walked it many times that summer because my parents had stacked up enough DUI's that the family car had been impounded. This enforced a modest rehab program, although they still would use the town taxi to take them to the bar or, more frequently, deliver a fifth of Crown Royal or Seven Roses to the house.

But in the Minnesota winter, the lakes froze, enabling an entirely new network of roads to form, crisscrossing the snow-covered lakes in a series of straight lines that connected any two points of interest. Want to go somewhere? Use line-of-sight reckoning and drive there. The informal road system even survived heavy snowfalls; pickups with snowplows mounted on the front would maintain the 'roads,' if for no other reason than to preserve access to the fish houses that dotted the lake.

That year, on the night of Kennedy's inauguration, snow was forecast for the next day, but so far the lake surface was pure black ice, twenty inches thick – much less in the channels due to the currents but still safe for walking on. For fifteen-year-old kids, especially Robert, Deborah and me, it was like having a thousand-acre skating rink.

So, that January, my parents could walk those hundred yards, the distance from our back door facing onto the channel to the small town bar on the other side, easily visible because of its large neon sign flashing "Hamm's Beer." The only hazard was the severe cold.

But then again, alcohol was the main ingredient in antifreeze.

Our neighbor, a Mrs. Johnson, was also my sociology teacher. Being a neighbor, she was well aware of my family's pathologies and had done her best to provide a haven when she could, particularly where I was concerned. She called that morning. "Mr. Kennedy's inaugural ceremony is on in ten minutes. You should come over and watch it with us. Robert Frost will be reading a poem."

The Johnson's had a television. It was black and white and very small, but I had watched each of the four Kennedy-Nixon debates on that screen and I still remember many of Kennedy's one-liners today and how pale Nixon looked.

I told Kristi where I was going and asked her if she wanted to come along, but she was thirteen, still in her pajamas. Plus, she was very snooty about older brothers and into pop rock.

"Watch a bunch of politicians? I don't think so!"

"Where's the old man?"

"Across the channel," a family euphemism for "at the bar."

"How about Mom?"

"Somewhere with Robert. Now go away and leave me alone."

I was gone for several hours and the sun was going down when I got home. I heard the back door slam as I came in the front and saw my father stumbling from the porch onto the channel ice. I remember hoping that he would stay away long enough to let me get to sleep.

The house was quiet and dark. When I turned on the single floor lamp in the main room, I was startled by a muffled, 'Don't do that. No light.' It came from Kristi. She was huddled in the space between the daybed where she slept and the wall, sitting with her knees up to her chest and her arms wrapped around them, as though trying to compress herself into the smallest possible amount of space. I could see the tendons in her forearms standing out like cords beneath her skin. She still had her pajamas on, fuzzy kid things with teddy bears.

"Kristi, what's wrong? Why are you –"

"Go away. And turn off the light."

But there was no animation in her voice, nothing of what was Kristi. It was neither an order nor a plea, spoken in an empty tone that I would hear again twenty years later, voiced by malnourished and abused refugee children in a war zone. One of the workers in the camp referred to it as a condition of 'learned helplessness.'

But back then, in January 1961, Robert, Kristi and I had a mutual defense pact that would rival NATO's. It was entirely tacit and deniable, but quite real. We had compelling reasons to unify. There is the natural affinity of siblings with shared genes and environment, helped by the tendency of the weak (children) to form alliances against the strong (parents). But the major unifying force was our shared need for a safe zone in the midst of chaos.

I once heard an interview with a gang member. When asked about his family, he answered, "Family ain't nuthin' 'bout blood. Family is 'bout people who got your back!"

So I did not go away nor turn out the light. I moved toward her instead. But she put out both hands to keep me away, and when she did, I saw that her legs were bare. She had her pajama top on, but not the bottom part. Then I saw them, the white cloth with teddy bears, on the floor near the door onto the back porch.

Christ, no! Not this! The son of a bitch! Not Kristi!

"Kristi. What happened? Are you OK?" *Stupid, inane, helpless questions! From someone that should have been there!*

"Leave me alone." This time a full-pitched wail.

"Not a chance. Not until I know what happened. And until I know you're OK." *Like there's some way to erase time or memory. Like I can make it all better. Like the bastard didn't do what he did to her.*

I knelt in front of her and said, "Tell me what happened. We can fix it."

I have replayed that dialogue in my head, hundreds of times. Always angered by my inability to say something – *anything* – that would make it better. If I ever visit a therapist for help with my emotional disabilities, I will start by describing the hour I spent huddled with Kristi, wrapped together in a coarse blanket and sitting against the wall while she sobbed and told me about what happened to her that day. And about the last two years of private hell that she had lived through before that.

Robert came home at about nine. He was supporting mother, who was clutching a pint bottle and muttering incoherently about 'the goddam bastard.' He saw the two of us in our corner, but didn't say anything until he had steered mother to the bedroom and pushed her down on the bed, still muttering and holding onto the bottle. He pulled the folding door closed and then sat down facing the two of us, sitting Indian-style on the floor.

The first thing he said, and the only thing for the next twenty minutes, was, "Tell me what happened. All of it."

We put Kristi to bed in our room. It had a door with a lock and we promised her that no one would come in the room, even us, unless she allowed it. She insisted on getting dressed and sleeping in her clothes.

Robert and I sat on the porch facing onto the channel. It was enclosed but barely insulated, so it was quite cold. We could see our breath.

I do not remember whose idea it was and I suspect that some deep down defense mechanism is at work to keep that particular memory out of reach. However, I do remember how the plan took shape, with each of us coming up with improvements to the other's suggestion. Robert thought of the ski poles and chisels standing outside of the Johnson's house, for example. I thought of the dark clothing.

We had the advantage of knowing our enemy's habits and could plan accordingly. And even the uncontrollables – those forces that later, as an economist, I would refer to as 'exogenous variables' – seemed to align with us. Over the years, I have read accounts, both real and fictional, of the hypothetical 'perfect murder,' but our simple plan, conceived in haste and executed with only the simple tools at hand, still seems to me to be the exemplar.

The bar closed at one AM and he came out within a couple of minutes, briefly backlit by the rear security light of the bar. He was staggering badly, but once on the ice itself, he moved slowly, taking very short steps with his arms spread for balance. Once he was out of the light, we could not see him, but we could hear him coming – the shuffling of feet, heavy breathing and the slurred speech with its endless recycling of self-pity and anger at 'them.' We did not need to see him, as we knew he was focusing on the imaginary straight line between him and the dim porch light that marked his destination and that he would come to us.

It had taken us about twenty minutes with both of us chopping to cut the opening in the surface. The ice was about ten inches thick at the midpoint in the channel and we had cut a slot that was about six feet long and two feet across. It was the size and shape of a grave. We had scooped out the slush ice and larger chunks so that the opening would be as smooth and black as its surroundings, nearly invisible both in its liquid form and when it returned to its solid state. Robert returned the chisels to the neighbor's shed and both of us were waiting, positioned at opposite ends of the opening in the ice and almost invisible to one another.

We had debated what we would do when he reached the critical point. I don't know about Robert, but I almost gave up on the whole idea when we thought about what might be required. But the old man took the problem out of our hands: he simply shuffled into the hole in the ice. He was there one second and gone the next.

It was over incredibly quickly. The hard part was that we had to use the ski poles to push him under the ice, away from the edges that he was frantically clawing at. It is an image that revisits me every night.

Neither Robert nor I have discussed that day with one another or anyone else, including Kristi.

Our father being missing was not unusual; he was well known for his periodic binges and long absences. The general feeling was 'good riddance.' It was an unusually cold spring and the lake ice did not go away completely until mid-April. His body was discovered about a hundred yards away from a hypothetical straight line drawn between our house and the bar, making it easy for everyone to assume that he had fallen through an unusually thin patch of ice or into one of the larger fishing holes left behind when a fish house was moved. In a strict sense, that was true.

Because of the cold, the body was preserved well enough that the coroner was able to verify that his blood alcohol level was 'extremely high.'

There was no formal funeral service.

The Secret Life of Robert

Kristi flew out from Minnesota for Robert's funeral. It was only four of us – Kristi, Melanie, Daniel and me. We met at the crematorium and then took Robert's ashes to the cemetery on Skyline Drive, to the highest point, where Deborah's grave was, and we buried the urn with his ashes alongside Deborah's.

It was a good place for a grave: a bright green open field that overlooked thousands of acres of trees and – in the distance – the Pacific Ocean. Melanie and I had begun meeting here every year or so on a Sunday morning, bringing flowers and telling random stories about Deborah. Neither of us talked about her murder or how Melanie had screamed at me, "You didn't love us!"

Kristi went off with Daniel, leaving Melanie and I at the side-by-side graves. It was only as we were standing there looking down on the two bronze plaques that I realized that Robert had killed himself on the anniversary of Deborah's death.

Melanie knelt down to brush away some grass from her mother's grave. Still kneeling, she said, "You were gone a lot," causing a shiver of apprehension to run through me. But then she added, "She missed you," so softly that I barely heard it.

Yes, I was gone a lot. Griggs was right about two things. First, he was right that the Soviet system was unsustainable. Nobody got the timing right and everybody was taken by surprise when it actually happened, but he saw it coming and pointed me to write my thesis about how to transition from communism to capitalism. Second, he said 'if you do it well, you'll be famous.' He was right about that too. The Berlin Wall opens up and suddenly I'm flying around the world designing the economic infrastructure for entire countries. It was hard to say 'No.' As Melanie said, I was gone a lot.

I could think of nothing to say to her. I couldn't when she was screaming at me in those first days after Deborah's death and I had no words today.

She stood up and looked down at the plaques. "Why did you put Robert's ashes here, next to her?"

So many reasons. Because she loved him, and he has been so lonely for so long. Because at one time he had an equal claim on her and she could just as easily chosen him rather than me. Because of those adolescent years where we swore childish oaths that we would always stay together. Because I did so little for him for such a long time. Because he said he needed her more than I did. Because it's the right thing to do.

"Dad?"

She was looking at me in a way that I had never seen, and I realized that I was crying. And that I hadn't answered her question.

"Why here? I guess it just felt right."

"It is right, more than you know." Melanie walked a few feet away and stared out toward the Pacific. "You were gone a lot. Sometimes, it felt like it was just Mom and me. And I was a difficult teenager most of the time, more of an adversary than a companion. And even when you were home, you were busy doing important stuff ... not much time or attention for us –"

"Melanie, I –"

She held out her hand to stop me, and resumed talking. "This is not about you. Well, maybe a little. Mostly, it's about them." And her hand trailed down to indicate the two plaques.

Suddenly, the ambient noise of a grassy hilltop on a California summer day simply stopped; the sound of the breeze in the trees, bird calls, the faint far-off voices of Kristi and Daniel ... all faded away. And my field of view narrowed until all I saw was Melanie's hand indicating the side-by-side graves. And I knew that I was about to learn something important; something that would change me.

"He came around a lot when you were gone. He would stay with us for a couple or three days and do things with Mom and me... movies, pizza, sometimes a hike."

She paused, and I wondered if she would go on … if she would think what she had said was sufficient. But she continued, and the tentativeness was gone.

"They were lovers."

It was if those three words, once said aloud, removed the last vestiges of her need to protect me. She went on in a rush. "They were careful. Always correct and proper around me and anybody else that knew us. I know that they thought I didn't suspect what was happening … that I was a self-absorbed kid who wouldn't pick up on all the clues. I never said anything to them … or to anybody else. But it was so obvious to anybody with eyes in their head."

Not to me. Even when she told me 'I want more of you.' Even when I would come home from one of those oh-so-important trips and we would make love but always revert to the same uneasiness with one another, as though we were the ones cheating on an unsuspecting spouse. Even when the three of us were together and I was glad that we were all close again … just like those days before we discovered that gender mattered.

I'll deal with this later.

Deborah always told me I was really good at compartmentalizing, at putting feelings into little boxes and closing the lid tight. Until I can think about it, analyze it. But the memoir won't let me do that. It's bringing out everything that matters.

I laughed out loud, causing Melanie to look at me with concern. She probably thought I was about to be hysterical. But the absurdity was so striking that I had to laugh.

You're writing a memoir! About your innermost life and thoughts, and you have missed most of what's been going on around you for the last fifty years!

Reminiscences of a KGB Agent

"Can we talk about Islamabad?"

Valentin looked at me closely, as if checking to see if I was serious. It was the kind of look that Deborah had when I asked her, "What did Robert say to you that day?"

"Are you sure you want to do that... talk about Islamabad? That was a long time ago."

Do I? This damn memoir! It's made my past into a scab that I can't stop picking at. And there's so goddam much that I don't know. Or, what's worse, that I thought I knew but had all wrong!

And he's got the same problem ... a past that he wants to understand.

"Valentin ... why are you writing about your past life? Why not let it be? Especially if they'll kill you to stop you."

He answered immediately and I envied him his certitude. But it wasn't the response that I expected.

"Because I decided that I was a Kazakh rather than a Russian."

I looked at him closely, but he didn't elaborate. So I said, "That's just a little bit too cryptic for me."

He smiled sadly. "That's because you're a smug rich white man in America. Let me try an analogy. Or is it a metaphor? Suppose you were a man... an everyday ordinary, middle-class man ... that sacrificed and worked to enable his wife and children to have whatever they wanted. You have no life of your own. But your wife and children despise you, think you're dull and uninteresting because you work so hard. And then you -- this hypothetical man -- are told that you have incurable cancer and will die in two weeks. What would you do?"

He did not wait for my answer. "Me? What I would do? I would rewrite my will and give all of my money to charities, the kind that give scholarships to left-handed orphans or take in unwanted kittens."

At Griggs house at Stanford, in 1974 … Jacob said to Valentin – 'Kazakh culture has been mostly eradicated by the Russians. Stalin has imposed forty years of collectivization, resettlement, gulags and nuclear tests on your country.'

"So, you have become a vengeful Kazakh patriot? For a way of life that last existed in 1936, before you were born."

"More like an avenging angel. For my parents and their parents who disappeared into those Russian gulags."

I thought about it and was depressed. *Is that what my memoir is, a petty form of posthumous vengeance by a crotchety old man? A way to get even without any fear of recourse?*

I'll worry about my motives later. Right now, I really do want to know about Islamabad.

"Why did you kill those two men – Akmal and Qasim -- in Islamabad?"

He shrugged, the way someone would if both the question and the answer were obvious. "Because they were important mujahedeen commanders. Very high up on our wanted list. And we thought … I was told … that killing them was important to our Afghan strategy. Anyway, wasn't it Kipling who wrote about soldiers in Afghanistan… Ours is not to reason why …etc.?"

Actually, it was Lord Tennyson. And it was Crimea, not Afghanistan.

"How did you know where to find them?"

Valentin paused, clearly trying to visualize names and faces from a quarter-century away.

"I had informants in the mujahedeen…. But this was different. I received a coded transmission from Moscow itself. About thirty minutes before your meeting."

"Saying …?"

"That a highly reliable source had intel about Akmal and Qasim meeting with a western agent at a certain time and place. That I should kill them."

"Kill all three?"

"The message was not explicit, but that was my takeaway."

"But you didn't. You left me alive. Why?"

He smiled, a most sardonic smile. "I have often wondered about that very question. I think it was because of those many times sitting in your kitchen with your Deborah."

"Did you get in trouble with your KGB bosses? For failing to kill me?"

"I worried about that. But in the end, it worked out quite nicely. We were able to use you as a hostage to get certain concessions from the Americans. So I ended up with a commendation."

Four days in that claustrophobic little room watching the guard fingering his gun and staring at me, wondering where Jacob was and whether I'd be dead in the next ten minutes.

Valentin mistook my momentary depression. "What? You thought that we just let you go? That there was no form of ransom required?"

"What was the ransom?"

He asked me the same question as before. "Are you sure you want to know?"

No, I'm not at all sure. But I can't stop. I nodded.

Valentin shrugged. "I was not involved, but I understand that we approached the CIA through a back channel. I was told that we offered to trade you for certain military information about their operations with the mujahedeen."

I asked Jacob. He said that neither he nor the CIA had anything to do with my release, that the Russians did not want to be seen engaged in kidnapping of westerners in Pakistan, especially if the hostage was obtained as a byproduct of an assassination mission. That I was let go because I was of insignificant value to them.

"And I'm here, so the deal got done. So, who finally put up the money? And how much?"

He shook his head. "Not money. Something much better than that. And I don't know who it was, but I know it wasn't Langley. You Americans had intelligence agents on the ground in Pakistan and even some in Afghanistan itself. The KGB found one of them and offered your release in exchange for certain information that he had. Very good stuff, too. We learned a lot about the timing and delivery methods for American arms shipments to the mujahedeen."

"You recruited him."

Valentin shook his head. "It wasn't me ... somebody higher up the KGB chain. And 'recruited' is too strong a verb. Let's just say that he agreed to help us in that one specific area."

He smiled and added, "Situational treason. There's more of that than you think. What they don't realize – until it's too late -- is that it gives us leverage the next time we call. And the next."

"And it was all done locally? No Moscow or Washington involvement?"

He nodded, watching me closely. "That's what I was told. And it's plausible. All of us in the business – Russians, Americans, Israelis, Brits – like to hoard their informants. The agents in the field don't trust the executives behind the desks. And it's safer for the agent."

There's something wrong with this story.

"Here's my problem, Valentin. Why would an active agent in the field become a traitor in exchange for the release of an unknown college professor? All he has to do is tell his handler and let him deal with it. Why would he risk his career... hell, his freedom ... for someone he neither knows nor cares about?"

Valentin turned away from me, looking out the window. "Maybe he – or she -- did know you, and care about you."

It took seven or eight seconds for the words to sink in and to be processed. Valentin could tell precisely the instant when the pieces fell into place, when his question *Are you sure you want to know about Islamabad?* became intensely meaningful.

My stupidity or ego – if there's any difference between them – caused somebody to betray their country ... to commit treason on my behalf!

Sheila & Jacob Connolly

Sheila was sitting in a blue sedan with a Hertz sticker on the back window, parked outside my front door. She got out and stood waiting when she saw me approaching.

"We need to talk. Hop in."

"Hello again, Sheila. I didn't expect you. I'm afraid I don't have much time. You really should have called first."

She opened the passenger side door for me. "I don't trust your phones. And I don't need much time. And you need to hear what I have to say."

I got in. She drove straight up into the foothills and parked at a scenic view pullout. One could see all of San Francisco Bay, from the city down to San Jose. There had been a light rain last night followed by a strong sea breeze, a combination that left the air crystal clear so that the Bay and hills took on new colors and distances seemed to shrink.

Sheila was quite obviously nervous. She switched the engine off and sat looking straight ahead, drumming her fingers on the steering wheel.

This is her meeting. She can decide when to start.

"Most of what people think they know about spies comes from the James Bond movies, so they're used to hearing about the *Official Secrets* Act and think that intelligence agents swear an oath written in blood not to divulge classified information. Most of the rules in the U.S. are derived from the Espionage Act of 1917, believe it or not. But rules aside, the CIA has a very strong culture, one that forbids the leaking of classified information. We don't talk about what we do. Ever."

It's interesting that she said 'we.' She's been retired for a dozen years. But she's speaking in the present tense.

"I get the feeling you're about to violate that code of conduct."

She glared at me. "Informally, information gets classified into three buckets. When we talked before? In your office? That was all public domain stuff, the kind of thing that any idiot could find on Wikipedia. I'll talk all day about that and nobody at the Agency would bat an eyelash.

"At the other end of the spectrum, there's –"

I tried to divert her, to get her out of the lecturing mode. "I know, the kind of stuff where you say, 'I could share that with you, but then I'd have to kill you."

She didn't even bother to smile. "Let's just say that some ex-CIA analysts are spending significant time in prison for talking at that level of classification. And they weren't even sharing the information with our enemies. Usually with politicians, in fact.

"But there's a lot of information that falls between those two extremes. And what I'm about to tell you falls into that category. If I had enemies – and I do – they could make life very difficult for me for talking to you."

"So why do it?"

"Two reasons. First, because you've blundered your way into the middle of a puzzle that needs to be solved ... and because I care, really care, about what the CIA is trying to do. It does stupid things, sometimes even things that are evil, but it's still our best line of defense in a nasty world."

There's that present tense again.

"And the second reason to cross the imaginary line?" I asked. *I think I know the answer to this one.*

"Because I don't' think I'm taking much risk in talking with you. You have more to lose than I do. You're an eminent academician and a consultant with an enviable – and profitable – client list. If it got out that you've been an errand boy for the CIA for the last thirty years ...."

She smiled in a way that reminded me of her description of her first days at the CIA, in a windowless basement room reading – not analyzing – purloined documents.

I waited, figuring she needed to talk herself into stepping over whatever line that – until now – marked an ethical boundary.

"You asked me to see what I could find out about three names."

I nodded.

"Valentin Aslanov is easy. He's exactly what he appears to be ... a high ranking ex-KGB officer who parlayed himself into a multi-millionaire status through his connections to Vladimir Putin, fell into disfavor and emigrated to the U.S. He's done a lot of dirty stuff, but nothing that we don't expect our own spies to do in the best interests of their country."

"Can't he help the CIA, given all that he's been involved in? Now that he's here?"

"I'm out of the loop on that one, and I won't speculate. As far as I know, all we're doing is watching and waiting. Frankly, I think Mr. Aslanov's life expectancy may be quite short. The Russian take a dim – and violent – view of defecting security officers.

'Retirement' is not part of their employment contract. And he isn't trying real hard to stay out of sight, is he?"

Deborah met him over thirty years ago and said that he was sad; that he didn't think anything good would ever happen to him. I said, "Actually, there was an assassination attempt a few days ago."

Sheila nodded. "I heard about that. The only surprise is that it failed. They're quite good at that sort of thing."

I started to speak, but she held up a finger to stop me and sat thinking. "It's funny, though, that they would care that much about him. Aslanov had a high rank – a colonel, I think – but they kept him away from Moscow Center. He worked mostly in the satellite states and was never one of the ones with access to the real workings of the intelligence apparatus. He specialized in assassinations."

"What about the other names?"

She smiled. "Wynken, Blynken & Nod? Old stuff, and mostly in the public domain. I'm surprised that you didn't come across it in your research into the Stasi files that were recovered. An East German cell that operated under Stasi's nose for four years. Gave us some pretty good stuff on Russian operations in the GDR. The Stasi shut it down in 1989 and the three conspirators were shot."

So I know more than the CIA does about the cell. And Valentin hasn't shared what he knows about the release of the three spies. Or maybe he has, and Sheila – being retired – hasn't been included in his disclosures.

I prompted her, "So that leaves our third name -- Mr. Jacob Connolly. And I'm guessing that a lot of what you may know about him falls into that in-between category of information."

She grimaced. "I've known of him for a long time. He's worked for us since the sixties. The Brits had him, didn't know what to do with him... kept him under wraps at first. They didn't trust him. They finally handed him off to us. We didn't trust him either.

Claimed to hate the Russians. Wanted to give us information to hurt them."

"Did he? Give you information?"

"We told him, 'Show us a sample of what you know. Then we'll talk.' And he did, in a big way. He helped us smoke out three major Stasi moles in Western Europe. Probably our single biggest success against Markus Wolf during the entire thirty-three years of his tenure.

"Richard Helms was the brand new CIA Director at the time and he used the Stasi setback to convince Lyndon Johnson to give the Agency more funding and latitude. We were still suffering from our bungling role in the Bay of Pigs invasion and badly needed a win. Jacob Connolly gave it to us."

I said, "So he becomes the fair-haired boy in the CIA at that time."

"Not exactly. Langley never has liked outsiders, no matter what level. So we made him an independent contractor. Gave him a CIA business card, title and a big enough retainer to keep him happy. He turned out to be fairly good at recruiting informants and – over the years – has acquired and run a small stable of them, mostly low-level civil servants on the fringes of Russia. But ..."

I waited, but she was clearly having second thoughts. *I feel sorry for her. This must be incredibly hard. Breaking lifelong habits. Risking imprisonment. But I need what she knows.*

I finally said, "But what?"

"He's produced a lot of what I would call 'small wins,' insights into Russian strategies and operations that led to some setbacks for them, but nothing like his original Stasi coup. And some of the agents he's recruited have caused us some serious losses with bad intel. But that's normal in this business. Win some, lose some.

"The real problem was his independence. Nobody inside really knows what he did or who the informants were. He just passed on the output. You hear a lot about rogue agents, throwbacks to the Wild West days? He was the working model."

"You keep saying 'was.' Has his status changed?"

She didn't respond, staring vacantly at me without seeing. Then she – literally – shook herself and refocused on me.

"Brian, the collapse of the Soviet Union was a cataclysm for the CIA, almost an extinction event. Our existence rationale required a strong enemy, and all of a sudden it was gone. And so was I, two years later. Since then, everything's changed."

"Has Connolly become an insider?"

"Yes and no. 'Yes' because he is one of our official conduits for some of the human intelligence coming out of Russia. Not the satellites or NSA phone tracking. None of that. 'No' because he still runs it as his own shop without any effective oversight from Langley. He's like the little boy on the playground, the only one with an actual football who threatens to leave unless they let him make the rules."

"And I don't like it. It's against all the tradecraft."

"Can I try out one more name on you?"

She nodded.

"Dieterick Schreiber."

"Him again?" When I nodded, she closed her eyes for a few seconds as if to scan a remembered document. "East German mathematician, circa the seventies and eighties. From the Leipzig area. Important to the Soviet ballistic missile program. Rumored to be a dissident. The Russians 'persuaded' him to move to Russia when the wall came down. To one of their missile facilities. Died shortly after that."

"He didn't defect?"

Again, she looked at me intently. "No. I already told you that." And then, "Why do you ask?"

"Sheila, this is important. You said that you got Connolly from the Brits. Was he a Soviet defector? What was Jacob Connolly's name? His real name, when you got him?"

She looked directly at me. "I can't … I won't … tell you that."

We had finally reached the line in the sand, the step she couldn't take.

"OK, just one more question. You're telling me all this stuff for a reason. What is it about Connolly that bothers you? Other than your generalized distrust."

She thought for a long time and then came a long sigh. "I didn't trust him in our first interview and I still don't. But there's nothing but my instinct, and instinct isn't valued very much in our new age intelligence institutions."

She's unhappy about her past. She should write a memoir. But I kept the thought to myself.

After she left, I sat at my desk thinking. *She said she came because I'd stumbled onto a puzzle that needs solving. And after a lot of talking, she only said one more thing of any substance.*

They don't trust Jacob Connolly.

Valentin – Three days ago

Valentin answered on the first ring. When I identified myself, he said, "So my caller ID tells me that you have a new phone."

"Yes. Two credible sources have suggested that my phones are tapped. So I took a cell phone from my office. It belonged to a graduate student who had been doing some research for me."

"So, what do you want? Another brunch in the countryside with cruising motorcyclists and flying bullets?"

"I was hoping for a less chaotic environment; one with just the two of us."

"The Vista Inn on El Camino. Room 301."

He answered my knock immediately. He was holding a large handgun in one hand and was wearing a Kevlar-style vest over a T-shirt. The vest seemed much bulkier than the one that had stopped the four bullets.

I gestured at the vest. "Looks like you've upgraded your equipment. And you've become harder to find. Will the FBI --"

He cut me off. "Thanks for your concern, Brian. But all this" – he poked at the vest with the muzzle of the gun still in his hand – "is, to use your American slang, 'whistling while walking past the graveyard.'"

"Don't we have programs for defectors? Give them a new identity, that sort of thing?"

He smiled gently. "I'm a visiting scholar, remember? Here by invitation. Not a defector. And I'm not that important. And it wouldn't work anyway."

"How can you be –"

He held up his hand to stop me. "Sit down, Brian." He tossed the gun onto the couch and we sat facing one another in the small room. He'd pulled the curtains, so the only light was from the desk lamp in the far corner.

"You were about to ask how I could be so sure that they will find me and kill me?"

I nodded.

"This vest?" He rapped on it with the hand that was clenched into a fist, holding on to some object. There was a distinct metallic sound. "The very latest in ceramics. It's good for small arms protection ... unless they're using armor piercing ammunition. Useless against most rounds from sniper rifles. And, of course, they won't be aiming at the torso in any case. And then there are the bombs, poisons and more personal weapons like knives and garrotes. As for finding me, perhaps they followed you here? Or monitored your cell phone call?"

I started to protest, but again he stopped me with his upheld hand.

"Brian, do you know what my specialty was in the KGB and then the FSS? What I was so good at that they kept promoting me and giving me more responsibility?"

I shook my head.

"You should know. You experienced it directly."

Islamabad. Akmal and Qasim. That room for four days. The pistol on the sofa cushion. And Sheila said, 'he specializes in assassinations.'

"You kill people."

He smiled as though I'd complimented him on a new tie. "They used to call it the Second Chief Directorate in the old days. It was mainly about counterespionage. The unit I headed was tasked with the elimination of the enemies of the state, a label that was construed very broadly, especially when Mr. Putin became president and so many citizens began to believe that our new democratic principles entitled them to criticize their leaders."

He's not a threat to Russia's national security. He won't know about missile codes, or double agents, or Middle Eastern strategies, or secret weapons systems. He's a threat to Putin himself!

Valentin nodded, as if reading my mind. "Yes. The only thing keeping me alive is their fear that if they kill me, I'll have made arrangements to release information that would make them uncomfortable."

"Have you? Made such arrangements?"

"It's harder than you think. I'll be just one more wild-eyed conspiracy theory in the paranoid never-never land of bloggers and psychics. Another Litvienko with an ax to grind. Another Khordokofsky offended by the expropriation of his billions of dollars."

He looked at me with an intensity that was unsettling. "Unless my story came from an unimpeachable source."

He means me! I didn't sign on for this!

He held out his hand and unfolded his fingers to reveal a small black USB drive.

"Here. For your memoir. And mine."

Half an hour later, we had moved to Starbucks. He didn't wear the vest and I wondered if that signified a decision of some sort.

"Tell me about Jacob Connolly."

He shrugged. "A mid-level contractor for the CIA. Up until the whole system collapsed, he was mostly involved in recruiting agents, usually low level bureaucrats working in satellite countries. He was well known to our intelligence services. We found it useful to leave him alone and watch to see who he was talking to. You probably know more about him than I do."

1974. Jacob and Valentin were with Deborah and me. A dinner at Professor Griggs to celebrate the completion of my thesis. There were some sparks about the Russian annexation of Kazakhstan. They left together.

"Did he try to recruit you? When you met at Stanford?"

He smiled, clearly visualizing some internal video. "Yes. But it was crude. No subtlety. The kind of approach that they warned us about before they sent us off to the U.S. He was just going through the motions."

"Did you have any contact with him after that?"

"Other than that time at Stanford, at that dinner with you and Deborah, I've never talked to him."

"Could he be a Russian agent? A double?"

That stopped him cold. He leaned back in his chair and stared at me, shaking his head. "Brian, even if I knew the answer to your question, why would I – a high-ranking officer ... ex-officer ... in the Russian secret service – divulge such top secrets to the very people that I've been trying to exterminate for the last forty years?"

I held up three fingers. "First, to quote you, because you're a Kazakh, not a Russian. And, because you're a Kazakh, you have ancient grudges to settle. Second, because the organization you call the Russian secret service is trying to kill you. Third, because I'm willing to bet that you ran off with some of those top secrets – that USB drive you handed me -- and are thinking of publishing them."

We looked at each other for a long time. Then I asked again, "Could Jacob Connolly be a Russian agent?"

He thought about it for a long time. Then he made a little shrugging motion and said, "I don't know. I would not have access to that information. However, I can tell you that if he was a spy for the Russians, he wasn't much of one. He didn't have enough access. It was a one-way relationship. He provided information to the CIA. They didn't share their secrets with him. The worst he could have done is to spread disinformation."

"And yet they—the CIA -- trusted him to manage a high level defector like Dieterick Schreiber? Doesn't seem very plausible."

Valentin sat up straight and stared at me for a long few seconds. I had finally succeeded in surprising him.

"Dieterick Schreiber? The German mathematician? He didn't defect. The Russians kept him at Plesetsk – their space center – until he died. In 1990, I think."

Nikolai Orlov said that Schreiber died in a KGB basement cell in Moscow. Sheila – and now Valentin -- have him working at a Russian missile research facility. And Jacob Connolly says he's alive in New Mexico.

Valentin was watching me closely. "Or maybe they didn't?"

I asked him, "How sure are you that Schreiber died at Plesetsk?"

"I have no hard evidence one way or the other. It was gossip in the FSS, a rumor ... the kind of thing that makes the rounds when a prominent anti-Soviet agitator is dealt with. The dissidents were not part of my job description, so I had no reason to question the information."

He looked at me with real concern. While he was talking, I had slumped lower in my chair and stopped paying attention. All at once, I was enormously tired. Tired of dealing with questions that ran in never-ending circles, tired of talking to people whose instincts were to lie, tired of secrets that would neither go away nor stop haunting me. Mostly, I was tired of myself.

It's this damned memoir. The more I learn about the past, the less I know. I've got to finish the thing!

Now

I placed the final sheet of paper facedown on the stack in the middle of my desk. The first draft of my memoir was complete. *Strange. There is no great warm glow of accomplishment. Sixteen months of intense introspection and wallowing in my past, and I feel nothing except distaste for what it has taught me about myself.*

I did not notice Jacob come in until he said, "So you have done what so many people have told you not to do. Congratulations. Now you must deal with the consequences." He took three more steps, placed the gun on top of the stack of paper, and said, "You can use it or I will."

He sat down facing me. I noticed that he was wearing gloves and that he kept his hands on the desktop within easy reach of the gun.

"You expect me to shoot myself?"

He shrugged. "Why not? You're despondent over your brother's death. You've just finished writing about your life. Discovered quite a lot that you don't like about yourself. Your friends will say that you've never really recovered from Deborah's murder. Your suicide is quite plausible, really."

I said nothing, just looked at him. *I first met this man thirty-three years ago. He's old and tired. It must have been a hard life.*

Jacob sat looking at me in the way he had, the flickering up-from-under glances that somehow gave one the impression that he could see what you were thinking; that the auditory part of the meeting was only for your benefit.

He gestured at the manuscript. "Did that help? Getting all that suppressed guilt off your proverbial chest?"

Where to begin? I can't compete with him for cynicism and he neither believes in nor practices pity for others or atonement for his own sins.

I didn't answer the provocation directly. "Guilt is a relative thing. For example, Plovdiv, Bulgaria. 1991. The central banker who wanted a townhouse in London in exchange for the list of 'special' accounts and the truth about foreign currency reserves. Some would argue that you should feel guilty about the four days that you kept me ignorant of the reality that Deborah had died? Was his information worth that?"

He didn't hesitate. "No. His information was worthless. You told me so yourself. He was either wrong or lying about everything we asked him. He was at the bottom of the Black Sea before your military jet was over the Atlantic."

At the bottom of the Black Sea! So. Another fatality charged to my account. And I can't even remember his name. I've been like a Typhoid Mary, going where Jacob told me to go. It began in 1976, in Varna, with Nikolai Orlov, and I've left this trail of bodies behind me. And I've been oblivious to it all.

"But you kept me there in Bulgaria, while Deborah was --"

"Your wife was dead. Murdered by a madman. There was nothing you could do. Your brother was there to comfort your daughter. Keeping you in Plovdiv was the greatest good for the greatest number. Isn't that a primary goal for economists?"

I murmured, "It's called classical utilitarianism. Econ 101."

"And Robert was your wife's lover as well. Better that he should be there rather than you, don't you think?"

How does he know that? And he's saved it until now, when he can spring it on me as another incentive to shoot myself in the head.

But the question was no longer important. Jacob's matter-of-factness and gratuitous cruelty was the final confirmation that the gun was not just a prop; it was to be used.

I asked in a voice that revealed more emotion than I intended, "What about Dresden? Wynken, Blynken & Nod. Whose 'greater good' was served by blowing up a few retired spies? Or maybe you got it wrong and they were the classic innocent bystanders!"

The question stopped him. I watched him think about how to respond. But in the end, he only shook his head and said, "A loose end that needed to be tied up."

"Was Deborah a loose end too? You killed her, didn't you?"

He was silent, his eyes fixed on the manuscript. For the first time since he had walked into my life, he looked uncertain. Out of all the injustices that I might throw at him, he had not anticipated that one. When he looked up at me, he opened his mouth to say something, but then stopped.

I said, "You left me in Plovdiv with the banker and were gone for four days. Time enough to get to the East Coast and back."

He responded tonelessly, an actor reading for a role that he had no interest in. "Brian, a paranoid schizoid named Anton Morris killed Deborah because his voices told him to. It was a random, senseless act."

I pressed him, leaning forward. "She overheard us talking in Toronto. Worked out that you were CIA. That was threatening to you."

"Brian, I'm open about being CIA. Remember, I even handed you a business card? Why would she be a threat to me?"

The reasonableness of his voice did more to undermine my confidence than the logic of what he was saying. I was beginning to feel foolish, but I could not stop. "Because of what she overheard. We were talking about Dieterick Schreiber. Where he was and what he was doing. Definitely not a topic you wanted to hear about in public."

It's like we're opposing attorneys in a murder trial. Direct testimony and then cross-examination. All of it around conjecture and highly circumstantial 'facts.' Except that I think he wants me to convict him, to use the really damning evidence that he knows is out there.

Jacob stood up and walked to the window, his back to me. His actions made the gun suddenly prominent, a factor that was going to require a decision. He said, "I liked Deborah," in a voice so soft that I barely heard him. Something in the way he said the words told me – as clearly as if he had said 'I killed her' – that it was him that had given Morris the knife and left him standing over her body.

But a voice from the doorway changed the entire course of the debate.

"Deborah was a threat to him, but not because of his CIA connection."

We both turned to see Valentin standing in the opening. He was carrying a pistol loosely in his right hand.

Reunion

The three of us sat, me in my executive chair behind the desk and one of them at each corner. We formed an equilateral triangle with the gun and that damnable stack of paper at its center. Valentin continued to hold his own gun, his hand resting on his knee and the muzzle slanted toward the floor.

Jacob immediately took the offensive. He inclined his head to indicate Valentin. "I suppose he's told you his hard-luck story. About the aggrieved Kazakh who worked his way up through the KGB ranks? Always working for Russians who weren't as good as he was. How Vladimir Putin expropriated his millions?"

Valentin was looking intently at Jacob, but his expression was unreadable. *It's the same expression as the one that he had at that dinner with Griggs in 1974. When he asked Jacob, 'What exactly is it that you do in Washington D.C.?'*

"The two of you are the genuine odd couple." Jacob spoke to me but looked directly at Valentin. "He was supposed to kill you. Twice. But he couldn't do it. It seems that our coldblooded amoral assassin has a residual spark of compassion somewhere in there."

"Not compassion," Valentin said. "I lost that emotion when my father and brother died in a Russian 'relocation camp.' One of those instant communities that the Russians didn't bother to evacuate before the nearby above-ground nuclear tests."

He turned to me. "You know what happened in Islamabad. The orders were from Moscow Centre. They said 'Kill the men in the meeting.' But they never said that you were one of the targets. You were a complete surprise to me."

Moscow wanted to be able to show the world a prominent American caught scheming with the mujahedeen. Preferably a dead one. But Valentin botched the assignment. Knowingly.

I nodded, and then gestured at Jacob. "But he said that you tried *twice*. To kill me. Is he lying?"

Valentin's expression did not change, but he did sigh deeply. "That night in Dresden? When the restaurant was firebombed? The orders for that came from Moscow Centre as well."

His words brought Nadia back with a rush. Not just her image, as she looked that last day when she left Dieter's house to visit her sisters, but her very *presence*, the uncanny physical ache that I felt when I woke up and she wasn't there. But thoughts of Nadia were driven out by an instant all-consuming rage.

I choked out, "That was you? The one who placed the bomb?"

Why am I having trouble with this? He told me that his specialty was counterintelligence. Assassinations.

He didn't answer directly. "Why weren't you there? At the restaurant? It was your party, after all."

I was on the way out the door when Valentin showed up. He was dressed like a laborer, with a nametag on his shirt and carrying a shoulder bag. If he hadn't come, I'd have been there, at the restaurant when the bomb exploded. He was there to stop me.

Jacob sat watching the back and forth between Valentin and me. He had an amused expression, knowing where the dialogue was going.

Valentin continued. "My orders – from Moscow – were to put a bomb in the restaurant, set to go off at fifteen minutes after eight. They didn't tell me the targets. When I left the satchel under the table, I heard the owner – Gunter? -- say something about the Brian Norquist party that was coming at eight. So I went to find you, to slow you down."

I wanted to ask him "Why?" But not with Jacob sitting there smirking at us. So instead I asked, "But you had ample chances to do away with me after that… and that was your job. You told me yourself that you were good at it."

Valentin shrugged. "There were no more orders from Moscow Centre."

Jacob said, "That's because I convinced Moscow Centre that you were more useful to me alive than dead. We had the world's leading expert on the transition from communism to capitalism working for us."

And, with those words, he ended his forty-four years of living as a mole. The spy had come in from the cold.

The quality of the air in the room seemed to shift, as if our five human senses had ratcheted up to a new level. Jacob sat quietly with his hands in his lap, seeming to enjoy my confusion. Valentin's ever-present skepticism even softened.

We both looked at him. Valentin said it for both of us. "So the orders from Moscow? They came from you?"

He didn't respond. Just kept smiling.

"You're Nikolai Orlov," I said.

Jacob looked away for a second and when he turned back to face me, he was unalterably sad, but all he said was, "Yes."

That single word transformed my understanding of the last forty years. It was like being given a powerful flashlight after being trapped in an underground cavern. But I was surprised by the first question that came to mind.

"Why did you pick me?"

"Your Professor Griggs was tight with the CIA Director. He watched for likely students, ones that would fit in with Agency needs. He said that you were one of the few that really understood what the post-Cold War world would be like."

"So the Director sent you –"

"Not him. The woman that debriefed me when I came across. Very young, but very smart. She knew that I was good with economics, so she sent me to make contact with you at that Stanford workshop." He smiled, as if at a private joke. "Her name was Sheila."

I keep thinking: No more surprises. But they keep coming.

"So those SALT II talks in Varna –"

"Were completely legitimate. We needed an economist and I thought it would be a good trial run for you."

"But a man called Nikolai Orlov got sent to Perm-36 because he talked to me there. Why?"

"Mostly bad luck? We didn't know he'd be one of the three Soviet economists sent to that meeting. And we couldn't afford to have the two of you in close contact. Markus worried that the two of you might learn what you had in common – an East German defector who was once named Orlov."

"What about Islamabad? Valentin tells me that the orders from Moscow were to shoot me as well as the mujahedeen tribal leaders. Were those orders from you?"

He hesitated only slightly and, at least in my imagination, sounded faintly apologetic. "It would have been nice to have a famous American professor killed while deeply involved in a CIA plot against Russia."

 "And Schreiber?"

"Poor Dieterick. He really thought that I was his exit visa to the west. But even then he didn't trust me, so I needed you as bait."

Valentin broke in, "Tell him about Deborah."

Jacob leaned back in his chair, but put both hands on the desktop, within easy reach of the gun on the neat stack of paper.

He spoke to me, but his eyes were on Valentin's pistol. "As you said, I killed Deborah."

Why doesn't his matter-of-fact admission bring about a blinding rage? Why don't I lunge for the oh-so-prominent pistol and empty the magazine into his face?

Instead, I asked, "Why?" *Valentin said that she was a threat to him, but not because she overheard us talking about Schreiber.*

But what he said next made no sense.

"Because she knew about your brother."

Robert?

The last time I saw him, he was talking about selling real estate to Valentin. "Russians. They're difficult to deal with. Expect real value for what they're buying. The kind of people you can't negotiate with. They'll be back. They always come back."

And Valentin told me the same thing. I was a hostage in Islamabad. He traded me for information about arms shipments to the mujahedeen. He called it situational treason. "They think, 'Just this once,' but we always come back for more."

I asked him who put up the ransom for my release in Pakistan and he said, 'Perhaps someone that knows you and cares about you.'

I looked at Valentin and knew that he was experiencing the same series of thoughts as I was. *Robert gave them the information they wanted in exchange for your release. And it wasn't a one-time betrayal. It went on, and on.*

I said to Jacob, "You weren't worried about Deborah talking about you. Or me. What you couldn't risk was her talking about Robert." I stopped, and then was surprised that I could say out loud what was now so obvious.

"Robert worked for the Russians."

Jacob nodded. "For me. He was my major asset for twenty-five years. At the end, he was a Brigadier General in U.S. Army

Military Intelligence, with direct access to Pentagon-level strategies. And I was the only one who knew .... None of your people, and nobody on the Soviet side except Markus Wolf. Until Robert told Deborah."

"Did you kill him too?"

He looked up at the ceiling, then shrugged. "Not directly. His suicide was quite genuine." He paused and then added, "But I was there, drinking with him. And I may have emphasized that he was a traitor and would be exposed as such. Oh, and I added the 'I'm sorry' note after he shot himself."

I almost picked up the gun. My right hand was flexing and reflexing and all three of us were watching it.

How blind can one person be? First, you insisted that Robert was murdered. Then you convinced yourself that he killed himself out of his guilt over our joint assassination of our father. Then you had another brilliant insight, thanks to Melanie's disclosures – that it was self-inflicted vengeance for his betrayal of you with Deborah. And now? You discover that he lived most of his adult life as a traitor. Until he couldn't stand it any more.

And you were the cause, the reason for all of his crimes. You were the bait. If you had not been in Islamabad, none of this would have happened and he would be alive today! If you had really loved Deborah as she deserved to be loved ....

Jacob was watching me closely. He leaned forward and his voice took on a faintly pleading tone. "It all changed when Markus Wolf retired and the KGB took me on. And you were there."

That night in Helsinki.

"Wolf let me do things my way. But from 1989 on, the new liaison ran the show. He was the one who ordered the executions – Deborah in 1993, and Nadia and her German friends in 1993. And then the fake Orlov and Robert in the last few weeks." He pointed at Valentin. "And you too."

"And he's put you at the head of the list." He very slowly slid the stack of paper three inches in my direction, with the gun on top, and rotated it so that the butt of the gun was positioned for me to pick up.

Both Jacob and Valentin were looking at me, Valentin with an expression that was almost sympathetic. Jacob looked as he always did – amused and cynical at the same time. And expectant.

This is what he did with Robert. This is why he's here. And why he's placed the gun there for me to use. So that I could atone for what I've done. To my father. To Deborah. Most of all to Robert. Because he knew that his disclosures would be devastating.

I looked directly at Jacob. "This" – I nodded at the gun – "has nothing to do with the memoir, does it?"

He shook his head. "Nope. Actually, I think it's a fine work of first-hand history. Hardly a mention of the CIA and certainly not a threat to me. I especially like the chapter on the summit conferences in the eighties. I think you titled it 'Futility With Top Hats.' A nice touch."

I could not help but look at the desktop computer on the credenza behind me, the one with that damned blinking cursor.

Jacob saw the direction of my glance. He smiled and said, "It sends me a copy of whatever you're working on every time you hit the 'Save' key."

More proof of my long-running gullibility. Another reason to pick up the gun and use it. Let him compose another suicide note. But then he would think he'd won. And I would have to forego my own revenge.

It's time for Jacob to face some of his own history. It's not a memoir, but it will have to do.

A Revelation for Jacob

I pushed back from the desk and slid open the middle drawer. I was pleased to see that the motion caused Jacob to reach forward toward the gun, and equally pleased that Valentin inclined the muzzle of his gun to track Jacob's movement.

Jacob is right to be concerned, but he has no idea of the weapon that I will pull out of this drawer.

With exaggerated slowness, I reached into the drawer and pulled out the manila folder. It was unlabeled and so thin that it could have been empty. I pushed the manuscript a few inches to the side and placed the folder in the middle of my desk. I folded it back to expose the contents, three glossy squares of paper, obviously the backs of photographs. Even at a casual glance, they were of different ages.

I turned over the first and newest one and pushed it to the edge of the desk where Jacob sat. It was the candid Poloroid photograph of Nadia and me in the courtyard outside the cathedral in the central square of Dresden. It was seriously faded, but her happiness and my shyness about cameras still came through quite clearly.

"That was fourteen years ago. Her name was Nadia. She was almost thirty-three years old and would be dead in a month." I added, "I loved her. She was going to come home with me as soon as the passport came through." It was somehow important that I include that fact, even though it was not essential to the story that I was telling.

I had their attention. Not that they were riveted. They already knew this part of the story, after all. Each of them had played a part. But they sensed that the other two squares of paper, still face down in the center of the desk, were important to what was playing out in this room. I was like a Las Vegas dealer in a high-stakes poker game turning over the last fateful cards.

I turned over the next photo and placed it alongside the one of Nadia and me. It was older by approximately fifteen years, but in better shape by virtue of being printed on quality photo stock. It was the picture of a family – a mother, father and daughter – that Nikolai had shown to me in Varna in 1978 and that Melanie had brought back from Moscow two weeks ago. Still, it was badly creased and worn, as one would expect of a document that had spent several years in Perm-36.

Neither of them reacted other than with curiosity. *So Jacob did not know his avatar Nikolai. Markus Wolf did not confide in others. Even if he cared for them.*

I put my index finger on the photo, pointing to the teenage girl. She was ordinary looking, a little bit sullen, like she resented having to sit for a family photo. Slightly overweight, with her dark hair arranged into intricate braids trailing to her shoulders. She wore thick glasses and leaned away from her parents.

"This is the same person. Nadia at age fifteen, although they didn't call her Nadia then. A typical rebellious teenager. Who grew into this remarkable woman," and I pointed at the thirty-three year-old Nadia in the first photo.

Valentin and Jacob looked back and forth between the two photos. Finally, Jacob asked the obvious question. "The parents. Who are they? What happened to them?" I thought I could detect a very faint note of dread, but I may have been imagining it. Longing for it.

"I don't know about the mother. The father went to an academic conference in Bulgaria and never came home again. Nadia said, 'He abandoned us.' He called himself Nikolai Orlov. He died just a few weeks ago, in Moscow."

I could see the awareness overcome him. First in his eyes, and then in his suspended breathing and stillness, and finally across his entire body, until he was slumped back in his chair.

"But then there's this last picture," I said to him. I turned over the last piece of pasteboard. It was new, with crisp edges. And it was blank.

"Oh, yes. I forgot. You already have this one. In your wallet."

Valentin was caught up in my stagecraft and both of us looked steadily at Jacob until he reached inside his coat and brought out the envelope-sized wallet that he carried. It was newer than the one I had last seen in the lobby of the luxurious Moscow hotel, and it was less overflowing with pieces of paper. But he reached into the innermost compartment and extracted the same photograph as on that day, the picture of the infant girl with such big dark eyes. He placed it carefully alongside the other two and the three of us looked at the trio of photos representing the life history of Nadia, the daughter that he left behind.

"She was a beautiful child, Jacob. What was her name?"

Very softly, "Elena."

Then he began his own story. He told it haltingly, in short bursts separated by long silences; the way one would expect a seventy-year-old man to describe a past that was so deeply cloaked in deceit and layers of secrecy as to be almost irretrievable.

"Wolf said that he would look after her for me. That I could come back in a few years as a Hero of the Soviet Union, once the decadent west collapsed of its own weight, that I could resume being myself, that he would take care of Elena …."

He talked without interruption for thirty minutes. Valentin and I listened as rapt as first graders at story hour. Or as priests hearing the last confession of a condemned prisoner.

He did not seek forgiveness, nor did we offer any. To the contrary, when he stopped talking, I said the cruelest thing I could think of. "So you killed her, your own daughter. With a firebomb. In Dresden. To – how did you put it – to tie up some loose ends."

Jacob wasn't listening. He picked up the photo of his daughter, and in his head, he was back in Wittenburg in 1961. "I put her to bed before I left to cross the border. I recited all of Wynken, Blynken and Nod to her before she fell asleep."

The three of us sat in silence, thinking of all of our losses. Three old men whose lives had been interwoven for so little benefit.

Both Jacob and I seemed to become aware of the gun on the manuscript at the same instant. Our eyes met and I said, "You can use it or I will."

He reached out very slowly.

Gunfight

"Something always goes wrong. The only issue is whether Plan B is any good."

Valentin had used those words to explain how he survived the assassination attempt on Skyline Drive, and they proved true once more.

There were two of them, probably the same two shooters that were on the motorcycles last week. They came through the door together, in the classic two-handed shooting stance, fanning out quickly to left and right. They looked identical, thick dark men in blue jeans and leather jackets.

Whatever their 'Plan A' was, it went to hell in a hurry. Their first problem was that there were three people in a room where they expected two. Another complication was that two of those three had a weapon in their hand, ready to use. And they were handicapped by their training, right out of the assassin's textbook. They came in fast, breaking right and left to cover the room, their eyes sighting along their extended arms and the muzzle of the gun. But the one on the right should have been looking down. One of the 'Deborah boxes' was in his path, and he went down hard.

They counted twenty-three shell casings in four distinct clusters. That seemed too few to me, but then again, I was on the floor, trying to crawl under my desk. All I remember is the incredible loudness of the gunfire and how silent it was when it stopped.

They also counted three bodies – Jacob and the two shooters. Valentin was gone.

Damage Control

My study was still off-limits, labeled a 'crime scene,' although it had been three days since the last white-coated specialist had been there. Caroline and I stayed mostly in the kitchen during the daytime, probably because it was brightly lit with few shadows. We did not talk very much.

When I came into the kitchen this morning, she was sitting at the counter staring at the wall. When I touched her on the shoulder, she said, "There are bullet holes in the walls and bloodstains on the rug. This is Palo Alto. What kind of house has bullet holes and bloodstains? TV news trucks in the driveway?"

A rhetorical question, the kind that serves as a prologue to a lecture. No response required.

She went on, still talking to herself. "I liked it that you were quiet, maybe even a little introverted. I thought my only worry was Deborah's ghost. I thought I knew you. But I don't, and I can't. Your past has a way of reappearing, and you have secrets that even you don't know about."

Do I? Even after all this? I didn't bother to respond to Caroline. She was right, and in any case, it wouldn't matter what I said.

She turned away and spoke at the wall. "I'm going away for a while. I don't know for how long. I don't think I'm coming back."

I just looked at her, saying nothing because there was nothing to be said. She nodded, as if acknowledging that my silence was in fact a complete response. And I suppose it was.

She left, leaving me with the bullet holes, bloodstains and television cameras. I decided to deal with it later.

Déjà vu all over again!

The same two serious men in dark suits with leather briefcases and shined shoes – the ones that said that they were representing an important but anonymous client in DC and warned me against writing my memoir – were waiting for me in the lobby of my Palo Alto office. They said nothing, just trailed along with me to my second floor office and closed the door behind them.

I remembered our first encounter. *Was it just eighteen months ago? I got all offended and righteous when they told me what I couldn't do. I was in their face, thinking that I could manage the past, that I knew the difference between right and wrong.*

They're different as well; not as assured and domineering as they had been at our first meeting. Like lawyers with a bad set of facts trying to work out a plea bargain. Their important and anonymous client has also been slapped with a few nasty truths about his own operations and belief systems. Plenty of shocks to go around. I wonder if any of us have learned anything useful.

The three of us sat at the conference table, the two of them facing me. This time, the older one spoke. "Dr. Norquist, I think that we want the same thing."

I thought that I was beyond aggravation at this point, what with Jacob's disclosures and the shootout in my home, but the man's presumption – that he knew what I wanted – provoked me, even though he was probably right.

I snapped at him, "What is it that you're so sure we both want?"

His answer was instantaneous. "Silence. Or, more realistically, a lack of legal and/or media attention. A quiet, cloistered life, free from scandal and censure. For both you and your family. An absence of drama."

"And your client?"

"The same as you. The chance to reflect on his mistakes and to adapt, rationally and effectively."

"And without any of those pesky Congressional inquiries or persistent journalists seeking Pulitzer Prizes for investigative reporting."

"Precisely. We think our interests converge."

"What about concepts like justice, transparency and truth?"

"For whom? All of the victims and wrongdoers are dead."

Not quite. There's the man from Helsinki, the one that ordered the deaths of my brother and friends. But, other than that, he's right. You'd have to stage the Congressional inquiries in the graveyard,

I said, "So we have a standoff, it seems." *That's as far as I'll go. They probably want a signed affidavit, but they'll have to live with the ambiguity.*

The two of them stood up and the other man spoke for the first time. "Think of it as détente... peace for the sake of our converging interests."

They were almost to the door when I said, "Mad." They turned to look at me with worried expressions.

I opened the door for them. "MAD. It's an acronym. The governing strategy for most of the Cold War period – 'Mutually Assured Destruction.' That's your so-called *détente."*

Melanie arrived two minutes later.

"Oh good! It's my favorite law enforcement officer. I presume you're here to tell me that the FBI has solved the Palo Alto crime spree that took place in my home? Maybe even identified the shooters?"

She grimaced. "Two brothers. On tourist visas from Albania. That's all we know. Apparently without families, prison records or past lives. As far as we know, they could have been dropped in from outer space."

"And Valentin? I assume he's in custody as a material witness?"

"Gone. No trace."

No surprise there. He's been practicing being gone for forty years. It probably helps to have a lot of large bank deposits scattered around those tropical islands.

Melanie said, "I saw two men leaving your office just now. They looked like the Blues Brothers without the sunglasses."

"Emissaries from afar. Bearing carrots and sticks. Selling détente."

She sat down heavily. *She looks tired.*

She smiled at me, but it was a sad smile. "I had a visit too. From a person who's about eight pay-grades higher than I am in the Bureau. Very unofficial, of course. Mostly generalities. Complimented me on my track record. Promised a rosy career path. Providing I don't get sidetracked, of course."

"Sidetracked?"

"An old railroad term. It means –"

"I know what it means. What does it mean for the career path of a relatively promising and female FBI agent with questionable relatives?"

"To stay with colloquialisms … 'Don't rock the boat,' 'Be a team player,' 'No grandstanding,' 'Keep your mouth shut,'–"

"Stop! I get the picture. *As my visitors just said, 'We think our interests converge. You want an absence of drama, for both you and your family.*

"What are you going to do?" I asked. *It's probably unfair to ask her to answer the same question that I can't answer for myself!*

She slumped even lower in her chair. "I don't know. My first instinct is to say the hell with them! I think about Mom and Robert ...."

Her voice trailed off and she looked miserable. I reached across the table and put my hand on hers. I tried to think of something to say, but only clichés came to mind. I patted her hand a couple of times, feeling hopelessly inadequate.

Then she asked me, "What are you going to do?" and I realized that she knew as well as I did that she was being held hostage, that my silence was the ransom payment in exchange for her career path. *No wonder she looks so miserable.*

I stopped patting and stared at her. She knew what I was thinking. "Dad, do what you think is right. I can live with the collateral damage."

We sat in silence, each with our own thoughts. Then she asked, "Who was he? Jacob Connolly?"

She never met him. Her first encounter was when she zipped open the body bag when he was being wheeled down the driveway to the coroner's van. How can I make her understand who Jacob Connolly really was?

Stick with simple facts. Just like when Daniel asked me, 'Were you in the war, papa?'

"He was a Soviet spy. His real name was Nikolai Orlov."

"The suicide in Moscow that I looked into for you ... his name was –"

"Horst Weber, but he had pretended to be Orlov for most of his life."

"Why?"

How can one word be such a complicated question!

"Why? At first, because he lived in a totalitarian state, and the state told him to do it. And then, after that state ceased to exist, because he was bribed. Not with money. With threats." *His daughter was about the same age as Melanie. How would I have behaved if a Markus Wolf had threatened to execute her unless I went along?*

As I knew she would, Melanie scowled at my non-answer. "Let me rephrase the question, why would the totalitarian state want to substitute Orlov for Weber? For forty years, for God's sake!"

"Because Markus Wolf needed a placeholder. When Orlov – the real one, Wolf's illegitimate son – defected to the West on Wolf's orders, Wolf promised him that he could come home again, that he would maintain a place for him, that he could resume his old identity. I think they both believed that, both then and later.

"And he left his daughter behind .... for the good of the party. Part of the deal was that she would be raised as Nikolai Orlov's daughter, with additional oversight from Wolf, who was her grandfather of sorts. She was a year old, the substitution would be painless for her."

"But why maintain such an elaborate scheme after Stasi is gone and Wolf is out of power?"

"Because both Wolf and Jacob insisted that the arrangement be kept in place. Jacob was providing a steady stream of first-rate intelligence and feeding disinformation to the CIA. When Wolf retired in 1986, Jacob insisted on a face-to-face meeting with Markus Wolf and his KGB counterpart. He demanded that Orlov stay in place in return for his continuing as their American source. Another part of the deal was that the KGB agent would take over from Wolf as his sole contact point."

And I was there when Wolf handed off Jacob to his new handler, at that meeting, oblivious to what has happening around me. Those two men in that square in Helsinki with Jacob and Schreiber were Markus Wolf and his KGB successor. And poor Dieterick Schreiber was thrown in as a sweetener!

Melanie said, "And that agreement held until last month, when the substitute Orlov committed his so-called suicide. What changed?"

Robert was dead, so Jacob no longer had any value to the Russians. He lost most of any negotiating power that he once had. But Melanie doesn't need to know about Robert's treason.

I lied, "I don't know. Everybody just got old and stopped caring, I guess."

She looked puzzled. "But he – Connolly -- could still threaten them. Blow the whistle on their espionage activities in the U.S. ..."

"Which is why we had the shootout in my study. Your so-called Albanian tourists weren't after Valentin. Their target was Jacob." *Both shooters were focused on Jacob. He was hit nine times. That's why Valentin was able to walk away.*

She seemed satisfied with my answer, so I did not have to tell the other, far more important reason. *Because Jacob's handler – the KGB agent I had met in Helsinki – had risen to a point in the Russian hierarchy that he no longer feared exposure. He was untouchable.*

An Official Visit

Sheila Weiner was next. She rang my doorbell the next morning. Just as the first time, she walked by me as soon as I opened the door, saying, "There are some things you need to know about Jacob Connolly."

I trailed her to my study. "What happened to the ... how did you put it ... the 'strongly held norms about information security in the Agency?' I thought that the subject of Jacob Connolly was not open for discussion."

"That was then."

"And this is now. But what's changed?"

"I had a call from the Director. He thought you should be in the loop."

The bureaucrats are using a full court press. They send two suits to see me, have the head of the FBI lean on Melanie, and – the carrot among the sticks – tell Sheila to give me enough of the story to make me feel good about my complicity in the cover-up. That might be difficult to do. I probably know as much – or more – than they do.

I have no stomach for this bullshit! "Sheila, I know all I ever want to know about Jacob Connolly, and probably at least as much as you do. In fact, there's only one thing that I'd like you to tell me."

She smiled in a way that I chose to see as condescending. It made me mean, so I said, "His name was Nikolai Orlov before it was Horst Weber before it was Jacob Connolly. He's been a Russian mole for the last forty-six years."

She glared at me, but I was suddenly enormously tired. It was as if all that accumulated willful ignorance, along with the deaths and betrayals was somehow transformed into a physical weight and dumped on me.

I cut off the protest she was about to make. "He was the godson of Markus Wolf. More than that, really. Wolf was a notable ladies man ... three wives and more than a few mistresses. I think Connolly was his son, illegitimate but important to Wolf despite that. That's what made him so attractive to the CIA ... his ticket to the west. And then he gave you three of Wolf's European moles to make sure that you brought him inside."

She said nothing, her frown growing deeper as I talked. I chose to imagine her thinking about the miscalculations of that era, some of them hers.

I went on, talking mostly for my own benefit. "And that's why there had to be an ongoing Nikolai Orlov for everyone to see on the Soviet side, so that Jacob Connolly could come home again."

I was into my story, wanting to offend Sheila and everything she stood for. I turned rhetorical.

"How much harm did he do?"

"Plenty." I answered my own question. "He was in place for more than forty years, most of it during the Cold War era. Essentially, he was running two covert operations. First, he recruited and handled dozens of informants in the Soviet Bloc who were feeding you bogus information about Russian operations and intentions."

Sheila tried a mild protest. "But that all ended long ago. Wolf resigned from the Stasi in 1986 and the Stasi itself was shut down in 1989. Connolly lost his favored status --"

I bulldozed on, "But Wolf handed his responsibilities – including Jacob -- off to his ex-KGB liaison officer. He also made sure that any Stasi documents referring to Connolly or any of his agents were permanently done away with. He even ordered the execution of some six or seven of those agents that he deemed unreliable without Stasi oversight."

Valentin said, "The unit I headed was tasked with the elimination of the enemies of the state, a label that was construed very broadly." I asked him if he had worked in East Germany. He told me, "Yes, counterintelligence assignments. But I was a specialist, never there for very long. The busiest time for me was in 1989, when the whole bloody system was coming apart. Hoenecker and Mielke were intent on preserving what they could."

"But he didn't get them all," I said. "Wynken, Blynken & Nod were still out there. And they knew of Connolly. They were feeding him information, mailed to his home address."

Sheila was hooked by my story, no longer trying to stop me. I think she was still living in the world where she was known as WWDN. She said, "Connolly never met them. And Wolf missed them."

That's close, Sheila, but wrong. Wolf did catch them. But when one of them turned out to be his granddaughter, he arranged for a new life for her. It wouldn't have been that difficult for him; after all, his own beloved German Democratic Republic was falling apart around his ears.

"And after the German reunification, Jacob decided to eliminate them, the last of his stable of informants. But they had covered their tracks quite well. So he enlisted me to find them. And used Valentin's bomb making skills to close the deal."

"All that happened almost fifteen years ago. Once the Iron Curtain disappeared …" She was speaking with a bitterness out of proportion to a retired analyst. Jacob's treason was something raw, personally offensive to her.

She hasn't retired from the CIA. She's still analyzing data at Langley. She lied about being a grandmother and she's lying about being part of the 'peace dividend' when the Soviet empire fell of its own weight.

She was going on. "… the dark ages for people like Connolly. America's primary enemy – Reagan's evil empire -- was defeated. And we had all those new toys -- satellites, drones, computer technology – so that we didn't need old-fashioned human intelligence. Or so we thought. But then Russia turned revisionist on us. Decided to reassert their rights as a global – and nuclear –

power. And we decided to go 'nation-building' in the Middle East."

Her disgust was thick in her voice and I wondered if it was aimed at Connolly or the litany of policy blunders she was reciting.

"So Jacob was back in favor in the CIA?" I asked it as a genuine question, not a statement of fact.

"With the Russians, yes. But now his primary value to them was because of the second covert operation that he was running."

"Robert, my brother."

"Yes, we now know – thanks to you -- that your brother was a major intelligence source for the Russians, starting with their Afghan adventure and continuing on through our Iraqi invasions in 1991 and 2002. He was our worst nightmare – a senior military intelligence officer with Pentagon-level access."

A silence settled in. *Sheila's probably told me what the Director authorized her to tell me. But she still doesn't know the whole story. She doesn't know about Nadia or why Robert became a traitor. And I'm not going to tell her. She has no need to know.*

I asked, "Anything else that the Director thinks I should know?" I put a lot of stress on the word 'should.' "Maybe a few tidbits about how Connolly had enough influence with Moscow to mount assassination attempts in Dresden in 1993. Or Palo Alto in 2007?"

She just looked at me.

"Robert retired from the Army in the year 2005. Not much good to them after that."

The silence continued. She knew where I was going.

"And Connolly's network of double and triple agents – if there were any still functioning -- would be getting a little long in the tooth by then, probably bored by the switch to commercial espionage that the Federal Security Service was emphasizing."

Still nothing. I choose to imagine that she is in her mind, running through a list of threats, trying to find the one that will be most effective.

"Markus Wolf finally dies, last year, leaving the pseudo Nikolai Orlov without any protective cover, and the FSS stages his suicide, no longer worried about what he might know or not know."

"Drop it, Brian. Let it die with Connolly." But her words had no force. She knew I wasn't going to stop. I had told her when she came in that there was only one question I needed her to answer and she knew I was going to ask it.

"Sure, I'll drop it. Just that one last question. Who was the KGB liaison to the Stasi in Dresden in 1989 when Wolf retired? When the Stasi folded and Wolf stopped managing Connolly, who took over? Who was the handler for Jacob Connolly after 1989? Who did Jacob call to send Valentin to Dresden in 1993? Why did those two gunmen kill him rather than me or Valentin? Who is that we can't afford to offend by naming them?"

That was more than one question. But they all have the same answer.

She didn't answer any of them. Or maybe she did, in the oblique style favored by those who lie for a living.

"Dr. Norquist. The American relationship with Russia is at a critical juncture. We're putting anti-missile systems with nuclear-tipped warheads in ex-Warsaw pact countries and Russia is threatening to do the same in Cuba. We're trying to get them to support us for independence in Kosovo. This is not ... *not* ... the time to dredge up ancient fairy tales about bogeymen."

Sheila stood up and walked out of my study. Just as she reached the front door, I answered the question for her.

"Vladimir Putin. The President of Russia"

Second Draft

I opened the Word file labeled 'Memoir: Current Draft' and it quickly filled the screen, two ordinary side-by-side typed pages, single-spaced. The scroll bar at the bottom of the screen informed me that I had written 95,437 words, covering 287 pages.

The USB drive that Valentin had given to me sat at the side of the keyboard. It looked deceptively innocent. Its capacity was thirty-two gigabytes and most of that was used. A small fraction – a couple of hundred megabytes – was for a document written in both Russian and English. It described Valentin's childhood, including word-portraits of his father and brother, who had died in relocation camps when Russia forcibly integrated Kazakhstan. The rest of the space was taken up by photos, mostly of documents pertaining to KGB operations during the Cold War, but some of them dealing with Russian politicians. It was particularly detailed concerning the career of Vladimir Putin, including his service as the KGB liaison to Erich Mielke during the last days of the Union of Soviet Socialist States.

I looked at the screen, thinking about the delusions that motivated the document and that were shed one-by-one in the course of writing. I thought about what I had learned – and unlearned – in the last year.

I closed the file and stared at the blank screen. Then I moved the cursor to drag the icon labeled 'Memoir: Current Draft" to the wastebasket icon in the lower left corner of the screen. A popup appeared, asking, "Are you sure you want to delete this file?" I clicked the 'Yes' box, and the machine made the cute little 'flushing' sound.

I opened a new Word file and the blank page appeared, nicely centered on the blue background. I typed 'Memoir: Draft II' at the top of the page.

I stared at the screen, thinking of Robert's note, "I'm sorry." And then of Deborah, Nadia, Jacob and Valentin. Finally, Ashley's words came back to me.

It has to be about you.

And Valentin's words, when he handed me the USB drive: *Here, for your memoir. And mine.*

So I began.

I never intended to work for the CIA.

The scroll bar read 'Pages – 1 of 1, Words - 8 of 8.'

Author's Note

You know the drill: *This is a work of fiction. Any resemblance between events or characters depicted in this book and actual events or characters is purely coincidental, etc., etc., etc.*

However, that is not quite correct in this instance. The idea for the book and some of the actual language is adapted from my experience in writing my own memoir. Therefore, some of the events and characters depicted will have shadings and emanations that may seem faintly familiar to readers with a shared history. But for those few, you will find only bits and pieces, not your whole self.

The major credit must go to my daughter Mary, who at one time believed – and told all her friends – that I worked for the CIA, that the professor/consultant trappings were camouflage.

I have tried to be accurate with respect to the Cold War timeline that runs through the book and when I have embellished, I have done so by adding dialogue, thoughts and actions that – for most of us – could be *plausible* twists to the historical record, or at least not obviously absurd.

And I wholeheartedly apologize to those friends of mine who are in fact Professors of Economics.

About the Author

Thomas Hofstedt is engaged in approximately his fourth career, each of which is partially reflected in the plots and settings of his writing. He has worked as a professor in major universities, as a management consultant all over the globe, and finally as an advisor and board member for not-for-profit organizations. He is the product of a Scandinavian heritage, a Midwestern upbringing, and a Northern California value system. He lives in San Carlos, California with his wife and most diligent critic, Sharon.

Other Books (Fiction)

The Hundred-Year Storm
A Convergence of Evils
A Conspiracy of Patriots
The House on Russian Hill
A Small War in a Far Off Place
They Call It Tinseltown

www.ingramcontent.com/pod-product-compliance
Lightning Source LLC
Chambersburg PA
CBHW062119170626
46813CB00002B/501